THE SPANISH INDECISION

The Jenny Abroad Series Book One

Sarah-Jane Fraser

To you, you can do whatever you want if you try.

CHAPTER 1

I stood in front of the mirror, still clutching my binder, drenched through to the skin. I couldn't shake the idea that Natalia had purposefully flipped the tray of drinks over me.

'Something ought to fit,' Pete had said as he gave me his locker key. I'd left him clearing up the mess; running off to a chorus of tuts and eye rolls from The Witches. Feeling like an entrant in a wet t-shirt competition, I'd grabbed my folder as I passed my desk, for a bit of protection.

The door squeaked and a waft of expensive aftershave puffed out of the locker as I opened it. Hanging up were some silk ties and two shirts; a blue and white striped double cuff and a plain white one. *Thank you, Pete!* I unhooked the white one and headed over to a changing cubicle.

Wincing, I remembered the feeling of clunky mugs and scalding coffee raining down on me. It was a horrible feeling, being soaked through to the skin. Peeling off my shirt I shivered. With a poke of my head out of the cubicle, I checked the coast was clear before I rushed to the door and slid the bolt across. Feeling rather exposed I stood, naked from the waist up, wringing my bra out and holding it under the hand-dryer. For the first time ever, I was pleased I had such a small chest. There wasn't too much material to dry.

The grunting started as I was hooking my bra back on. Wide eyed, I whipped around to see what was happening. My boss, Mr Thompson, and another man, quite frankly the most attractive man I've ever seen, suddenly shoulder barged through the door. *Why me? Why now? Why when I'm looking like this?*

With speed to rival an athlete I scuttled back into the cubicle, banging the door shut.

'Ah, sorry about that. We thought the door was just stuck...' Mr Thompson blushed like a plum tomato.

I made an indistinguishable squeaking sound, humiliation choking me.

'So, ah, this is the staff room, where people mad enough to walk or cycle to work come and get changed.' I could hear him giving the other man a tour as I rapidly tried to get some clothes on and recover a modicum of dignity.

Surprisingly, Pete's shirt looked okay once I had tucked it in to my high waist, pencil skirt. Even though the slight headache from all the grips around my head told me my large doughnut was securely in place, I still smoothed my hands over my blonde hair to double check. Then, gathering up the ruined shirt and my folder, I gingerly left the safety of the cubicle.

'Ah, young Jenny,' said Mr Thompson.

I cringed. I hate it when people call me young. I was twenty-seven for goodness sake, but I looked about seventeen, and not in a "you're ageing well" way, but in a "you're clearly too young and inexperienced to have anything useful to add" kind of way. *And why did he say "ah" all the time?*

'This is…ah…Mr Henson, who will be your… ah…new line manager. He just transferred in from the ah… Chameleon Group head office.'

'Nice to meet you…' I trailed off, deciding to avoid using his name, sure I'd say handsome instead of Henson.

Clutching the coffee-soaked shirt with one hand, I stuck out the other to Mr Henson, which he gave a firm shake. His eyes struck me first, steel blue and sparkling. His thick crop of dark brown hair was cut close at the sides and longer on top, there was a faint trace of stubble on his jaw. Deep creases around his mouth hinted at a nice smile, although his face was quite straight and serious. I made my excuses and rushed back to the office, feeling acutely mortified.

It was only when I was walking out of the staff room that I noticed the sign telling me that CCTV was in operation. *Oh no!* I thought of our resident security guards, Stan and Bill. Heat prickled my face as I pictured them huddled around their little TV screens, enjoying the show. I prayed that they'd been on a break as I pulled the door open and returned to my office.

The corridor was empty and as my cheeks cooled, thoughts of my gorgeous new boss floated around my head. I was sure that things were only going to get better at work. Surely, they couldn't get any worse?

Catching Pete's eye, I nodded what I hoped was a message of gratitude in his direction. As I sat down my eyes were drawn to the clock. Only a few hours to go and I'd be jetting off to Spain for my best friend's hen do. I could barely contain my excitement when I thought of everything I'd arranged. It took a lot of effort to drag my attention back to focusing on work.

Consulting the to-do list in my trusty organiser, I let out a quiet huff of irritation as I scanned over the first point.

1) MOVE ON FROM JAMES!

The less said about him the better. Lazy, selfish and chauvinistic. He wasn't a nice guy and I could do so much better. The trouble was, I hadn't. I was on the lookout for a new boyfriend; someone interesting and driven. The opposite of James.

2) Email mum.

Since her accident, I'd taken to checking in with her every day. I worried that I wouldn't be around for her while I was away, even though she insisted she was fine. I think she was getting a bit fed up with me but I couldn't help it, it was as if our roles had suddenly been reversed. I'd done her an online food order, so I forwarded her the details.

Then I made myself feel better by scribbling down a few tasks I'd already completed- purely for the satisfaction of ticking them off. Feeling suitably productive, I decided I'd earned a break and went over to see Pete.

'You okay darling?' he asked as I got to his desk. He inclined his head over towards The Witches, reminding me of the coffee incident.

'Never better,' I replied. I was aware that we were being observed and I didn't want to show any weakness.

He gave me a deep, understanding look and then said, 'You're looking fabulous today, chick, you must give me the details of your designer!'

'Oh, I don't think you could afford him.'

We chuckled and I felt some of the weight lift off my shoulders, it was so nice to have someone on my side. He's one of the nicest guys I've ever met. Shame he's in a very serious relationship with Jeremy from Finance.

Pete leaned in closer and whispered, 'Don't go on holiday and leave me here with The Witches.'

I laughed and said, 'There's no chance I'm missing it, even for you!'

'I know,' he replied and grinned. 'You're gonna have so much fun in Marencanto. Don't forget to go to 'Breeze' the beach club and tell them 'Posh

Pete' sent you.'

'*Posh* Pete?' I questioned.

'It's cos when I first went there they tried to ban me because I wasn't posh enough, darling, but they relented. Ooh how they relented!' Pete sounded as if he had to overcome some sort of dramatic persecution and made a show of mock outrage.

'Ha! It sounds like they'll probably try and ban me too but we'll give it a go. I'm so excited about going to Spain, I've never been before.'

'There's a reason I go at least twice a year. You'll have the best time! Are you all packed?'

'No, I'm leaving work at lunch time so I can go home and pack. Actually, I best crack on and finish everything before I go.'

'Your legs look fab in those heels by the way,' he called as I walked away.

The compliment gave me a lift and I headed back to my desk with a lighter heart.

CHAPTER 2

The sound of The Witches quietly snickering drifted over to me as I typed up some minutes. Paranoid, I was sure it was about me.

'...Such a loser,' I heard Natalia say.

She was the leader of the coven. Eve and Chantelle appear to worship her in a petrified kind of way. They all have dyed red hair and wear only black. I used to think they were all intimidating, now I've decided it's only Natalia who's terrifying.

Convinced they all hate me, my mind wandered. I'd been at this job a while, but I'd always had the sense that I didn't really belong here, and the bitchy girls had knocked my confidence. I didn't want to admit that it was a dead-end job, but truthfully, I couldn't see where I was going with it. Being distracted with arranging the hen do probably wasn't helping.

More sniggering snapped me back to the

present and I began typing up the minutes of that days meeting with renewed vigour. My work title was *Office Assistant*, it should have been *PA* but as I assisted all the managers in the office there was nothing "personal" about it. The moment I sent the finished document to email, my phone buzzed.

'Jenny George,' I answered.

'Miss George, it's Michael Henson. Could you step into my office?'

The phone clicked off before I could reply.

As I headed over to his office, I smoothed my skirt down against my hips. Aware that the first impression I had made was that of a startled, soggy loon who stunk of coffee, I resolved to make a better one this time.

I knocked on the door and while I waited to be called in I began to wonder why I was being asked to see him. My ability to feel automatically guilty, regardless of whether I had done anything wrong, kicked in. *Maybe I was in trouble for work place nudity?*

My heart was pounding and I was certain that anyone nearby could hear it. By the time I was summoned in I was so nervous I had started to sweat; I was stewing in panic and angst.

As he shut the door I breathlessly babbled out, 'I didn't know there was CCTV in the staff room. I didn't mean to cause offence to anyone I just needed to dry my bra.'

Mr Henson raised his eyebrows, clearly taken

aback. The word 'bra' rang through my ears as I quickly realised being naked wasn't the reason I had been asked to see him. My face flushed and my previously thumping heart sank.

'Thank you for that, Miss George, but that's not the reason I called you in here. Don't worry, you're not in trouble.' His warm smile and gentle tone soon calmed me down. 'I'm not even starting here properly until next week, but I wanted to come in to familiarise myself with the staff and the office, and lay out some expectations so we all get off on the right foot. I'm going to be speaking to everyone individually.'

His deep eyes met mine and the corners crinkled as he smiled. As I relaxed I let go of a deep breath.

'Okay.' *Smooth line Jenny.*

With a welcoming gesture, he extended his arm out to the empty chair opposite his desk. I endeavoured to sit down elegantly without ruffling my carefully arranged outfit, I could feel his gaze burning into me, studying me. *He's probably thinking about my bra right now,* I thought to myself. I had no idea how much he'd seen in the staff room and at that moment it felt like he was undressing me with his eyes.

'There're going to be some changes around here. Everyone's output is going to be subject to review, it's a case of toe the line or get out.' He paused to chuckle at his cheesy metaphor.

'Which brings me to my first point, you should remember that personal emails are to be kept to a minimum. Perhaps you could send out a reminder of this to all staff, I know you are familiar with the process of sending out an email to multiple recipients.' He gave me a coy grin as he said this.

Confused, I responded, 'Yes, sir.' *Really eloquent today Jenny.*

'And I'd like to get up to scratch with everything that's been happening as quickly as possible. So, I'd like the minutes from today's meeting to be typed up in the next hour so I can review what was discussed.'

'Yes, Sir. About the minutes, I...'

'I'm sure you're more than capable,' he said while drumming a pen on his desk. 'You've got lots to be getting on with so I won't take up any more of your morning.'

He stood up and ushered me over to the door. As he held it open for me he reached out and engulfed my hand in his, giving it another good firm shake. My skin zinged from his unexpected touch.

He continued to hold my hand as he said, 'I've got a good feeling about working here. I think we'll make a good team.'

Warmth spread up from his strong grip as he gave me a final squeeze and then let me go. I could feel my cheeks pink up as I squeezed past him, inhaling the scent of cedar and mint as I brushed against his immaculately tailored suit. I sighed at the thought of what might be underneath; he was tall and built like a swimmer, all lean with broad shoulders.

As I headed back to my desk I did my best to repress the memory of babbling on at him about my underwear; if I didn't think about it, it didn't happen. Focusing instead on the bubble of excitement I could feel expanding inside me. A new face may shake things up around the place, and what a lovely new face it was too.

An image of my ex flashed through my mind briefly and I considered how different he was to James. It had been one year, three hundred days and two hours since he had broken my heart and left me. I pushed all thoughts of him aside, and repeated to myself, *I deserve better than that.* I wondered if maybe, just maybe, Mr Henson might help me move on. Smart, motivated, extremely handsome; perhaps the polar opposite to James. In fact, he's exactly what I've been looking for. It had been nearly two years and despite my best efforts, I hadn't managed to find someone else. As he was my senior, I was fully aware that absolutely nothing would happen between me and Mr Henson, but a girl can dream.

Pete caught my eye and mouthed, 'Everything alright?' across the office.

'Yes,' I mouthed with a big goofy smile, and tried to beckon him over by waggling my eyebrows.

'You seem more upbeat, I think I know what's put a spring in your step!' he said when he arrived.

'I've met our new boss, he seems...like a good addition,' I said, picking my words carefully. Then lowering my voice, I added, 'I totally embarrassed myself earlier but he was so nice about it.'

'He was totally flirting with you! I was watching him fawn over you as you walked out the office,' Pete told me, leaning in, his eyes dancing. 'You must have done something right, he seemed a bit stern to me. Grilled me about everyone working here. Gave a speech about things changing and that he ran a tight ship and such. He likes a metaphor that one.'

'No, he seemed lovely. He had some suggestions for me, but nothing that I can't handle. I've done half of it already.'

A flicker of panic passed over me, *I had sent the minutes, hadn't I?* I checked my outbox. Yes, I had. And there below it was my email to my mum, with the words "send to all contacts" written in the recipients' column. A feeling of sickness passed over me. No need for Natalia to embarrass me when I'm quite capable of humiliating myself.

I looked at Pete and pretended to bury my head in my hands.

'Oh, don't you worry about that email; we've all done something like that before. Natalia once sent out her online order of diet pills to the whole office, it's easily done.'

I stifled a snigger, not wanting to draw any more attention to myself.

Everything Mr Henson had said to me suddenly made sense. 'Now I know what he was talking about, I've made such a prat of myself.'

'No, you haven't and anyway, you're one of the best workers we've got here; he'll soon see that.'

'I best get back to work and try and leave the new boss with a good third impression before I go off on holiday.'

Pete laughed and said, 'Absolutely, the first and second ones are overrated. Now, you have a fab time, darling, and we'll do lunch when you're back, yeah?'

'Looking forward to it already,' I said, truthfully.

He gave me a big hug before he headed back to his desk.

A message pinged up on my phone and I smiled when I saw it was from Kirsty.

YO! HEAD BRIDESMAID, ARE YOU READY TO PARRRRRTY?! K X

She's a bit bonkers but I love her. We've been best friends since we met in secondary school and bonded over our mutual love for a too embarrassing to mention boyband and us both having a mortal fear of sewing machines and other textile related equipment. We've been pretty inseparable ever since. Not wanting to miss a chance to wind her up, I fired back:

There's no need to shout. Now, what's all this about a bridesmaid and partying? Is someone getting married? I was planning a quiet weekend doing some knitting, did you have something else in mind? Xx

EEEEEEP! NOW I KNOW YOU'RE JOKING, YOU CAN'T KNIT FOR SH!#. HEN DOOOOO WOOP WOOP! XXXXXXXXXXXX

Chuckling to myself, I tossed my phone aside and then turned my attention back to work. Diligently ploughing through the rest of the to-do list so I didn't implode with excitement. With great satisfaction, I set my email auto-reply to say that I would be out of the office and then strode out, only glancing back to wave at Pete.

As I passed the security desk in the foyer I got a little cheer from Stan and Bill. Rolling my eyes, I gave them a mini bow like an actress at the end of her performance, figuring that getting all flustered about it would only keep them entertained longer. I bumped in to Mr Henson again as I got to the doors.

'Miss George,' he said by way of greeting, nodding slightly to me. His smouldering gaze locked on to mine.

'Hello, Mr Henson.' I struggled not to seem

overwhelmed by his powerful good looks as I scurried by. The heat from his stare followed me as I walked away.

CHAPTER 3

'**P**ut your foot down!' yelled Kirsty, as her
fiancé Steve weaved in and out of the
traffic.

I'd gone over to their place to get a lift to
the airport and when I'd arrived I'd found that
Kirsty hadn't even finished packing. She was just
stood surrounded by all her clothes, wearing a
sun dress, a denim jacket and a big floppy hat.
Arguing with her over what she did or didn't
need had slowed us down further, so I let her
pack everything in an effort to get her and her
giant suitcase in the car.

Now we were on our way. Kirsty wound down
the window and gave a loud, 'Woop woop!' as we
sped down the road.

Kirsty and Steve have been together since
college. He's just like a brother to me, so I've
never felt like a third wheel which makes a
refreshing change. Being single and hanging out
with friends that are couples isn't always so

comfortable.

'Now, Jenny,' Steve announced, 'I want you to take good care of my Kirsty and bring her back in one piece, you hear?'

I could see a mischievous grin on his face in the rear-view mirror.

'Absolutely, Steve, she's safe with me.'

'Errr, thanks *Dad*,' retorted Kirsty, 'you two can talk about me as if I'm not here if you want.'

'And don't do anything I wouldn't do,' added Steve.

I struggled to stifle a laugh. 'We both know that there's not much you won't do, Steve.'

'Oh yeah,' said Steve, laughing along. 'In that case then, Kirsty, I think you're in trouble.'

'Just pull it,' Kirsty groaned at me.

We were slap bang in the middle of the check in area, she was perched precariously on her bulging suitcase as I desperately strained to zip it up.

'I think...you need...to take...something out...' I grunted and panted as I continued to heave.

'Absolutely not, I need to be prepared for all eventualities. You haven't told me what to expect or what we're doing or anything,' said Kirsty.

'You're the one who gave me a list of people and said "*Let's get some sun, I don't want to know anything else*"!' I retorted as I considered bracing myself with my foot up on the case, like they do in films. 'I think trying to fit that hat in is the last straw.'

With a sudden ripping sound, the case relented and zipped up.

'Oh no, my suitcase!' wailed Kirsty.

With a snort, I informed her that it wasn't her suitcase ripping that we'd heard, and then, for dramatic effect, spun round and stuck my bum out to show her the giant tear down the seam of my jeans. Kirsty let out one yelp of laughter and then whipped her jacket off and tied it round my waist before I could blink.

'That'll stop you getting chilly while we sort out your wardrobe malfunction.'

We both got the giggles as we tried to salvage my decency.

'I'll lend you some of my jeans, they'll look better on you than me anyway,' said Kirsty. Then with a nervous chuckle she added, 'They're in… the *case*!' She erupted into hysterics and we both had to hold our ribs we were laughing so hard.

'Might make it easier to *close*!' I managed to say, as another wave of laughter rolled over us.

Kirsty is about the same size as me, but she has a brunette bob in contrast to my blonde curls. I quickly nipped to the ladies' toilet to change into her jeans. She was taking three other spare pairs as well, *just in case*. The suitcase had closed a little easier this time, to Kirsty's chagrin.

As I came back, I could see Kirsty had the hat back on her head again. I managed to suppress a growl when she told me she'd decided to keep it out of the case so it wouldn't get squashed. We checked our cases in and Kirsty did her best to smile sweetly at the airline staff so she didn't need to pay the excess luggage fee.

'What have you got in your case, Jen?' she asked. 'Yours is almost over the limit and you normally pack so lightly.'

'Just you wait,' I answered mysteriously. 'There're no clothes in there, just things for you. Some people may call them surprises but I like to think of it as being chocka-block full of blackmail material!'

'Oh don't!' she said laughing, and we headed over to security.

We went through and dutifully got our liquids and electronics out and removing shoes, anything metal and of course the big floppy hat for the security scanners. I briefly wondered why I bothered getting fully dressed before we arrived.

We made our way to the back of the departures area, towards the airport bar.

'Your first mission, should you choose to accept it, is to pick a drink at the bar, but it has to begin with K.'

'I love this already.' She gave me a squeeze. 'Kir Royale, please,' she sung to the barman with excitement.

'Make that two, please,' I said and handed over the money. 'To Kir-sty Royale!' I toasted her as she grinned.

We didn't have to wait long until the rest of the hens joined us. First to arrive was Suze, Kirsty's best friend from work. We've been out several times together since her divorce. She's slightly older than us but don't read that as her being more mature, she's a lot of fun.

'Love the new hair, Suze,' I said as I hugged her. It's different every time I see her. On this occasion it was looking distinctly Cruella de Vil-ish, jet black with a white stripe and fringe.

'Hiya girls,' she cooed, 'on the cocktails already? I'll join you, let's start as we mean to go on!'

'I'm so glad you could come,' said Kirsty. 'I'm surprised work let us both take the time off.'

'I told them I had to have the time off too, so I could make sure you came back safely.'

'You're not the first person to worry about this,' said Kirsty.

We chuckled and nattered together, sipping our cocktails and waiting for the rest of the group to arrive.

Next tottered in Kirsty's little sister, Jade. I like to think of Jade as my little sister too, I'm an only child so she's the closest thing I've got. She's Kirsty's doppelganger, but her style really sets them apart, that and she's almost ten years younger. Jade has a unique look and firmly believes no one should hide away. She's the only person I know who can get away with wearing double denim and still look gorgeous.

Jade's a bridesmaid too, however, as organising is virtually my middle name, Kirsty decided I should be head bridesmaid. Plus, Jade had only recently started going to university, so it may have been a little overwhelming for her. I didn't mind at all, it was such an honour and luckily Kirsty wasn't a bridezilla.

'Love the heels, Jade,' Kirsty and I chimed in unison.

They were absolutely killer black patent stilettos, at least five inches high and they went beautifully with the forest green jumpsuit she was wearing. We caught sight of a glimmer of red sole and Kirsty grabbed at her ankle, causing Jade to sit down rather abruptly. Thank goodness there was a stool right there.

'They *are not* Louboutins, Jade, tell me they're not?' Kirsty's eyes were wide.

'Well...' hesitated Jade.

'What did you do? Spend all your student loan? Mum's gonna freak out!' Kirsty promptly downed her drink.

'Of course they're not, K, I'm a *student*. I painted the bottoms to make them seem like Louboutins, all the fashion students have done it,' gasped Jade, exasperated.

'You had my heart pounding then, Jade. Now get us both a drink to make up for it, you made me waste my last one in a fit of panic.' Kirsty made her demands with a cheeky smile on her face. 'I could really get used to being chief Hen.'

At that moment, the last two in our little party arrived, Beth and Annie, the glamorous city girls. Once the shrieks of excitement died down there were hugs all round and introductions to Suze. Beth kept coming back for seconds and thirds of hugs, she pulled me into a tight embrace, her long wavy hair tickled my cheek.

'You okay, Beth?' I asked. She isn't usually so affectionate.

'All the better for seeing you, chick,' she replied. Her big green eyes staring deeply into mine.

I gave her a tighter squeeze and thought, *Something's wrong.* I couldn't ask her there and then so I decided to press her more later.

'Thanks so much for coming,' said Kirsty. 'It's been too long since we all got together.'

'You guys need to come out in London again soon, don't they Beth?' said Annie.

Beth nodded quietly and Annie made a face as if to say that she had been nodding quietly a lot recently. The four of us used to be inseparable, but since Annie and Beth moved to London for university and then never left, we don't see as much of each other as we'd like.

After rallying the girls' attention, I announced the first of the hen games was to only drink things beginning with letters from Kirsty's name, there were six days so it was a letter a day. Penalties would be severe. Helping Jade get the next round in, we chose Kahlua and Coke for everyone and brought six brimming high ball glasses back to the table. As we sat around chatting, laughing and sipping our cocktails, I took a moment to drink in the wonderful feeling of contentment you get when you are with good friends and loved ones.

Annie patted her afro checking its shape and then gave a little cough to get everyone's attention. 'Our flight boards in ten minutes, ladies,' she announced. 'Now, before we go and raid duty free for a last minute spritz of perfume, there's something we have to do...' As Annie was speaking Kirsty looked nervous. 'And that's *take a selfie!*' cried out Annie, pulling a selfie stick out of her oversized handbag.

We cheered and goofed around posing for photos, with her phone extended out on the silver pole in front of us. The barman offered to take a nice one for us but we politely declined, this way was much more fun.

We eventually arrived at the boarding gate, but suddenly there was a squeal from Kirsty, 'Has anyone seen my hat?'

'It's probably back at the bar,' said Annie. 'I think I saw it on a chair.'

Kirsty teetered as she moved to go back and get it.

'I'll go, please can the rest of you make sure Kirsty gets on board okay? Don't let them leave without me,' I called over my shoulder while I headed in the opposite direction from the plane.

The barman gave me a knowing smirk when he handed it over, having picked it up from under our table a moment before.

As I headed back I shouted out, 'Thanks.' The giant hat flapped as I ran.

I was the last person through the gate. Bounding down the rickety air-walk, I skidded to a halt at the entrance to the plane. I smiled to the air-hostess on board and took a deep breath to compose myself. Then I tried to glide elegantly on to the plane and find my seat. As elegantly as anyone can look when they are bright red, sweating and toting a huge floppy hat. Suze's black and white barnet caught my eye and then I saw Kirsty and Annie waving. Holding my head high I aimed for them, deliberately avoiding any eye contact with my fellow passengers. I hate being centre of attention and the hat was certainly eye catching.

Tossing Kirsty her salvaged hat, I flumped down in my seat between Beth and Jade.

'You missed the hottest guy in the queue at the boarding gate,' whispered Annie as she leaned over from her seat in front.

'Yes, he was yummy,' giggled Kirsty.

While Suze, who had swivelled around as well, piped up, 'I wouldn't say no.'

The air-hostess walked past checking seat belts and then begun the safety briefing. Being responsible, I reached down to my handbag to turn my phone off for the flight. As I pressed the power button on the top, I noticed a missed call from Pete. I wondered if he'd come up with some more recommendations of places to go near our resort, I figured I'd message him when we got into the apartment's Wi-Fi. Sitting back in my chair (with it in an upright position and the tray table stowed) I took a deep breath, relieved that we had all made it this far on the hen do in one piece. It was no mean feat organising six ladies.

Seizing the moment of quiet, I turned to Beth to ask her if she was okay. Her eyes flicked to Jade, who was sat quietly next to me, and she gave an almost imperceptible shake of her head before insisting that everything's fine.

Sensing I needed to change the subject quickly I asked, 'So where's this hottie?'

Craning their necks, the girls couldn't see him from our seats. We decided to keep our eyes peeled for him when we landed.

It was an uneventful flight and soon the captain was announcing our arrival in Malaga. While plodding along following the stream of passengers, I wrestled the taxi information out of my binder. I'd picked up Kirsty's forgotten hat again so I was struggling with my hands full when Annie nudged me hard in the ribs.

'It's the hottie,' she mumbled through a shut mouth.

'Huh? Where?' I glanced up.

'You missed him again. I can't believe you're

still toting that folder around everywhere.' Annie rolled her eyes.

My organiser was a simple A4 folder, but it was brimming with information about everything I had planned; my life was in those pages and I don't know what I'd do without it. I clutched it protectively.

'Hey, I gave her that!' said Kirsty. She looked fondly at the cute red cartoon elephant printed on the front. 'Doesn't it remind you of Jenny?'

'Well, they say elephants never forget,' said Suze, 'and that's true for you too, you're bloody good at organising things.'

'Thanks, you're always so thoughtful, Suze, but I think Kirsty was implying that I have all the grace of a blundering elephant.'

'I think you're both pretty accurate,' replied Annie and everyone chuckled. Everyone except Beth, who remained quiet and subdued.

A glass wall divided the arrivals gate from the outside world. Seeing the taxi queue on the other side, I was relieved I'd pre-booked something. While we waited for our luggage I dialled the taxi company and, in my very bad Spanish, let them know we'd arrived.

'I didn't know you spoke Spanish,' said Kirsty.

'I don't, I tried to learn as much as I could before we came away, but I'm not very good.'

'Well, you're better than the rest of us.'

Feeling the pressure of being in charge, and not wanting anything to go wrong, I had confirmed all the bookings for the trip at least once. I wanted to make sure they knew we were a hen party too, as I'd heard horror stories of people being turned away once the terms "hen" or "stag" were mentioned.

As we walked through the arrivals door I could see a friendly looking, shortish man, possibly in his sixties, with deep lines creasing his face. He was holding a hand-written poster saying *Kristy and the chickens.*

'Here's our ride, girlies,' I announced.

I gave our chauffeur a warm smile and went in for a handshake. He had other ideas and went for the continental double cheek kisses, which led to a rather awkward half embrace.

Our driver was called Antonio, and I found out a lot about him on that journey. The girls had decided I should be the one to sit in the front with him.

'You speak the most Spanish,' they'd all argued.

He had a minibus so managed to fit us and all our luggage in quite comfortably. I normally avoid sitting in the front of a taxi, it's a strange phobia of mine, it makes me feel weirdly uncomfortable making small talk with a complete stranger, this is probably why I suck at dating too.

This, however, was an interesting journey. He haired around the bumpy roads and took roundabouts without either slowing or checking for other drivers, yet all the while kept up a gentle chatter in pretty good English, and politely tolerated my terrible Spanish. The girls were looking a bit green from being thrown around in the back so I was quite pleased with my spot up front.

Big white letters spelled out the name of our destination, Marencanto, on a roundabout. Antonio swung the minibus around it, taking the last exit, and after a minute pulled into the carpark of our resort complex. From my research, I knew this was a sprawling hotchpotch with everything from self-catering holiday lets, basic hotel accommodation to fully serviced penthouse apartments. It had a pool, a bar and was only a stone's throw from the beach, absolutely perfect for what we needed.

Antonio was so lovely he insisted I take his home number in case we had any problems, he said we seemed like nice girls. I didn't know whether to be flattered that he wanted to take us under his wing or worried about what possible trouble he envisaged us getting in to.

Later, I decided that Antonio must have had some sort of prophetic power.

CHAPTER 4

O nce we had checked in at reception, I entrusted Jade with keeping Kirsty well hydrated at the bar. They sat under one of the many leafy palms that were dotted everywhere, while Suze, Annie, Beth and I blitzed the apartment. We strung bunting between the light fittings in the living room and above the French doors to the balcony, we then framed this with some bunches of balloons and streamers. To avoid the risk of this being confused with a classy affair we fixed up a giant 'pin the cucumber on the hunk' poster on the door, I'd blown up a photo of Steve's head and stuck this on top. My photo printing skills had also been put to use gathering some embarrassing photos of Kirsty with us all over the years, so we placed these around too. Then we piled up her gifts by one of the armchairs and laid a sash and veil out to dress her up with.

Annie held up a packet of willy confetti and

said, 'Anywhere in particular you want this, or should I throw it around... *willy-nilly?!*'

I groaned at the pun as she cackled and flung it around liberally. I instantly regretted that purchase, thinking of the cleaning up I'd have to do when we left.

'It looks like we've set off some sort of hen do bomb,' commented Annie as we admired our handy work.

'I wanted to make this trip classy and demure, but Kirsty would hate that.'

'Yep, some silly fun is perfect for her,' replied Annie.

'This place looks great,' said Suze, 'You've done a great job.'

Suze and Annie wandered through the open plan living area and out onto the balcony. The smell of baked terracotta wafted through from outside as I put away the shopping I'd pre-ordered in the kitchenette. To avoid too much washing up I had bought some willy adorned paper plates, cups and napkins. The piece-de-resistance for any hen do, the willy straws, were located and finally we were ready. For a while after I was sure that every time I blinked I could still see willies.

The girls were lying on a couple of sun loungers, the balcony was so big it had space for one each as well as a dining table. Our view looked out to the sea.

'Don't you want to choose your rooms?' I asked

and they scrambled up to explore the rest of the apartment.

There was a double bedroom with an en-suite and two twins plus two more bathrooms. We decided to give Kirsty and Jade the double, and giggled as we set about blowing up an inflatable man to greet her in bed. Suze and I stashed our stuff in one twin room and Beth and Annie bagsied the other.

The four of us joined Kirsty and Jade at the pool bar and I secretly switched Kirsty's next drink for a soft one. Jade had been thorough in her job and I didn't want Kirsty to peak too soon. We ordered some tapas to have with our drinks and sat there, soaking up the wonderful atmosphere. The sun had already set over the pool and we could hear cicadas singing in the grasses and the competing basses of a few nearby bars. It was still lovely and warm with only a slight salty breeze off the sea. Thinking of the breeze suddenly reminded me of Pete and his club. Having left my phone in the apartment, I made a mental note to contact him later. *Keep it together Jenny.* There was so much going through my head for the hen do I kept forgetting things.

Kirsty gazed hazily at me. Slurring her words, she said, 'Can I see the apartment now, pleeeeease?'

'Eeek!' the four of us yelped.

We were so carried away with enjoying the wonderful Spanish evening we'd quite forgotten about it. Poor Kirsty and Jade were still sat there with their cases. We merrily made our way back up, all helping to carry the bags.

We showed Kirsty in first, she stood in the centre of the living room and spun around and around, taking it all in.

Clapping her hands together she exclaimed, 'I loves it!' and hiccoughed.

Kirsty teetered and I managed to get her sitting in her armchair before she fell. We gathered around her and got her dressed in the special sash and veil.

She sat there absolutely beaming and loudly whispered, 'It's soooo tacky, I really love it.'

Kirsty was thrilled with the gifts we'd all given her. I bought her some of her favourite perfume and had made her a photo album of her life as a "single" lady with lots of memories of all our antics over the years, everyone wrote a little note in it too.

'Open my gifts next,' said Jade, bouncing with excitement.

Kirsty peeled back the paper of an oddly shaped packet and out fell some flip flops which left "Just Married" prints in the sand as you walk.

'These are fab,' exclaimed Kirsty.

'Well, they're hardly high fashion but I thought *you'd* like them,' replied Jade, with a cheeky twinkle in her eye.

'I'm taking that as a compliment,' said Kirsty. Jade grinned back at her, mischievously.

Kirsty then unwrapped a square shaped gift, as the paper fell away, a pocket guide to the Kama Sutra was revealed.

'What the?... oh no... not from my little sister!'

Jade doubled over in silent hysterics. She eventually spluttered out, 'I couldn't wait to see your face,' before creasing up again.

Kirsty remained stunned, while the rest of us giggled at her reaction. Kirsty struggled with the fact that Jade wasn't such a *little* sister anymore.

Annie grabbed the book and thumbed through it. 'I always wondered who on earth would have this ready in their pocket, you know, just in case the situation *arose*?'

I caught Kirsty's eye and she finally relented and fell about laughing with the rest of us.

When we'd all caught our breath, she opened another present, this time some luxurious silky wedding night undies from Beth and Annie. Finally, she opened Suze's gift. Peeling back the crisp, creamy, paper she found a recipe binder.

'Oh, thanks,' said Kirsty in what I knew was her "I hate it but need to be polite" voice.

'Open it,' said Suze, with a knowing look on her face.

Inside, instead of recipes, it had been preloaded with all the local take away menus and in a pocket at the back there was a voucher for a meal for two at Kirsty and Steve's local gastro-pub.

Kirsty grinned, relief evident on her face, 'Oh,

thanks! This is awesome, you know me so well.'

Suze replied, 'Well, it's no secret that you're ....'

'*A terrible cook!*' cut in Annie, Jade and me, all at once.

'Hey, I was going to say "still learning",' said Suze, kindly.

Kirsty batted at us with the binder and smiled warmly at Suze. 'It's perfect, thank you. I'm a terrible cook, but Steve loves me anyway.'

'Ahhhhhhhhh,' we all sighed.

'Right, before I chuck up my tapas, let's get the party started,' announced Annie, ever the romantic.

We'd all contributed to a playlist of tunes that remind us of good times with Kirsty, so we put it on and had a little dance in the living room. It became the soundtrack to the holiday. Kirsty really loved all the little hen do touches, I'm pretty sure she even went to sleep in her sash and veil.

CHAPTER 5

Despite a late night, I awoke feeling pretty good. We'd spent a lovely long evening dancing around and then fell exhausted on to the sun loungers and chatted on the balcony for hours. Nevertheless, there was plenty more catching up for us all to do; I hadn't got to the bottom of what was upsetting Beth and I hadn't shared my humiliating experiences at work either.

Once we'd all freshened up, I thought it would be fun to go and explore Marencanto a bit to help get our bearings. Never having been to Spain before, I couldn't wait to see some proper Spanish culture. We strode out in pairs looking very much like tourists, with me, Kirsty and her floppy hat leading at the front of the pack.

The day was already heating up but there was still a fresh zephyr in the air and we skipped across the cobble stones to walk in the sunny patches of the road. I loved the feeling of the warmth playing on my back. Rangy weeds grew out of cracks in the terracotta coloured walls and bougainvillea tumbled over the tops giving vibrant splashes of pink and purple along the way. The air was laced with orange blossoms and sea salt, I breathed in, content.

Our first stop was at a little chiringuito, a cosy, ramshackle, structure on the beach, which served us strong dark coffees and some fresh churros. I burnt my fingers as we dug into the sweet treats, hot from the fryer.

'This is the life!' said Kirsty, smiling.

We stood at the raised table and gazed out at the sea, the fishing boats were already out on the distant horizon, while the colourful floats and lines from the water sports company dipped as they were being strung out for the day. I couldn't quite believe we were finally there, after months of planning. The barman kept plying us with coffee and churros, claiming that we were good for trade but eventually we decided we had to move on, there was so much more to explore.

We ventured inland in search of the old town district, and as we plodded uphill we came across the old bullring.

'Poor bulls. I hate the idea of bull fighting,' I said.

'It doesn't look like they do it here anymore,' said Suze, staring up at the half-ruined shell of an old amphitheatre. 'Shall we pop in for a little look?'

It was unmanned and completely open to the public. We put some euros in a donation box and went in. Through a dark, dank smelling tunnel we emerged out into the piercing light, and, as our eyes adjusted, we could see the crumbling stands spanning up and away from us. We stood on the edge of the sandy ground, dwarfed by the towering ruin. The ancient architecture was stunning.

'Let's climb up to the top,' suggested Kirsty, and bounded eagerly upwards.

'Careful with your step there,' said Suze, as some dislodged stones skittered over the edge.

We climbed up through the stony remains, carefully sticking to the designated path and reached the very top.

'What a view,' said Kirsty, slightly breathless.

From here we could see out of the bullring and across to the beach and the sparkling bay beyond. Wandering around the edge to the other side we peered over and could see into the heart of Marencanto old town.

'Oh, something's going on down there. I wonder what's happening?' squealed Jade.

People were busy unloading trucks, erecting stalls and stringing up decorations. At one end of the square there was a stage being set up. We craned over the edge of the balustrades to get a good look.

'It looks like they're setting up for a fair,' said Annie.

'That sounds fun,' said Kirsty.

'There were posters for a *feria* in the street, this must be it. Let's go there next,' I suggested.

Everyone seemed excited by this plan, except for Beth who had been loitering at the back of the group. I tried to catch her eye to see if she was okay but she kept her head down. We took a few snaps of the spectacular view and of course Annie took an obligatory selfie.

We crossed back down to the bottom of the stalls and headed out through the opposite tunnel; the gaping black mouth which would have been the bull's entrance. It was damp and eerie underground, the grime from years of disuse was dripping from the ceiling. I was relieved when we emerged back out into the daylight.

'Where's Beth?' asked Annie and tutted.

'I'll go and find her,' I said, feeling responsible for everyone's welfare as I'd organised the trip. I was worried for my friend, she didn't seem herself.

I went back into the grim tunnel to look for her, trying to ignore the spooky feeling it gave me. My skin prickled and I shivered until I came back through into the daylight. I found her sat on an old, tumble-down wall, in the middle of the ring.

'You okay, Beth?' I asked, 'We're heading off now.'

She rose up and nodded with a weak smile.

'Seriously, Beth, what's wrong?' I asked again, but she didn't say anything as she moved slowly to the exit; I followed her back through the dark tunnel in silence.

Shuddering, the dank passageway gave me the creeps for a second time. A coldness crept over me and I wasn't sure if it was Beth's odd behaviour or the gloomy nature of the tunnel. When we emerged into the light Beth gave everyone a big grin and apologised.

The girls were all a flutter about a group of guys that had just walked past and were babbling like immature school girls.

'I think one was the guy from the airport again,' said Suze. 'It was hard to tell without that fine suit on.'

'He was hot,' said Kirsty.

'You're a taken lady!' protested Jade, laughing.

'I think the sun's getting to you lot, you're like dogs in heat!'

With everyone excited about the feria and the fine-looking men that had passed by, I didn't manage to speak to Beth any further. I berated myself for still not managing to talk to her.

We left the bullring and headed round to the old town where all the action was. There was a vibrant buzz in the air, some Spanish party tunes were pumping and there was a clang of scaffolding as the last of the stalls were being set up. Several hunky men were swaggering around in ripped jeans and slightly grimy white vests, muscles rippling.

Strolling in and out the maze of stalls, we sampled some local delicacies. I ate about half a ton of caramelised almonds, they were so sweet and moreish. I was addicted. Kirsty cut me off from my supplier, a toothless pensioner, when I was about to go back for my third box.

'It's for your own good, J!' she scolded me, and laughed as she dragged me away.

The sun was heating up, so we got some cool drinks from a bar on the edge of the square, right by the stage. Watching all the bustling around, we soaked up the atmosphere. The barman insisted we all come back later that evening, telling us that's when the party really got going.

Despite the heat, a couple walked proudly on to the stage dressed from head to toe in black and red, the man wore a suit and the lady was in a magnificent flowing gown. The music stopped and they began rhythmically clapping their hands in the air and stamping their feet. Before we knew it, we were treated to an up close and personal flamenco dance; the dress rehearsal for their performance tonight. It was poised yet passionate, almost hypnotic. We whooped and hollered when they finished and they turned to bow to us at the bar. The couple beckoned to us and before we knew it, they were giving us our own flamenco masterclass.

Kirsty pulled me up on stage as I was reluctant to make a fool of myself so early in the day.

Despite my regular mishaps, I'm not comfortable making a spectacle of myself. They showed us some basic steps and some of the intricate handwork the ladies do. The gathering audience made me nervous but, Jade, as confident as ever, shone out as she strutted her stuff, she was a natural. Kirsty seemed to love it too. We got a big applause at the end but I couldn't wait to get off the stage and go and have a large drink.

After calming my nerves and quenching my thirst, we spent the rest of the day exploring Marencanto, only briefly returning to our hotel to get changed before heading back to our bar on the main square. We were ready for a cocktail or two.

CHAPTER 6

In the evening, the site of the feria looked completely different. The dark sky enhanced the bright lights of the rides, which blinked and flashed; there was a radiant display of colours, even when I shut my eyes I could see them; the neon scorched on my retinas. The sweet smell of caramelised nuts and candy floss mingled with the sickly smell of fried food, a delectable combination only found at fairs and carnivals.

Our bar hosted tables that spilled out onto the pavement and we chose one of these to sip our drinks and soak up the atmosphere. A procession of floats and dancers waltzed through and we started to bob in our seats.

'Let's join in!' said Kirsty, as she bounced up and down in time with music.

We finished our drinks and stood up, getting swept along with the crowd dancing in the street.

'Look at those rides, let's do the bumper cars,' squealed Jade.

So, with the hyper excited sisters leading the way we hit the rides. First, the bumper cars shunted us side to side. Then the teacups whirled us around and around, followed by a crazy octopus one that flipped and flung us upside down. I have no idea what "scream if you want to go faster" is in Spanish but I think me yelling out "Noooooooo!" was giving mixed signals. We were whipped into a frenzy and when we finally got off, I all but staggered back to the bar for a much-needed cocktail.

Before we knew it, the flamenco dancers were back on the stage. I clung to the bar trying to regain my equilibrium but watching them weave around each other was not helping. Then my worst fears came true. After their rousing performance, they signalled for all the crowd to join in, beckoning our group up on to the stage again. Still woozy, I desperately wanted to decline.

'Come on,' yelled Jade, eager to get in the spotlight.

'You guys go, I'll watch from here.'

'Don't be daft,' said Kirsty. 'You'll be fine once we get going.'

'If I can do it, you can,' encouraged Suze.

'I'm not nervous,' I protested, 'I'm just feeling really...'

They never found out how I was feeling,

because, despite my objections, Annie somehow managed to pull me up on the stage and I found myself at the front next to Kirsty. I tried to follow along with the moves but it was a struggle. The flashing lights were spinning, the rides were weaving, the audience was rocking, and I was pitching forward. I was doing my best to keep up and keep myself steady but with a lurch I suddenly found myself tripping. I tumbled over the edge of the stage. Falling. I shut my eyes expecting to crash, but instead of landing in a painful heap, some strong arms caught me, softening the blow considerably. The forceful collision took us down to the ground but my landing was definitely more comfortable than I'd been expecting.

I opened my eyes, but shut them again quickly. Saying that I felt dizzy would be an understatement. There seemed to be not one, but three crazy octopus rides spinning above me, that's far too many tentacles. Lying on my back, I cautiously blinked. Six eyes were twinkling over me, the bright lights shining off them, three mouths moved and a slurring noise came out. I squeezed my eyes closed.

With a zipping noise my hearing snapped back to normal and I could hear a babble of Spanish voices sounding concerned. Risking opening my eyes again, I found there was just one of everything, but it was very blurry. Kirsty, Suze, the flamenco guy and a couple paramedics were craning over me. I sat up to try and see who had saved me, but they pushed me back down. Kirsty grabbed my hand and shoved her face in front of mine.

'You okay, J?'

'What's going on?'

'Well... You kinda fell off the stage. They're checking you're okay. Are you okay?'

'I think I'm fine.' It hit me. 'But this is...this is mortifying!'

'Don't worry,' she called as she was bustled away to give the paramedics more room. They sat me up and my blood pressure was taken while I was prodded all over. Then I had to remember my Spanish numbers and answer how many fingers were being held up. It was declared that I didn't have concussion, I was just extremely dizzy from all the rides and then the dancing; the paramedics advised me not to drink anymore and said to take it easy. Carefully, I stood up, and as I'd managed not to swoon, I attempted to take a couple of steps. I was absolutely fine. Except for the scald of humiliation, which was sizzling my cheeks.

The flamenco man came up to me and gave me a triple cheek kiss, and then, as I walked shyly in to the bar, I got a cheer and a high five from the barman, which made me laugh, easing my awkwardness immensely. There was no sign of my saviour anywhere and I wasn't sure how that made me feel. I wanted to apologise and thank him, but equally, I was so embarrassed it was a relief I didn't have to see him again.

'I'm so sorry, but I've been told to take it easy. No more drinking for me tonight I'm afraid,' I said to the hens.

'Don't worry,' said Kirsty, 'we're just glad you're okay.'

'But I'm ruining your night,' I replied, feeling truly awful.

'No, you're not. The barman keeps giving us free drinks 'cos of what happened to you. I think he's trying to calm our nerves,' explained Suze, full of glee.

'Let's have one more here and then head back,' said Kirsty.

'Let's make yours a water though,' suggested Annie, smirking.

'Sorry you're having to cut your night short because of me.'

'Stop worrying, it's no problem. I'm just happy having fun with you lot, it doesn't matter where we are.' Kirsty reassured me while the others agreed.

'Okay,' I said and smiled at the group.

They all enjoyed reliving their version of events to me, repeatedly. The stage looming up in the square right by our bar was a constant and unwanted reminder of the incident.

'I can't believe I fell off the *stage*!' I laughed, 'I'm such a dick!'

'Yeah, but you're our dick,' said Annie, warmly.

'Did you see who I landed on?'

They shook their heads.

'It was quite hard to see down into the crowd with all the lights pointing at the stage,' explained Jade.

'All I could see was you flat on your back on top of someone, your dress had flapped over their face,' said Annie. Seeing me look aghast she hastily added, 'Don't worry, no one could see your knickers!'

'By the time I'd climbed off the back of the stage and run around to the front he'd been led off by some other paramedics, I think,' said Kirsty.

'I should go and look for him,' I said, standing up.

'I already checked with them,' replied Suze. 'He'd already left. There was no sign of him.'

'Oh no, what if I've given *him* concussion?' I said, burying my head in my hands.

The barman came over and offered us more free drinks but we declined, worried we'd probably send the poor guy out of business.

Jade asked him, 'Did you see who caught Jenny?'

'Si, si!' He nodded and glanced around. 'I can't see him now though.'

'What did he look like?' I asked, feeling excited.

'English.'

'No really, what did he look like?' I begged.

'English!' repeated the barman then laughed again. 'He must have left with his friends.'

'What if he's had to go to hospital?!' I said, getting worried again.

'Non! I saw him after, he was fine!' The barman grasped my shoulders in a friendly shake, 'Vale?' he asked if I was okay.

'Vale!' I replied, relieved I hadn't hospitalised anyone yet.

The barman grinned at us and then called out, 'Vale!' again, as he headed back behind the bar.

We meandered back through the old town and passed the even spookier seeming bullring, heading back to our apartment. The streets away from the feria were quiet, in stark contrast to the lively old town square. It had got quite late so we headed straight to bed. I checked my phone before going to sleep and cursed as I had another missed call from Pete, the poor guy, I still hadn't managed to get in contact with him. That was the top of my list for tomorrow I thought and then smiled to myself about the surprise I had in store for Kirsty.

CHAPTER 7

I boiled the kettle to make coffees all round and did a quick clean-up of the apartment, getting rid of empty bottles and paper cups from the night before. My phone was charging and I heard the bleep of a new message coming in. When I walked over to check it I remembered that I still hadn't got in touch with Pete.

The text was a confirmation message for today's plans. I grinned as I consulted my organiser to double check the arrangements. Wrapped up in thoughts of the day ahead, I forgot about contacting Pete as I placed everyone's hot drinks on a tray.

Delivering the steaming mugs to my friends, I issued strict instructions that they only had forty-five minutes to get ready.

Passing the balcony door, I could see Beth perched on the edge of a sun lounger. She was alone so I seized the chance to chat with her.

'How are you feeling, chica? I'm worried about

you.'

'Don't be silly. I'm fine,' she replied, curtly.

'No, Beth, I'm not brushing over this anymore. Things haven't been right all holiday. Not since you arrived at the airport. I'm not taking no for an answer!'

Beth looked at the floor intensely, then after a few seconds, she took a deep breath and said, 'Oh Jenny, it's all gone wrong.'

'What's happened?' I asked gently. We sat shoulder to shoulder, clutching our cups of coffee, and she revealed everything.

'I've been made redundant.'

'You can get another job,' I tried to console her.

'Not in a law firm like that, those positions are like gold dust.'

'You could do so much with your legal knowledge. It'll be okay in the end.'

'It's not just that, there's other stuff too.'

'Sorry, you talk, I'll listen.'

'I can't afford my flat anymore, not without my previous income. I was stretching myself anyway.'

'What about Craig? He pays the rent too, can't he...' Beth shot me a glare which told me to hush.

'Craig's left me. We had a stinking row and it turns out he was only interested in me for my legal connections and pursuing his own career. What a jerk. So, I phoned mum to tell her and ask if I could go and stay for a bit...' Beth paused.

'What did she say?'

'I didn't actually tell her in the end. She was already really upset and said she was about to call me because...' Beth sniffed loudly. '...Because my grandma's really ill. Like, seriously ill.'

Tears silently flooded down her face and my heart reeled for my friend's anguish. I didn't have any words that were good enough so I simply hugged her close, feeling useless.

Eventually I said, 'What can I do to help?'

'Nothing,' she said flatly.

'Have you told anyone else all this?'

'No, you're the first person. I only found it all out myself three days ago and I'm still trying to get my head around it, plus, I didn't want to ruin this for Kirsty.'

'You should've said sooner, you wouldn't be ruining anything,' I said, desperate to reassure her. 'We're all here for you, and any one of those things is too much to deal with on your own, let alone all of it. Seriously, what can we do to help?'

'Don't say anything to anyone, promise me,' she suddenly demanded.

'But...'

'Promise me, Jenny. You asked what you can do to help and that's it,' she snapped at me, her green eyes flashing as she scowled.

Bewildered, I hastily agreed. Beth wiped her face and turned to me, pasting on a smile.

'Good. I'm just gonna have a shower,' she said as she skipped through the balcony door and into the apartment.

Stunned, I sat there, not knowing what to make of it all.

My phone bleeped again, signalling that my surprise for Kirsty and the girls was about to commence. I called everyone into the sitting room and announced that I had a game for Kirsty to play. We sat round in a circle and I blindfolded the chief hen.

'For the next hen game, you have to guess what these different objects are, no peeking! You have to do a shot for every one you get wrong.'

'Oh, hello,' said Kirsty cheekily, as she fondled a banana.

I left her to work through a variety of other phallic shaped household items, while the other girls sat around laughing, and I slipped out to the front door. I opened it up to greet the visitor but my hello got stuck in my throat. *Oh my goodness!* This was not what I was expecting.

In front of me stood a six-and-a-half-foot tall roman warrior. He was wearing nothing but a helmet with a strip of red feathers across the top, a pair of knee-high, laced, sandals and what can only be described as a pleated leather skirt. And nothing else. Nothing. Not a stitch.

'Huh…' I managed to get out.

'Hola, Señorita!'

'Wh…who…what are you?'

'I am your Roman in the Raw!'

'What? This is not what I organised!' I hissed trying to keep my voice down so the girls wouldn't hear me.

'Si, Si, you are Jenny, non?'

'Yes, but I made a booking for a butler, *not* a Roman!'

'My butler costume got stolen last night, so now I'm your Roman. Now, where is the lucky lady?'

'Stolen?! Oh gosh...'

'Si, it was a crazy party last night. The ladies wouldn't give me my clothes back,' the Roman shrugged and smirked. 'It's all part of the job.'

I ushered the guy in and shut the door quickly, hoping none of the other people in the resort had seen. I could hear the game drawing to an end in the sitting room so I decided to roll with it. My plans for a hunky, semi-clad butler to serve us brunch were dashed, but at least the guy had turned up and hopefully Kirsty would see the funny side of it. Although, I did wonder what on earth would be in store for us if having your costume stolen, when near naked already, was merely "all in a day's work"?

The Roman towered over me in the narrow hallway. 'This is *not* okay,' I hissed. 'But I guess you'll have to do. Kirsty's the one in the blindfold. You need to attend to her every command and make us brunch please. Follow me and don't say anything just yet.'

I feared saying "please" probably ruined any

assertiveness I had, I really wasn't good at bossing people around. Putting a finger to my lips, I beckoned the Roman into the sitting area. There was a sharp intake of breath from the other girls as we walked in.

'There's one more thing you have to guess!' I called out to Kirsty.

What a picture, I wish I'd filmed it. Jade's eyes were popping out, Suze and Annie were desperately trying to suppress some giggles, hands clutched to their mouths. Even Beth had one eyebrow raised in an appreciative smirk. Maybe a Roman wasn't so bad after all.

I led the warrior to stand in front of Kirsty. 'Put your hands out and see if you can work out what this final object is.'

Under the blindfold, we could see that Kirsty's face was the picture of confused innocence, she had obviously heard a slight stir from the girls but had no idea. Hands stretched out in front of her she reached out for "the object" only to be met with the hard, smooth, ripples of the Roman's waxed body.

'Erm...' she said as she patted around, clearly bewildered. 'Eeeek!' she squealed as the guy shrieked loudly; she had found, and tweaked, a nipple.

We all spluttered with laughter unable to suppress our giggles.

'It's not Steve, is it?' asked Kirsty.

'Non, it's not Steeeeeve,' the Roman called out,

as he grabbed her hands and pulled her over to him.

When she was close enough he squeezed her hands onto his butt. Kirsty squealed again and wiggled her arms away so she could manically rip off her blindfold.

'Oh my... what the... *Jen*?!'

'Surprise!' I sung, giving my hands a little wave. 'So, I wanted to get you someone special to cook us a little brunch in the apartment, but he couldn't make it, so a Gladiator came instead.'

'You can call me Brutus,' called out the Roman as he scooped Kirsty up into his strong arms and twirled her around.

Brutus was a handful to say the least, not content with getting a grope of Kirsty, he paid everyone a lot of attention, kissing us on the lips, pinching our bottoms, I even caught him fondling Beth's boobs but she really didn't seem to mind. Try as I might I couldn't convince Brutus to cook us brunch, he was not the debonair waiter type I thought I'd booked. Instead, Suze and I knocked up some bacon butties and a fruit salad, while Brutus ran amuck.

Beth was getting very carried away, she even let him open some bottles of Cava by firing the corks onto her behind; I figured it was helping her to forget her woes at home. Any innocence that Jade had left after starting university had certainly been shattered. Kirsty was taking it all in her stride and giving as good as she got; she was clearly determined to embrace the full hen do experience. Annie, who had a fiancé herself, was enjoying watching the others lark around and was snapping some, hopefully never to be seen, candid photos.

The bacon butties and Cava were an amazing combo. I did my best to tuck in while Brutus leapt around me. He put a foot up on the back of my chair, his leg over my shoulder, and swiveled his hips, gyrating right in my face.

'Brutus, this isn't really what I had in mind.'

'You're no fun, Jenny. You need to loosen up,' he said as he suddenly spun around me and started enthusiastically rubbing my shoulders with his giant hands. I caught Kirsty's eye and made an *I'm sorry this really isn't what I planned* grimace, she gave me a big grin and a head shake back, letting me know that she was enjoying it nonetheless.

CHAPTER 8

There was no chance I was going to get Brutus to agree to the washing up either. He was having far too good a time, what with trying to corrupt Jade, and Beth fawning over him. So, I suggested that we play a game out on the balcony. Our gladiator tried to insist on strip poker but Suze threatened to throw our bag of ice over him if he made her do that, which stopped him in his tracks. I was pleased one of us could control him, this guy was loose. We ended up playing "clink and drink", which was revealing to say the least.

'Clink and drink if your name is Kirsty,' I said to get the game underway.

'Cheers!' said Kirsty, taking a swig from her Cava. 'Are you trying to get me drunk?'

'Maybe!'

We all chuckled and I gave her a wink.

'Clink and drink if you're getting married,' said Jade.

Kirsty and Annie clinked their glasses together and both took a sip.

Then Brutus said, 'Clink and drink if you've ever had a threesome...' He looked around, disappointed, as we all remained silent. He shrugged and took a big swig of his drink. 'I can arrange it if you want, Señoritas, I am here.'

'This has gone from zero to X-rated pretty darn quickly,' said Suze.

Getting the game back on track I called out, 'Clink and drink if you're English.' Us girls all bumped our glasses together and took a sip.

With a knowing glint in her eye, Annie said, 'Clink and drink if you've ever had sex in the college car park.'

Mortified, Kirsty exclaimed, 'Annie!' as she slapped the air in her general direction. She was about to take a sip, but she stopped suddenly as she caught Jade gingerly lifting up her glass. 'Nooooooo!' wailed Kirsty.

'Noooooo!' we all shouted gawping back and forth between them, as Jade's eyes bulged and nodded.

Kirsty screamed, 'Not my little sister!'

Not blinking, Jade gingerly nodded, and then visibly relaxed as Kirsty laughed and reached out to clink glasses. After they had taken their sips we demanded their stories.

'John Cook. After my English A-level. Bonnet of his red fiesta,' confessed Kirsty.

'Peter Green. Last night of the school play. On

the steps of the fire escape,' said Jade cagily. She hesitated and then added, 'and in the back seat of his car.'

We all gave a big, cheesy, teasing 'Whooooo-ooooo!'

'The Jones sisters - more alike than just in looks,' said Annie, laughing.

'I wonder what else you've got in common that you don't know yet?' asked Beth.

'No!' said Kirsty, 'we are *not* going there! My sister is still little and loves dolls, thank you very much. I don't need that illusion to be tarnished any further!'

Brutus was sat looking particularly entertained, he had a cheeky sparkle in his eye. A bit later, as our game carried on, we found out he was enjoying it a little too much. As he got up to go and get another bottle of Cava we could see his pleated leather skirt sticking out more prominently than it had before.

'Oh. My. God.' Annie mouthed. 'He totally has a boner!'

'Noooo,' whispered Suze and I, simultaneously.

Seeing this, Beth jumped at the opportunity to "help" him open the bottle. While she was bending over, Annie asked me quietly if I knew what had got into her. Not at all comfortable with lying, I tried to reassure her that everything was fine, all the while thinking that things seemed the very opposite of fine.

Our Roman didn't seem to have made any other plans and after three hours had gone by I hinted that it was time for him to go, but there was no shifting him. I found him completely odious and was desperate to get rid of him. He seemed very happy messing around with Beth. Kirsty seemed tired but clearly relieved that he was finally leaving Jade alone.

'I think I've had enough party games now,' she said. 'Shall we do something else?'

'Let's go down to the pool and chill out in the sun for a bit before we go out later,' I suggested. Staring pointedly at the Roman I said, 'I'm sure you're a busy man, Brutus we don't want to keep you from getting on with your day.'

This didn't get rid of him.

'I don't need to be anywhere, I'm having fun with you lovely Señoritas,' he replied.

'You don't have to go,' Beth said to him.

'Why don't you girls go and we can stay here and chill out on the balcony, we can join you later,' said Brutus with a naughty gleam in his eye.

Beth giggled. The rest of us were keen to get away from him so we agreed. Finally Beth seemed happy.

I managed to text Pete when I went to my room to get changed into my bikini.

Sorry I keep missing your calls, everything okay? Xx

I left my phone behind when I went down to the pool, not wanting to get it wet by accident, so I didn't see his reply.

I ordered a water from the bar to try and combat all the Cava we had consumed.

'Cava doesn't begin with 'R', Jenny, what's the forfeit?' said Jade, smugly.

Thinking on my feet, I quickly retorted, 'The winery's name does though, so I guess I'm in the clear.'

'Oh, she's good,' said Suze laying back on her sun lounger, as Jade rolled her eyes.

'You're scared of losing your own game,' Jade teased.

'I'm scared of an epic hangover and liver damage,' I replied and Jade laughed.

We all lay in a row and carried on bantering away happily. I slapped on some sun cream not wanting to burn and got Kirsty to do the bits I couldn't reach.

When I felt the water had counteracted the alcohol in my bloodstream I went for a gentle swim. The pool itself was empty although most of the sun loungers were occupied by people reading, sleeping and chatting. Self-consciously I dived into the water but, as the coolness engulfed me, and I got into the rhythm of breathing and swimming, I zoned it all out. I could feel the tension ooze out of every muscle. I hadn't realised quite how much stress I'd piled on myself. With each length, it felt like I was taking off one layer after another; an onion unpeeling.

Breathe in, breathe out. Stroke, stroke, stroke. Breathe in, breathe out. Stroke, stroke, stroke. The misery at work that The Witches had inflicted on me floated away. Breathe in, breathe out. Stroke, stroke, stroke. Embarrassing myself in front of my new boss drifted off into the distance. Breathe in, breathe out. Stroke, stroke, stroke. The loneliness I'd been feeling flowed freely away. Over the last few months I'd been getting really disappointed that I was perpetually single, wondering if I would ever find anyone; some people are happy one their own but I wasn't one of them.

The swim was cathartic. I reassured myself that I'd done all I could for my mum and I mentally sorted through the next few things I had in store for Kirsty and the girls. This wasn't a bad stress, but a pressure I'd put on myself for wanting everything to go well and worrying that everyone would enjoy it. The rhythmic movement helped me to organise my thoughts and I was happy with the next few plans. I had a little laugh when I thought of the unexpected *Roman in the Raw* who had appeared on the doorstep and how it had turned out alright in the end, even though it wasn't at all what I'd organised.

Laughing and swimming was a bad idea and I rapidly came out of my Zen-like state and spluttered over to the edge of the pool, the chlorine scorching my lungs. I looked over to our group and the four of them were happily chatting and sizzling in the sun. Thinking about the Roman made me realise that Beth and Brutus hadn't emerged. Now my mind was clear, I began to get worried. I gripped the edge of the pool and heaved myself out with water gushing everywhere. I splatted over to the girls.

'Jenny, you just missed him again,' said Kirsty as I arrived.

'Who? Brutus?'

'No, the hot guy. He must be staying here too.'

'He was yummy,' confirmed Suze, while Annie nodded.

'Not really my type; he's a bit old. But you can have him,' said Jade.

'Thanks very much, Jade, very kind of you. So where did he go? How have I *still* not seen him yet?!' I went up on my tip toes and peered all around but I was unable to see anyone in particular.

'It must be a sign, if he is staying here too,' said Suze, winking.

I wondered what the sign was that meant I kept missing him, but I kept my snarky comment to myself, there was a more pressing issue.

'Anyone heard from Beth?' I asked.

Everyone shook their heads dismissively.

No one was particularly impressed with her behaviour, but not knowing the full story as I did, they weren't worried, only a bit fed up.

'Do you think she's okay with that Brutus guy?' I asked.

'She's a big girl,' huffed Annie. 'I'm sure she'll be fine.'

Kirsty looked awkward, as if she was trying not to be annoyed with Beth for going off, but I could tell she was feeling a bit let down that the group had split up so soon. Jade seemed disappointed too, although I suspected it was more because she was overlooked by Brutus, than anything else.

I felt torn, I'd made a promise to Beth not to say anything, but her behaviour was clearly annoying the girls. I wanted to tell them that it was probably to try and make herself feel better after an avalanche of upset, or possibly even a cry for help. *Oh God, a cry for help*? That thought made me feel queasy.

'I'm getting worried about her, I'll head back up to the apartment to check she's okay. Meet you up there in a bit?' I suggested and walked off.

It was a good job I did.

CHAPTER 9

As I approached the apartment I could see the door was open, this was an ominous sign. We had definitely shut it behind us. A feeling of dread sunk deep into my stomach.

I drew closer. I could hear muffled voices and what sounded like sobbing.

Quickening my pace, I dashed through the hallway and into the lounge, following the sound.

The Roman was stood in front of the patio doors, wearing only his sandals, clutching his feathered helmet in front of his groin. His face was red and his muscles bulged as he shouted. Poor Beth, who was almost completely starkers, had had the presence of mind to try and drape Kirsty's Hen do sash strategically around her, she stood slightly away from him, tears glistening on her face. In front of him, with his back to me was a complete stranger wearing a beige cap, shirt and trousers. He was shouting. Unfortunately, it was in Spanish so I had no idea what was going on. Worried for Beth, I bowled into the mix without thinking.

'*Stop!*' I yelled at the top of my voice, as I jumped into the middle with my arms raised out to the side.

Both men were taken by surprise and did, unexpectedly, stop. Beth's sobbing lessened and she took big raking gulps as she composed herself. I chucked her my soggy pool towel and led her into her room. When I returned, the men's discussion was heating up again. I didn't understand most of what was being said but 'Policia' stood out and I could hazard a guess at what 'exposicion indecente' meant. *Oh lordy.*

I rubbed my forehead; a dull headache was forming above my nose. *What had happened?* I was clearly out of my depth. I decided to ignore drunk, naked Brutus and focused all my attention to the guy in beige, quickly deducing that he was a security guard. He stood with legs apart, both hands braced on his hips, he wore sun glasses, had a walkie-talkie, a tab on his bicep that said 'Seguridad', oh yeah, and a gun. This freaked me out, I'd never been so close to a weapon before, not in a volatile situation such as this.

Steeling myself and in my best, yet still terrible, Spanish I said, 'Perdon. Hable Ingles, por favor?'

'You give me money or I call police,' challenged

the security guard.

Oh good, I thought sarcastically, *he's not only armed, but he's bent too.* At this Brutus started yelling in Spanish again and their argument continued.

At a loss for what to do, yet determined to keep calm, I thought through my options. Normally, in a bad situation, I would head to the police, or perhaps a security guard for help, but this was out of the question. I was in a foreign country where I knew nothing and no one. *Crap.*

I slipped away from the argument to grab my organiser, I hoped I'd had the presence of mind to put in the number for the British Consulate or something but I hadn't. While shutting the folder I caught sight of the airport taxi details. Relief swept over me as I remembered the lovely driver Antonio insisting I take his number. My hands shook as I searched through the contacts on my phone. Finding the right number, I pressed dial, and held my breath. Bless him, he answered on the fourth ring.

'Hola, is that Yenny?'

I quickly explained all I knew and Antonio said he was on his way to help, luckily, he wasn't due to begin his shift for another hour and he was only ten minutes away.

Relieved that help was on the way, I went to find Beth. She had passed out on her bed, I moved her into the recovery position and sat for a moment beside her, my head in my hands.

When Antonio rang the doorbell, I leapt up to let him in.

'Thank you so much for coming, Antonio. I need a bit of help with translating and...'

'And a bit of muscle to get rid of these men,' said Antonio, smiling. 'It is my pleasure to help, Yenny.'

I led Antonio to the living room, I wasn't sure what to expect, but it wasn't Antonio greeting the security guard like a long-lost brother.

'Raymon!' cried Antonio, grasping him into a big manly hug.

'Antonio! Antonio!' replied the security guard slapping him on the back.

They had a brief exchange in Spanish which went straight over my head, and I took the opportunity to throw Brutus his uniform and tell him to keep quiet and behave; this was his only chance of getting out of the situation.

I caught Antonio's eye and he must have read the perturbed expression on my face as he said, 'We will talk in English, non? It is only polite for Yenny here.' Gesturing to the security guard, he said, 'Raymon and I go way back, we are old amigos from *escuela*.'

'Si, si, we were in the same class.'

Antonio braced Raymon by both shoulders. 'You are looking good, amigo. Life is treating you well!'

Raymon beamed and stuck his chest out while Antonio continued to shower him with compliments. I was sceptical about how exactly this was helping my current blackmail situation but I trusted Antonio, and besides, he was the only help I had.

Eventually Antonio said, 'I am so pleased you are here to help look after my good friend Yenny and her friends, I know you will show them our wonderful Spanish hospitality.'

Raymon nodded, but I could almost see the cogs whirring in his brain as he realised where this was leading.

Antonio spotted it too and quickly continued by saying, 'I understand they were having trouble getting this man here to leave them alone; he even took advantage of one of Yenny's friends. I am so grateful it is you working here and that you can help escort him from the premises.'

'Si, si,' said Raymon, patting his weapon. 'I was about to call the police when you arrived.'

'That is a very good idea,' replied Antonio. 'Ah, but, it is a shame we cannot go get a drink and reminisce about the good old days if you have a busy afternoon with the police. I thought perhaps we could go and get some brandy on your break. You remember we used to sneak out at lunch time and do that?'

'I remember, and we never got caught!'

'No, we did not! Well, it has been nice seeing you again, Raymon, I must leave you to your work.'

'Whoa, Antonio. Not so fast. So, are you buying the brandy?'

'Of course.'

'Well, it would be a shame to miss catching up with my old amigo. Let's get rid of this *perro* and carry on.'

Brutus, who had been keeping very quiet this whole time, looked affronted at being called a dog, but I shot him a fierce stare and he kept shtum. Realising it was his opportunity to escape he followed Raymon to the front door.

Antonio followed and as he went by, leaned in closely to whisper, 'No need to worry, I can handle Raymon. I remember him well from escuela. He was a bully then and best handled carefully. I will make sure you girls are okay.'

I heard Brutus being hustled out and there were more raised voices, finally the door shut and Antonio and Raymon came back in laughing.

At least one creep had gone. I wasn't sure how much longer Antonio and I would have to endure Raymon's company for. Not wanting him in the apartment, I ushered Raymon onto the balcony to admire the view. Antonio managed to secretly tell me that the indecent exposure charges were phony and that Raymon wanted to con money out of tourists. By associating with us, Antonio had changed us from faceless tourists into family. I felt the weight lift off my shoulders.

'My brother, Jaime, is a police officer,' said Antonio. 'I can tell him about Raymon's scam but it is unlikely he can do anything.'

'You've done more than enough already, thank you,' I replied, earnestly.

'I think I will wait until after your holiday, I do not want to cause you more trouble.'

'I don't know how you've got us out of this mess, but I'm so grateful. I don't think I can ever repay you.'

'You need a taxi, you give me a call. That is how you repay me,' said Antonio giving me a friendly wink.

As we headed out to the balcony, Antonio muttered, 'Flattery will get you everywhere,' before calling out to Raymon, 'There he is, the top man.'

The men carried on bantering and eventually Beth emerged and I got her some tea and toast. Wanting rid of Raymon and remembering Antonio was due on shift at any minute, I said, 'I'd hate to make you late, Antonio.'

At that moment the girls came back.

'Everything okay?' asked Kirsty, looking confused as they all piled unwittingly onto the balcony.

'Isn't that the…?' Annie started to ask.

'Kristy!' called out Antonio, 'How is your chicken holiday?' Then before she could reply he launched into giving everyone the double kiss on the cheeks and introducing them to Raymon.

'Raymon is an old amigo of mine, this is Kristy and the chickens.' I hadn't managed to correct

Antonio on how to pronounce our names yet and now really didn't seem the time.

'Now, you look after these chickens for me, eh?!'

'Si, si, claro!' responded Raymon, warmly.

Antonio checked his watch. 'I really do need to be getting to work myself, so we will leave you now. Raymon, we must have our brandy another day. Yenny, you have my number so you call me if you need, si?'

'Si, gracias, Antonio. Muchos gracias,' I responded, hugging my hero.

With a cheery, 'De nada,' Antonio and Raymon left.

I shut the door behind them and turned to find the girls stood in the middle of the living room, staring at me.

'What the…?' Annie asked.

'It's a long story,' I sighed and slumped down next to Beth, stealing one of her slices of toast.

CHAPTER 10

Sensing an epic tale, Suze put the kettle on for us all and I began to fill them in.

'Antonio is a legend, a hero and a lifesaver,' I said, emphatically. 'I came back to find that revolting bastard security guard blackmailing Beth and Brutus.'

Annie almost spat out the tea she had just sipped. 'What?!' she said.

'I'm not sure really, he was trying to say that he'd call the police about some sort of indecent exposure charge unless they paid him off. He'd caught them...in the act...on the balcony.' I wanted to explain everything delicately to save Beth further distress. 'I had no idea what to do, so I called Antonio and thankfully he managed to completely defuse the whole situation.'

'I can't believe you had to deal with all this while we were sunning ourselves by the pool,' said Kirsty.

'I'm glad you didn't know what was going on. I

didn't want to ruin this trip for you.'

'I wish we could have been there for moral support though,' said Suze.

'That would have been nice,' I said, smiling. 'But no harm's been done, except, well maybe to Kirsty's sash.' I tried to joke and break the tension with Beth but she continued to sit silently, looking very sheepish.

'It sounds like a drink's in order,' said Jade. 'Red wine anyone?'

She opened a bottle and offered it round to everyone, extolling its stress relieving virtues.

'No thanks,' said Beth meekly, clasping her tea.

'What's gotten into you Beth?' demanded Annie. 'You've been quiet for days and then you were completely out of control this morning. You dumped us as soon as you could to be with that guy, and now you're being all pathetic. You're doing my head in!' She threw her arms up to either side of her head in exasperation.

We all sat very still, stunned with the sudden explosion.

'Whoa, now Annie...' I started to defend her but Beth interrupted.

'You're totally right and I'm sorry.' Beth turned to Kirsty and said, 'I'm really sorry if I've ruined your hen do.'

Kirsty shook her head and smiled. 'You haven't ruined it, don't be daft. You've...' she paused glancing between Annie and Beth. 'You've not been your usual self.'

'Pffft!' said Annie, sitting back with her arms crossed.

We sat awkwardly for a bit, I didn't want to tell Beth's news for her, nor force her to tell it before she was ready. The other girls sat there expectantly, waiting for a bit more, but Beth had clammed up again. It was Jade who salvaged the situation in the end.

'Did I tell you about the Uni fashion show last month? On the final night, I walked up and down the catwalk three times with a feather boa stuck in the heel of my stiletto. I just couldn't shake the bugger off. It was horrendous… in front of all those people! I went back stage and howled.'

'Whaaaat?!' screeched Kirsty, trying to stifle a laugh.

'Yep, it was completely humiliating and yet hysterical all at the same time. I'm only saying this because we've all done embarrassing stuff, Beth, so don't worry. For the finale, all the other models tied feather boas to their ankles and paraded up and down stage with me. We got a standing ovation.'

Beth hugged Jade. 'You are such a sweetie, but I don't think that you all getting off with a Roman is going to help much.'

'I'd give it a good go for you though,' said Suze with a wink.

The tension eased again. After taking a deep breath Beth confessed her tale of woe, about her job, her boyfriend and her nan, and, to her credit, managed to get it all out without crying. Annie grabbed her hand and when she'd finished, pulled her into a big embrace, burying Beth's head in her hair.

'Why didn't you tell me?' Annie asked.

'I just couldn't, it's all going so well for you, I was... embarrassed. And I didn't want to make everything about me, it's Kirsty's moment.'

Kirsty took Beth's hand. 'You're being daft again. It's not all about me, this is a holiday for everyone. You simply have to treat me like your queen and do what I say at all times!' she joked.

'Group hug!' I yelled, pulling Suze into the huddle.

Jade jumped on us all yelling, 'Bundle!'

'Seriously though,' said Kirsty pulling away to face Beth. 'You can tell us anything, we would always help if we could.'

Beth pursed her lips together in a small smile and nodded. Her eyes had welled up again. When she composed herself, she decided to phone her mum to see how her nan was. She came back biting her lip, worried.

'It's not looking good, girls,' she said in a tight voice. 'They're talking about days and hours...I thought we might have months but...' She broke down again.

Kirsty pulled her in to another hug, rubbing her back and soothing her. The rest of us sat there feeling horrible and useless.

'You know what you have to do, B?' said

Kirsty quietly. She gently pushed Beth so she was slightly away from her, looking in to her eyes. 'You need to go see her and give her a hug from all of us, okay?'

Beth nodded eyes streaming. We were all welling up.

'Go get your stuff packed, I'll sort out the rest,' I volunteered.

Annie followed Beth to their room to help her. I found my trusty binder which had all the details I needed at hand; I phoned the travel agent and managed to get her on a flight that evening at an alarming fee, which Annie insisted on paying. Then on Kirsty's instruction, I phoned Steve and arranged him to get Beth from the airport and drive her to the hospital. Finally, I called Antonio, in his professional capacity, and arranged for Beth's taxi to the airport.

'We've got a couple of hours before you need to go, right?' asked Suze.

Beth bobbed her head.

'Well, I saw a lovely looking place around the corner. Let's go and get some food, then we know you've eaten something proper too.'

'Thank you, I'd really like that,' said Beth.

'Suze, are you trying to feed me up?' asked Annie.

Suze had ordered a huge paella to share and it came out steaming in a dish nearly the size of the table. We all tucked in to it, elbows flying.

Jade chased a mussel around her plate with a fork until I showed her how to pluck out the yummy part using an empty shell as a pincer.

'Oh my goodness, these prawns …' exalted Kirsty as she shovelled food into her mouth. 'You've got to try it,' she said to Beth who was picking at it gingerly.

'I think I'll stick to the chicken,' replied Beth, still looking a bit green.

'This is such a lovely idea.' I grinned at my friends as I plonked my glass of wine down heavily. 'Good food, good people…good idea Suze.'

'Are you getting tipsy?' asked Kirsty.

'Perhaps,' I replied.

'Good 'cos I am,' Kirsty said, laughing.

We carried on chatting happily until Antonio came for Beth. I helped him load her bag into the vehicle then paid him in advance for the journey plus a hefty tip. Beth had said all her goodbyes so after a squeeze from me she hopped into the minibus and away they drove.

We stood in the sun baked street for a moment, the cobbles and dust radiating the day's heat.

'Phew! It's been quite a day,' I said and everyone nodded solemnly.

'This evening's gonna go one of two ways,' said Annie, 'either we go back to the apartment and call it a night…'

'Or go and get absolutely wrecked!' chimed in

Suze.

Kirsty shouted, 'Woop!' and pointed high up into the air. Collaring Annie and Suze with an arm around each neck she said, 'Show me the way, Ladies!'

Jade and I followed behind them.

'So, tell me all about Uni,' I prompted her.

Jade giggled and filled me in as the other three searched for a bar. The flaw in our plan was that it was still early in the evening and nowhere was open. After the fifth bar we tried, and failed at, Kirsty suddenly had a brain wave.

'To the pool bar!' she shouted, pointing down the street.

Jade and I laughed and carried on following them.

She linked arms with me and then peeking around she whispered, 'You know you missed him again?'

'Who?' I asked in a loud stage whisper, leaning in closer.

'Mr Hot,' Jade said under her breath. 'I saw him a while back.'

'Where?!'

I started to glance around but she grabbed me.

'Don't look, it'll be super obvious if he's watching.'

'But there's no one there,' I said.

'I know, he's gone- but he might be back and you should play it cool.'

'I've not even seen this guy yet!'

'But he's seen you and he was check-ing you ouuuut!' she said in a sassy voice. 'When you were leaning into Antonio's window, sorting out the fare, he walked past staring, he was totally in to you.'

I grinned and thought, *I still got it!* Curiosity was starting to nag at me, I kept missing this supposedly gorgeous guy and my friends kept going on about him; I was intrigued. Little did I know that I was soon to find out exactly who he was.

CHAPTER 11

'It's time to glam you ladies up,' declared Jade, wielding a bumper pack of false eyelashes.

We were back in the apartment getting changed to head out for the night. Already in a little black dress and heels, I felt a bit too posh as it was, but Jade insisted.

'I feel like a baby giraffe,' I said blinking in the mirror and then turning to peer at Jade through the long black lashes.

'You all look great,' said Jade beaming at us.

'Right, is everyone ready to go?' asked Suze.

'I need to check my phone. I'm waiting for a reply from Pete.' I called back over my shoulder as I went to rummage around in our room.

There were clothes everywhere, my bed was covered in outfits and my toiletry bag had spilled open, adding to the chaos. In my searching frenzy, I tossed my binder aside to see what was underneath and it fell off the bed. Across the floor came skidding a piece of paper with a game I'd downloaded from the internet. I thought it was a silly bit of fun when I printed it and then I forgot all about it until it slid across my path. On a whim, I grabbed it and folded it into my bag.

I found my phone and saw Pete had replied.

CALL ME!

That was one short message sure to reap dread in your bones. I pressed dial and let it ring. There was no answer.

'Come on Jenny.' The girls were calling to me.

'Hurry up!' shouted Jade. 'The rest of us are all ready.'

Giving up on Pete, I slotted the phone into my little bag and trotted out, my concern soon forgotten.

I came back from the bar with a tray full of drinks; five cocktails and five shot glasses.

'You're on a mission,' said Annie.

'Yep, to get Kirsty drunk! I found this in my bag.' I held out the now drink spattered game I'd printed off.

'What is it?' said Kirsty, nervously.

'A kind of treasure hunt,' I replied.

'Do I get some expensive jewellery at the end?' she asked hopefully.

'Better than that. You have to complete these challenges, and for every one you fail you have to do a shot. If you complete it, you nominate who does the shot.'

'I know who's getting the first shot,' she replied dryly. 'I can't be the only one doing the challenges, I'll feel like a right lemon. As Chief Hen, I demand you all do them too.'

'Why don't we all do a shot and whoever puts their glass down last does the first challenge,' I suggested.

Kirsty nodded and said, 'That sounds fair.'

With a wince, we all threw back our shots, the last to slam their empty glass down was Jade.

'So, it says here that your task is to find a man and swap an item of clothing with him,' I read aloud from the top of the sheet.

'No problem,' said Jade as she sassily walked off.

She was really only wearing a tiny dress and heels, and I wondered which she would forfeit. It didn't take her long to find a chap willing to hand over his boxers and in return she planted a big kiss on his lips.

Jade strutted back to the table and threw down the boxers.

Before any of us could say anything, she said, 'Lipstick is one of the most valuable items in my wardrobe.' She sat down, crossing her legs and looked at us smugly.

I wished I had her balls.

Too slow to capture Jade in action, Annie moaned, 'I can't believe I missed it.' Her camera was poised in her hands.

With a flick of our wrists the next shots were downed and it was now Kirsty's turn. She needed to find a guy with the same first initial as her and get a kiss. Both a Kyle and a Kevin were in the bar. They were happy to oblige, simultaneously kissing a cheek each while Annie managed to snap an action shot.

'What's the next round?' I asked Kirsty, as she placed another tray of shots on our table.

'It's after midnight so I swapped to drinks beginning with S. This is a Sambuca,' she replied. 'Ready, girls, after three.... one, two, three!'

The smell of aniseed was strong as I lifted the sambuca to my lips. It scorched as it burned down my throat, and I must have breathed in wrong because I spluttered as it seared into my lungs. My coughing fit slowed me down and I was the last to put my glass down. My turn.

Kirsty grabbed the paper and gleefully read out, 'Your next challenge is to put on a blindfold and kiss a stranger that we're gonna choose for you.'

'Oh no!'

'No complaining. You were perfectly happy to inflict all of this on me,' retorted Kirsty.

'Very true,' I said, abashed. 'But you have a sash and veil to hide behind.'

'We'll use the sash as the blindfold and then you can hide behind it too.'

'Thanks, Kirsty,' I said, cringing. 'Urgh, you

know I hate stuff like this.'

The girls were bickering over who it should be as I sat there with the sash tied around my head.

'Take your time, don't worry about me,' I said.

'Let's just grab whoever steps into the bar next and then thrust him in Jenny's general direction,' suggested Suze.

'I don't want any old strange bloke!'

'Do you want us to be picky or quick?' snapped Annie. 'Oh, someone's coming iiiiiin!' she sung and then said, 'Hmmm, it's a couple. Stand down.'

'Ohhh, there's a whole group,' said Jade excitedly. I heard her chair scrape as she stood up.

'I'm not kissing all of them!' I said.

'Chill out J, it's only a bit of fun.' Kirsty tried to soothe me as I waited for Jade to hoodwink one of them into kissing me.

I was silently starting to panic that none of them would actually want to and that would be more embarrassing than the actual kiss.

Jade must have been rushing around, high on the hijinks. I could hear her panting as she came back.

'It's a mixed group of boys and girls... they're nearly all with someone... they're celebrating a birthday... but they're gonna blindfold the single guy in their group and bring him over.'

'Can the blindfold come off while I wait?' I asked.

I got a unanimous 'No!' in response.

It seemed to take forever, but it was still too quick for my liking. There was a rumble of laughter and I could hear the girls giggling and 'wooo-oooing'. I felt like a sacrificial virgin being lowered on to an altar as Kirsty led me forwards.

I could hear cheers of 'Go on Mike!' from the other group. I felt sick and it wasn't only the hideous variety of spirits curdling in my poor stomach. Putting my hands out, I felt towards the figure in front of me, finding a very solid, warm chest. I was quickly engulfed around the waist by some strong arms that felt very foreign but comfortingly at home all at the same time.

A deep, 'Hello,' reverberated very close to my face.

'Hi,' squeaked out of me.

If I was a hashtag kind of person, this would have been #awkward, but I'm not, so let's just say I felt very self-conscious.

'So, we should…' said the male voice.

'Erm… I guess,' I replied, berating myself for my lack of witty one-liners.

I could hear a swelling rumble from our audience, and then suddenly out of the darkness I was consumed. Soft wet lips planted firmly down on mine and moved like chocolate melting. I could feel his hot breath and a scratch of stubble as he overwhelmed me, it was all I could do to keep standing and I clung around his neck, my fingers twisted into his hair. He began slowly at first, as if he was going to pull away, but as my lips tingled against his, he devoured me, kissing me hard and deep. It was incredible; I think I actually swooned. This wasn't the quick peck on the lips I was anticipating. I must have blocked out the whole world, I was so lost in the moment, and as it drew to a tender end, my awareness of the bar and all the people returned, a tumultuous roar swelled around us.

My cheeks coloured and I felt hot under the sash and suddenly very uncomfortable. I pulled away and stripped off the blindfold, mussing my hair. Peering up to give the unsuspecting conscript a shy smile, my mouth gaped and my stomach pitched. Standing in front of me was the most striking man I'd ever seen. Although I *had* seen him before. It was my boss-

'Mr Henson,' I whispered.

His eyes crinkled as he smiled at me, 'Miss George, what a nice surprise. I think, given the circumstances, you should call me Michael.'

Michael's mob of friends came over, cuffing him on the back and scruffing his hair. As he turned to them, they grabbed him around the neck.

'Sorry...' he called out, as they dragged him off to the bar.

I was left standing there with flushed cheeks and a craving for more.

'Go Jenny!' cheered Kirsty, as I moved back towards our table.

'See, it wasn't that bad,' said Annie. 'All that moaning and whinging!' She shook her head and tutted at me.

Jade had already acquired the next round of shots and was drumming on the table impatiently so I sat back down. I lost track of the game as I kept glancing over at Michael and his group of friends, they were now partying on the other side of the bar. Shot after shot went down but I was oblivious to anything going on. Everything was drowned out by one thought; *did he feel that too?*

CHAPTER 12

My mouth tasted of dead kittens. I blearily opened one eye and froze, holding my breath. My mouth may have tasted of dead kittens because there appeared to be one on the next bed.

Oh. My. God.

Before panic really set in, the kitten snored. *Phew it's not dead!* I went over to get a closer look, with just the one bleary eye open. The kitten began to roll over and I tried to pick it up but for some reason I couldn't get a proper hold of it. Then the kitten screamed. So, I did too. Then I realised the kitten sounded an awful lot like Suze.

'Ow my hair! Jenny get off! Why are you attacking me?!'

'Whaaa?' I managed to say, through the fur in my mouth.

It slowly dawned on me, it wasn't a kitten at all. It was Suze's crazy hair. And I was still a little drunk.

'And why do you look like a pirate? Crikey, Jenny, you almost gave me a heart attack.'

I dumbly sat on the floor by Suze's bed, a little bewildered and slightly gutted that there was no kitten.

'Funny dream,' I managed to mumble. 'Sorry.'

'Not used to sharing a room yet?' she asked, chuckling.

I tried to open the other eye but it wasn't working.

'You feeling alright, Jenny?' she asked.

Only able to raise my eyebrows, the eye still wouldn't open, and with a dry mouth gluing up, I managed to grunt in response.

'I'll make us a brew,' said Suze and leapt spryly from her bed.

The sounds of Suze rummaging and clinking in the kitchenette filtered through to me. Soon Suze bounded back in with a steaming cuppa. *I could get used to sharing* I thought as I heaved myself back up on to my bed, the terror of the dead kitten incident slowly subsiding.

The tea revived my senses, well, everything except my vision and I began to feel a lot better. Although the good mood didn't last for long.

'How are you not suffering too?' I asked when I was finally able to string a sentence together.

'I switched to soda after midnight,' she replied smugly.

'Was that allowed?'

'It began with 'S' so I presumed yes.'

Suze had woken up in a chatty mood, despite the fright I'd given her and she wasted no time in reminding me of last night's escapades, most of which I'd forgotten. As she filled in the blanks I carried on trying to open my eye. I cautiously prodded it and could feel crusty lashes, bristling out at funny angles.

'I think you fell asleep with your falsies on,' Suze commented, watching me fiddle with my eye.

A stingy pain scorched through my eyelid as I struggled to prise it off. I decided to leave it for a bit, at least now I knew what had happened to my eye. Now I just needed to work out what happened the rest of the night.

'So, what do you remember?' asked Suze.

'Nothing,' I moaned, 'only the eyelashes... and the pool bar, ... did we do shots?'

'Yes, you worked your way through the bar's entire repertoire of 'S' named drinks! There was sambuca, sour apple, scotch and of course sangria...'

'Ohhhhhhh,' I groaned. 'I feel sick just thinking about it.'

'You were sick my love, all three of you, it was like some grizzly domino effect on the way home.'

'Oh, yuck.' A flash of the dusty road lurching towards me and the sound of cicadas shrilly singing screeched through my head. 'I remember that now, how disgusting. I'm sorry, you can't take me anywhere.'

'Don't worry! It's a good job you were or you'd be feeling a lot worse now.'

'Umpff' I grumped incomprehensibly, clutching my tea like a comforter.

'I've got a sneaky suspicion they water-down the shots too, so it really could have been worse. Has anything else come back to you?'

'There's more?'

'Yes, well, you girls got playing that treasure hunt…'

Slam! It all came rushing back to me, slapping me in my already pounding head. Feeling queasy, I made a dash for the bathroom. Lying on the cold tiles I tried to get my head around what exactly had happened, the trouble was, it was spinning from too much alcohol. I clutched my head and hid behind my hands, not wanting to admit that I'd snogged my boss on holiday. Not only my boss, but the man I had first met when I was soaking wet and covered in coffee, who I then proceeded to continue humiliating myself in front of. Not only my boss, but the most beautiful man I'd ever met. I groaned as I rolled onto my side and wished the floor would swallow me up.

When the waves of nausea calmed and I could hold my head up again, albeit without dignity, I heaved myself up and staggered back to bed.

Suze took one look at me and then said, 'Yikes!

I'll pop the kettle on again.'

With fresh cups in our hands, Suze sat down opposite me and smiled awkwardly.

'So, the pieces are falling into place?' she asked. I nodded solemnly. 'I noticed you went awfully quiet after your challenge, is everything okay?'

'Yeah, I guess I've got a lot on my mind. I want everything to be okay for Kirsty.' I wanted to tell Suze that the stranger I'd kissed was not a stranger at all, but something was stopping me.

Suze held my gaze, clearly unconvinced by my evasive answer. Then she said, 'You know he was the hot guy we've been seeing all holiday?'

Taking a big swig of tea to give me a chance to think, I winced as I swallowed it in one scalding gulp. My mind was racing. *Did he know it was me the whole time? Did he WANT to kiss me? Or have I once again made a fool of myself?*

'Suuuuze....' whiney voices called from Kirsty and Jade's room, interrupting us. 'Did we hear the kettle?'

Suze rolled her eyes, but jumped up to help them anyway. *Saved by the belles.* I breathed a sigh of relief, I wasn't ready to talk about it yet. Talking about it would mean fully accepting that it had happened and I wanted to cling to denial for as long as possible.

CHAPTER 13

I didn't quite know how to tell the girls the truth but knew I must, it was simply a matter of picking the right moment. Hopefully they could help me strategically avoid Mr Henson until I had worked out what to do about everything. Or at least until I'd found a new job. Preferably in a different country.

I felt much better after my third cup of tea and set about making us some breakfast. The other girls were rousing by this time, probably lured out by the rich smell of buttery toast, so Suze and I got to work nursing their hangovers too. No one mentioned the events of last night but when they all felt sufficiently better they started noticing my eye. Noticing and joking about it.

'You coming on to me, Jen? You've been winking at me all morning,' said Annie, laughing.

'Hey now, she was giving me a good grope this morning,' chimed in Suze. 'I'll get jealous.'

'Yeah, laugh it up you lot. As soon I can see straight, I'll get my own back,' I pretended to be fierce. 'Right girls, let's chill out this morning so we can recover a bit more. Then later we'll head out to a beach club. I've heard it's amazing.' I felt a bit like a teacher rounding up a naughty class.

When everyone was distracted, I scuttled off to the bathroom to wash my face and try and open my eye. It was so painful, I was pretty sure it was somehow welded shut. I peered into the mirror and tried to peel the lash off, it wouldn't budge. The pain was making my good eye water so I stopped; I didn't need impaired vision on both sides.

Jade knocked and stuck her head around the door.

'Ay, ay, Cap'in,' she teased me. 'Still not got the lashes off?'

I huffed jovially. 'You and your falsies. I look like a right plonker.'

She waved her toiletry bag at me and said, 'I'll sort you out in no time.'

And she did. Jade did a professional job at prizing the little bugger off. I sat on the closed toilet and let her get to work. She applied a warm compress and then gently wiped over some make up remover, and, with the delicacy of a surgeon, peeled the lash inwards, I'd been tugging at it the wrong way. Finally, she cleaned off the last of the glue with baby oil. No wonder I'd been struggling on my own.

'Ta-dah!' she sung as I blinked my eye open into the bright light. 'Hmmmm, it's looking a bit dodgy,' she confessed as she peered at me.

A searing pain was shooting through my head and my vision was blurry but I could see that Jade was concerned. I peeked at the mirror, I was grimacing back at myself with a very swollen, blood-shot, eye.

'I think the glue's irritated it,' said Jade.

'I look horrendous. What am I gonna do?'

Jade rummaged through my bag then tossed me my sunglasses, 'Cured you!' she cheered.

'Genius!' I grinned and donned my shades. 'Can you find some ibuprofen while you're there, please?'

Jade pulled out a large packet of pain killers and rattled them saying, 'I think we all need some of these.'

Suze had been giving me funny glances all morning but no one had brought up my odd behaviour last night, I wondered if perhaps they were also too drunk to remember. I was getting a bit fidgety about putting it off any longer, so when I found everyone lounging out on the balcony I decided to take the bull by the horns.

'So, we packed away a bit last night, didn't we?'

'Urgh! I'm not ready to talk about it yet,' moaned Kirsty. 'Each time I think of what we drank it's like I'm re-drinking it all over again.'

'Whose idea was it to drink scotch?' Annie enquired. 'I think I can still taste it!'

'It began with S!' defended Jade and Annie flicked her magazine in her general direction.

Suze was keeping a steady gaze on me, clearly wondering if I was going to open up. I wasn't really sure how to tell them, but I didn't want to do a Beth and start clamming up.

'I don't even remember how we got home,' said Jade.

'Oh, I do!' said Suze laughing. She caught my eye and said, 'I've got something important to say.'

A lump rose in my throat, was she going to grill me before I had worked out what on earth to say?

'I swapped to soda after midnight,' Suze confessed. 'I did the shots with you but I stopped drinking cocktails. You young things are making my liver ache!'

'I'm so jealous!' said Kirsty. 'I should pace myself more.'

'I've been feeling bad all morning, I thought you might be mad at me.' She sounded relieved. 'It means I remember weaving back up the road with you lot in the wee hours of the morning.'

I decided to seize my moment and 'fess up too, before people started remembering things on their own.

'In the interests of full disclosure, I've got a little confession to make too,' I said and inwardly cringed. Everyone was staring at me and I could feel myself pinking up. 'Do you remember playing the little treasure hunt game last night?' Not giving them time to answer I plunged on. 'Well, at one point you blindfolded me and made me kiss a stranger.' I'd been looking everyone in the eye up until this point but now I fixed my gaze steadily over the balcony rail, and out to sea. Quickly, I blurted out, 'Except it wasn't a stranger it was my boss.'

I glanced at each of them in turn. I didn't get the response I was expecting, that was for sure. Kirsty and Annie were swapping suspicious looks, Jade seemed generally confused and Suze was smiling, looking a little bit proud of me.

'So... say something,' I urged them.

Jade carried on looking puzzled and said, 'Did you say your *boss*?'

'Yes.'

'The hot guy?'

'Yes.'

'Thank goodness for that,' said Kirsty and she swapped another glance with Annie.

'What?' I glanced between Kirsty and Annie, not sure why they were so relieved.

'We thought you were acting so weird because of James.'

'James? James, my ex?' I asked, irately.

'Yes, we've been worried you were still in love with him or something...' mumbled Kirsty.

Annie interrupted, saying, 'It's just that it's

been a while since you've dated any one, there's not really been anyone for a couple years since him. We started to wonder...'

'*Still in love with him?*' All thoughts of embarrassment turned to fury, 'With that dick!'

Annie and Kirsty swapped a look again. 'Sorry, Jen, we were only thinking... it's been ages... and then you went all quiet and weird after that guy last night.' They had the decency to look a bit ashamed.

'James hasn't even been in my head for months. Can we get to the real issue here. I. Snogged. My. Boss. My boss. My actual boss.' My voice got higher pitched.

'Well, I wasn't expecting you to say that,' said Suze, 'that *is* a surprise!'

'What were you expecting me to say?'

'I was wondering if it was about this James guy too, especially after our chat earlier,' she replied sheepishly.

'How do you know about James?'

'Well...' Suze hesitated.

'We were kind of discussing it this morning while Jade was working on your eye,' admitted Kirsty with Annie guiltily nodding along.

'I've spent all morning wondering how to bring this up with you guys and you got started without me!'

'We spent all morning trying to work out how to ask you about it,' confessed Annie. 'We didn't want any more melt downs this trip.'

Jade, finally catching up, said, 'So, the hot guy is your boss?'

'Yes!' we all replied in unison.

'Eeesh!'

'So, what am I gonna do about it?' I implored. I was stunned that they weren't all freaking out about it like I was.

'Just have a little chat next time you see him and clear the air,' said Suze, the calm voice of reason. 'You were both blindfolded. It was an accident. A coincidence. Why's it upsetting you so much?'

Realising I'd only told them half a story, I decided I couldn't avoid talking about it any longer and filled them in on what had happened on my last day at work.

'These girls have been bullying you for how long?' demanded Annie, when I'd finished.

'I wouldn't call it bullying per se, but I've never really clicked with them.'

'It's bullying, Jen, and it's not on,' she replied, seething.

'You should have told us about them sooner,' said Kirsty

'I'm a big girl, I can take care of myself, don't worry about that.' I tried to dismiss how The Witches made me feel, not wanting to give them power to ruin my holiday as well as my work days. 'Now, what I'm more bothered about is how I've made a ridiculous first, second and now third impression on Mr Henson.' I counted it off on my fingers. 'I'm pretty sure it's career suicide.'

'Is there anyone at work you can tell? Or get some advice from?' asked Suze.

'I'd be careful though, you wouldn't want any office gossip,' said Annie.

'Actually, yes, there's Pete. I need to phone him anyway.'

Leaving the group bathing in the sun, I went back indoors to ring Pete. Locating my phone, I noticed another missed call from him. I felt a bit guilty about neglecting him all this time and then phoning him in my moment of need. I began to get nervous again as I waited for him to answer.

'Finally, darling! It's like you've been in deepest Brazil, not Spain!'

'Hi Pete, sorry I kept missing your calls. How are you?'

'Never mind me, now you've got to listen in case we get cut off or something and you become unreachable for days on end again! You'll never guess who's going to the same resort as you...'

'Pete, I...'

'No, you won't guess, it's only Mr Henson, the new boss!'

'But, I...'

'Can you believe it? You should look out for him in his speedos, he's quite handsome if you like that sort of thing. Anyway, he...oh hang on a sec love...'

'But...' It was no use he couldn't hear, I hung

on with my concerns burning my lips, desperate to be reassured. The phone clicked back on.

'Look, darling, I've got Jeremy on call waiting. I've got to take this but I'll call you back when I can, there's so much I need to tell you!'

And with that Pete hung up. I stood there with my phone against my ear for a few seconds more, while my brain caught up with what had happened. At least I knew why he'd been trying to get hold of me urgently, I considered the irony. My unspoken query was left bobbing on my tongue like the buoys out in the bay. I went back on to the balcony, hastily clawing my sunglasses over my eyes in the glare.

I flopped down on to the empty sun lounger next to Kirsty and huffed.

'What did he say?' she asked.

'Nothing I didn't already know.'

'Huh?' She peered at me inquisitively from under her floppy hat.

'I couldn't get a word in; he was too busy telling me to look out for Mr Henson, as he was here too.'

We caught each other's eye and suddenly couldn't suppress our giggles.

'Better watch out for him then.' Kirsty sniggered.

'Thank God Pete warned me,' I spluttered. 'Can you imagine what I'd have done if I'd known he was here!' I was laughing so much that my eyes watered as the emotion and stress released itself from me.

The sun-bed quivered, shaking from my laughter then promptly collapsed over into Kirsty's and we both landed in a dusty mess of hysteria on the balcony floor. I felt so much better for having a good laugh, my stomach hurt, my cheeks stung and my bad eye throbbed. I hadn't felt this good for a while. When we finally composed ourselves, we decided to head to Breeze, that way if I managed to speak to Pete again *and* get a word in, I could at least tell him that we'd been.

CHAPTER 14

Jade looked like a goddess. She wore a coral pink bikini, a gold chunky necklace and strappy gold heels, a stunning combination set against her perfect tan. She took one glance at the rest of our little group and sent us all back to change. We didn't meet her idea of beach club chic.

'Kirsty, you can borrow my white bikini; you're the bride to be after all,' said Jade.

'I'd rather not wear white, I'm too pale,' she replied.

'Well, I'm not letting you go wearing that,' said Jade, eyeing her baggy faded swimming costume.

'But, it's comfy.'

'No,' she replied sternly. 'Beach clubs are all about glamour, and this...' She pointed her finger up and down at Kirsty. '...is not glamorous. And you're the bride, you need to look better than the rest of us put together!'

Plucking at a strap, Kirsty said, 'If I can't wear this, then at least something with colour- not the white one, please.'

Jade rummaged through her things and then held up a bright red all in one swimsuit with a plunging neckline. 'This will look amazing on you. And use my lipstick, it matches.'

Moving on, Jade plunged into Annie's suitcase and pulled out a luminous yellow two piece.

'Why have you been hiding this? It's fabulous!'

'I don't know why I bought it,' said Annie. 'I'll feel like a pineapple, all bright yellow with crazy hair.'

'Don't be silly, it'll look great,' said Jade, while we all nodded our encouragement.

Annie changed quickly and came back in the bikini, seeming hesitant..

'That looks awesome,' said Jade.

'My hair's a wreck though, I can't do anything with it in all this heat and humidity.'

'Haven't you got that bright yellow flower hair clip, that'd go, wouldn't it?' I said and glanced over at Jade who eagerly agreed. She was clearly surprised by my sudden fashion savvy.

Annie slid the tropical flower into the side of her hair, sweeping it slightly off her face.

'I think it looks amazing like that,' I said and she grinned.

'Selfie time then,' she replied and ran off to pose for photos in her new ensemble.

Jade sized Suze and I up and down, and then a

smile crept across her face.

'Suze, I know you've got a black swimsuit, go and change into that,' she said bossily.

Suze saluted and went into our bedroom, leaving just me to Jade's critical eye. 'It's got to be the monokini for you,' Jade said.

'Mono what?'

'Monokini. This will look fab, accentuating your curves and legs. Monokinis are huge this season. Here you go,' said Jade, after sorting through her suitcase.

'Wow, how many have you got in there?' I asked, seeing at least four more swimming costumes and bikinis sliding over each other.

'You can never have enough,' she replied.

'Are you sure you don't mind me borrowing it?'

'Of course not, you're like family. And you should keep it anyway, I was given it after doing the fashion show and I don't think I'll ever wear it.'

As I thanked Jade, Suze walked back into the room, this time in a simple, black, swimsuit. Jade wafted out a chiffon poncho and fanned it over Suze's head, then she draped a long golden beaded necklace around her neck and stood back to admire her handiwork.

'Heels,' she said, her head tilted to the side. Then she shouted over her shoulder, 'Everyone, you all need to wear heels.'

'Oh no,' said Suze. 'No, no, no, no! I'm not

wearing heels to a pool.'

'Everyone else will be,' replied Jade.

'I'll be like mutton dressed up as lamb with all you young things. Perhaps I shouldn't go,' moaned Suze.

'Hey, don't say things like that. How does the saying go? Age ain't nothing but a number... you're a clever, beautiful woman. I'm just trying to give your confidence a boost so you can show it,' said Jade.

'I'm not sure,' hesitated Suze, 'I won't be confident if I'm not comfortable.'

'Trust me, you'll be your most confident if you feel amazing, and if you look your best you'll feel amazing!'

Suze looked at me for reassurance.

'I trust Jade, but you've got to be comfortable. Pete goes every time he's here and he's assured me it's a lot of fun.'

I left the girls all arguing over whether or not they were wearing heels and went to change into what Jade had insisted on calling a monokini. She was right, it did accentuate the best bits of my figure; it had cut out bits at the side and seemed like a bikini from the back. I was as pale as ever, having been slapping on the sun cream all holiday, although my hair had really lightened in the sun's rays. I curled it so it hung down my back in big waves.

I came back to find that Jade had compromised, letting Suze wear what she called "sexy sandals". Although I could hear Jade mutter, 'Sandals really aren't sexy,' under her breath.

Now she was satisfied with how we looked she allowed us to leave. Much to Jade's dismay, we threw on some sundresses over the top of her creations so we could travel in comfort. As we jumped in a taxi I felt a pang of guilt that it wasn't Antonio's.

Arriving at Breeze, we headed to the reception desk, I chickened out of name dropping "Posh Pete" in case they didn't know what I was talking about and then didn't let us in on account of me being mad. The receptionist appraised us carefully, but we were obviously deemed posh enough as they allowed us in. Baulking at the prices we all chipped in and got a big round sun bed on the edge of the pool which came with a couple bottles of Cava.

We could hear the mellow sounds of the DJ pumping out a chilled vibe as we walked through the foyer. I was glad of my giant sunglasses as we turned the corner and the expanse of the huge complex lay gleaming in front of us. There was a dazzling topaz pool in the shape of a figure of eight, the sunlight danced off the surface. Dotted around it were large white parasols with equally large round beds underneath. Fanning out from this were smaller, turquoise, sun beds mirroring the colour of the sea which lapped at the white sandy beach along the left side of the club. The DJ was at one end of the pool by the entrance, while at the very opposite end there was a raised decked area cordoned off behind a red rope. Amongst all this was a throng of very beautiful people.

We were led towards a bed at the narrowest part of the pool so it felt like we were almost surrounded by the water. The smell of coconut sun lotion was laced through the air.

'Wow!' said Kirsty. 'This place is stunning.'

'These people are stunning,' retorted Annie.

'So are we,' said Jade, looking right at home.

While we were getting settled, the waiter brought out our Cava in huge buckets of crushed ice. Toasting to Kirsty, we all took a cool sip and I found the bubbles gave me a boost to take my dress off and parade around in my swimwear.

'Aren't we only supposed to drink things beginning with S today?' cried out Annie.

'It's sparkling wine, does that count?' answered Suze.

'You're getting far too good at bending the rules,' replied Annie.

I lay back on the huge, pillow soft, bed and soaked in the ambience. It was so relaxing. I could hear the gentle tink of ice in glasses chime out over the low chatter and the deep bass of the music, while the waves swished over the sand. The Cava must have gone to my head and I drifted off.

Suddenly, I was aware of Suze asking me a question. 'Jenny, so what have you decided to do about your boss?'

There went my lovely relaxed state. I tensed up thinking about the embarrassing situation with Mr Henson, my stomach churning.

'I don't know. I guess I'll have to talk to him if we bump into either other again. It'd probably be better to do it here than back at work.'

'You're right there. Just remember you didn't do anything wrong.'

I nodded, feeling less confident than I portrayed.

Inspired by my relaxing swim the day before, I decided to go for a dip. It felt like years had passed since then, and I wanted to recapture the stress-free sensation I had with the last one.

Perching on the edge of the glassy pool, my legs gently kicked forward and back sending ripples spilling out to the far edges. I twisted my hair up into a knot on top of my head. Then thrusting my hips over the edge, I slipped down into the water, careful to keep my sunglasses dry.

Paddling over to the far end of the pool, I tried to get a better look at the ribboned off VIP area. I was at an awkward angle to get a good view but I could hear the sound of water falling and bubbling somewhere up on the decking. Intrigued, I swam back to our base, intending to people watch from afar.

'What on earth are you doing?' Jade confronted me.

'Sorry?'

'You're swimming!'

'Yeah, what's wrong with that?'

'No one actually swims in the pool, Jenny. We're merely supposed to drape ourselves around it looking fantastic. Or perhaps dance in it but that's when the DJ heats up.'

'Why can't I swim? It's a swimming pool!'

'It's just not what you do.'

Suitably abashed and a tad confused, I reached my arms onto the edge of the paved edge and floated my legs up behind me. I contemplated how absurd it all was.

'This place is great but, I don't get it; it's called a beach club but no one goes on the beach. We sit around the pool... but you can't go in the pool...'

'Yep, you've got it,' said Jade as she winked. 'You can stay there, you look suitably draped now.'

'Thanks very much.'

I slowly kicked my legs to stay afloat and chatted with the girls on the lounger. Our bridesmaid dresses were the hot topic of discussion, Kirsty was still to decide exactly what colour to plump for, Jade was keen on sunshine yellow but I wasn't so sure. Trying to be a good bridesmaid I decided that I'd wear whatever Kirsty wanted me to, except orange. I really didn't want to wear orange.

We ordered a round of cocktails and the waiter brought them over on a large silver tray. I slurped contentedly at my frozen strawberry daiquiri through a straw, humming a song about tequila in my head.

Conscious that Jade had banned me from swimming, but keen to explore a bit more, I decided to walk to the ladies' room taking the long route so I could have a good nose around. I rose out of the water and towelled myself down, I felt deliciously refreshed from being in the cold water and could feel the sun sizzling my skin as soon as I was in its rays. Holding my stomach in and my head high, I went off for my tour.

I passed some men talking business and profits on one of the beds. There was a twenty-first birthday celebration in another section. I could see at least two more hen dos, the brides to be in tell-tale white bikinis. Kirsty would be happy that she was a bit different.

The raised decked area seemed very secluded and exclusive. I could see several members of staff going in and out, working attentively to the unseen customers. A cheery babble of water and the sound of people chatting drifted down the high steps, but I couldn't sneak a peek at what it was like up there.

Carrying on so I wasn't accused of lurking, I located the sign to the toilets and followed it around the far edge of the pool continuing to scan my surroundings; I didn't want to miss out anything. As I walked through the door into the shady interior I collided into a firm, warm mass. Large hands steadied me and lingered on my skin. I could feel their strong grip as they held on to me, where my swimming costume cut away to my naked sides, it had been quite a while since I'd been held so intimately.

'Oh, I'm so sorry, I didn't see you there,' I gushed, blinded from wearing my sunglasses inside.

'It's fine...oh...Miss George...I...'

'Mr Henson? Oh my goodness ...I'm sorry,' I stuttered, aghast. As I pulled away from his grip, my eyesight adjusted and I took in his magnificence. Panic overwhelmed me.

'Hey, Mikey, hurry up.' A different male voice called out and another tall figure loomed into view.

While he was distracted I dashed through the nearest door, shaking. Luckily, it was the ladies' toilet and I breathed a sigh of relief, my pounding heart throbbing in my ears. Taking off my sunglasses, I steadied both hands on a ledge and rested my head against the large mirror.

Pull yourself together Jenny.

I could have kicked myself, far from being demure, I could now add "running away" to my list of ways I'd embarrassed myself. I glanced into the mirror, my swollen eye peeking back at me. I wanted the guy to respect me, I wanted to be able to look him in the eye, but I didn't want to do it looking like this. A girl's got to have some pride.

And, what was worse, he was smoking hot, with his white linen shirt open at the collar, revealing down to a smooth tanned chest. The sleeves had been casually rolled back to his elbows and I'd seen the muscles on his forearm bulging as he supported me, stopping me falling. His stubble had grown in some more over his chin, cutting a rugged profile. Something sparked in his eyes, was it bemusement? Irritation? Lust? I mentally scolded myself; he was my boss for goodness sake. Nothing could really happen. Could it?

Looking down I could see I was covered in goose-bumps and chicken-skin, perhaps from the air-con as well as the shock. I rubbed my hands over my arms briskly to warm up. I peered in the mirror again, critically giving myself the once over. Other than my eye, I didn't look too bad. I was thankful to Jade for making me wear a different swimming costume. Undoing the top knot, I zhuzhed my hair and then replaced my sunglasses, this was as good as it was going to get. Determined to cling to whatever self-respect I had left, I decided to head back out and enjoy the rest of the day. I had no idea how this whole farce was going to pan out but clearly, looking as hot as possible could only be to my advantage.

CHAPTER 15

As soon as I was back out in the sun I started to warm up, although leaving the safety of the ladies' room meant I was far from relaxed. My eyes were fixed firmly on our group, a smile pasted on my face, as I walked back over to them.

'Hi, ladies!' I chirped as I reached them.

'Where've you been?' asked Suze. 'I was going to send out a search party.'

'I was only sorting my hair out,' I said loudly. Then as I clambered on to the bed with them all, I quietly added, 'My boss is here, I've just bumped into him again.'

'Noooo,' they all whispered.

'Like, actually, physically, literally bumped into him.'

'What happened?' asked Kirsty.

'I didn't see him, what with this bloomin' eye, and I ploughed right into him. When I realised who it was I panicked and scuttled off. I'm such an idiot!'

'Don't be so hard on yourself,' she replied, rubbing my arm supportively.

'I feel like I keep making a very bad impression; I hardly excelled at work! And even out of work, I'm just blundering around. Do you think he can fire me for being a plonker?'

'Not for anything you've done out here.' Annie replied confidently. 'Although work's another matter. Did you ever get hold of Pete again?'

'Not yet, I'll try again later.' Changing the subject, I asked, 'So, what do you think of this place then?'

'It's amazing!' gushed Kirsty. 'I love it.'

The others nodded in agreement. 'How did you find out about it?' asked Annie.

'Pete recommended it, he comes here a lot. He said to name drop "Posh Pete" at reception but I chickened out.'

'Posh Pete?' Interrupted our waiter, who had been hovering, eyeing up our empty glasses.

'Yes, do you know him?'

'Si, si, why didn't you say so? Let me tell my boss; we have been looking out for you.' He trotted off before we could respond.

Soon he came back with a glamorous looking lady in a white skirt suit. She had a little gold badge pinned to her chest.

'Please let me welcome you, ladies,' she said in perfect English. 'I must apologise. We hadn't realised who you were. Your associate has arranged for us to take very good care of you, should you come and visit us. Please, follow me, and, once again, I apologise on behalf of all of us at Breeze for the misunderstanding.' She held out an arm indicating we should follow her.

'I'm sorry...' I started to say that I didn't understand.

Annie jabbed me firmly in the ribs and spoke over me. 'That's quite okay,' she said, 'these things happen. Please lead the way.' Annie raised up off the bed demurely and made to follow the manager.

The rest of us began to gather up our things but the manager stopped us. 'We will take care of this for you, please, just bring yourselves. I am Isabel and if there is anything at all I can do to make your stay with us more pleasurable please let me know.' And with that she strode off with Annie gliding along behind her.

Trying to stifle surprised giggles, we all followed, feeling rather excited. We were led around the edge of the pool and up to the decked area. A man, also dressed completely in white, unhooked the red rope and Isabel led us through and up the steps. The five of us struck our best postures and filed behind her, trying desperately to look completely natural; of course we belonged in the VIP area.

A sumptuous sight greeted us; plush white loungers were grouped around the decking, each with their own fluffy towels and champagne coolers. A private bar, bedecked in gold, spanned the back, with leather clad stools dotted along the edge. Succulent fruit was tumbling over the edge of large gold pitchers, flanking either side of the bar. The babbling I'd heard was from two huge hot tubs, one on either side of the area. Both were steaming, with huge chandeliers suspended above them. Large leafy shrubs provided some natural shade and privacy. The centrepiece was a beautiful dipping pool clad in topaz to match the pool below, flecks of gold were shimmering throughout the stone work, and a waterfall feature tumbled down the back wall.

A small group had taken over one of the hot tubs, we were led to the one opposite. Isabel made a hand gesture towards the bar and one of the waiters popped open some champagne.

Isabel said, 'I hope you will be comfortable here. Please, if there is anything we can do, don't hesitate to ask,' and then she swept away leaving us speechless.

Still trying to act as if I belonged, and hoping they wouldn't suddenly decide this was all a terrible mistake, I swiped one of the glasses. Thanking the waiter, I held it aloft.

'To Kirsty!' I said and grinned at her.

The other girls followed suit and we toasted the bride to be.

Our possessions had been brought up and laid out by the sun loungers so we settled down there. Unable to really believe what was happening, we all swapped excited glances and some heavy eyebrow waggling.

Under hushed breath Kirsty said, 'Jenny, was this your doing? It's amazing!'

'No, I wish I could claim it was. I have no idea what's going on.'

We giggled and sipped our champagne, nervous that someone would change their minds and chuck us out at any minute.

'I'm going to phone Pete,' I announced. 'He must have organised this, I need to thank him.'

Moving over to the leafy palms at the edge, I stood in their shade and dialled Pete. While it rang, I gazed out on the sparkling sea. There was no answer so I left a message and went back to the group. We decided to take advantage of our private hot tub so we all sunk into the bubbles clutching our drinks, the outside of the glasses steaming up.

We chatted leisurely about Kirsty's and Annie's wedding plans and Suze reminisced on her big day. When our fingers and toes had gone all crinkly and prune-like we reluctantly got out and lay down on our loungers to dry.

Filing out from behind the bar came Isabel and five men. They walked purposefully over to our little area.

'I have arranged some complimentary treatments for you, ladies,' said Isabel. 'I hope you will enjoy some back and shoulder massages.'

We all swapped looks and grinned, a little overwhelmed.

'Yes,' said Kirsty, answering for all of us. 'I think that would be acceptable.'

Twenty glorious minutes later I had been moulded and melted into a blithering blob. I was so relaxed, I was incoherent. The masseuse's hands kneaded and pummelled all my knots away leaving me feeling floaty and free.

'Urmmmmmmm, fanks,' was all I managed to mumble when he was finished. *I have such a way with words.*

The five of us lay face down soaking in the sun and letting our relaxation seep down into our bones. When we finally came-to and sat up, we could see that even Jade had let herself go, hair askew and smudged make up.

Kirsty laughed and nudged her. 'Don't get too comfortable. They might chuck us out looking like that! Come on, let's go and get tidied up.' The sisters headed away.

I ensured my sunglasses were in place and then approached the bar. The combination of the hot tub, the massage, and all the fizz had really woken up an appetite. I ordered the Chef's Special Combo Platter for the five of us and some jugs of water.

I heard the DJ switch up the music and some thumping beats reverberated through the complex. I could just about see over into the pool area, so I perched on a stool and people watched.

Sipping on some lemon infused water, I gazed down at the party below.

The hairs on the back of my neck pricked up as I could feel myself being watched. Turning towards the other hot tub I could see a group of guys in there with a couple of scantily clad, gorgeous girls, screeching and giggling with them. I cursed those false lashes; I couldn't see properly but I could definitely feel someone's eyes on me. I turned away again, but pulled my stomach in and breathed in, lifting my chest, giving the voyeur something more respectable to study.

A minute later I felt a presence at my elbow and twisted around to see who was casting a shadow over me. My breath caught in my throat; it was Mr Henson, and he looked spectacular. Chest glistening with water, he dripped onto the decking. He was so close I could feel the steam coming off of him.

Be cool, Jenny, be cool.

'Hello, Mr Henson,' I spoke up, clearly and confidently.

'I told you, I think you should call me Michael, we are on holiday.'

'In that case, you should really call me Jenny.' I said, raising my head to face him square on.

I was acting a lot more self-assured than I felt, it must have been the champagne.

'What do you think of this place?'

'It's great, perfect to celebrate my friend's hen

do.'

'I'm pleased. It's great to see you here, so, do you like the upgrade?' he asked with a coy eyebrow wiggle.

Taken aback, I wondered how he knew. 'Yes, it's fantastic, how did you…?'

'You came up in conversation with Peter in the office. He mentioned you were coming here and that he'd pulled some strings. I wondered if I might *bump* into you.' His eyes twinkled mischievously.

I didn't know what to say, and I was feeling very foolish for acting like such a doofus the entire time.

'Please excuse my indecency.' He glanced down at his near naked self, I couldn't help but look too. 'I wanted to speak to you while I had the chance. Our recent encounters have been…' he paused to choose his wording carefully, '…brief.'

'Mr Henson, I mean, Michael, I want to apologise if I've seemed rude; I was taken by surprise the other day, and again earlier.' I was quite proud that I'd strung an almost succinct sentence together.

'I hope you don't feel uncomfortable. It was, of course, a complete coincidence, are you okay with it all?' he asked as he leaned in.

'Yeah, of course.' I beamed and tried to laugh as if snogging strangers with a blindfold on was totally normal for me. 'I was hoping to bump into you again before we were back in work.

I thought that it might have been awkward otherwise.'

'Not at all,' he replied. 'In fact, I was hoping to bump into *you* again, I thought maybe we could go for a drink?'

'A drink? That'd be lovely but I'm not sure I should leave my friends. Plus, I've organised everything- they kinda need me.' I wanted to leap at the offer but I felt awful at the thought of ditching the girls for a guy.

'That's too bad, but I'm not surprised that you're indispensable. Maybe I'll have more luck if I ask you another time?' He raised his eyebrow provocatively.

Before I could answer Kirsty and Jade emerged by the steps and called over to me, while the waiter appeared, informing me that our food was ready. The universe was telling me this conversation was over.

'Please excuse me,' I said and stalked off trying to ooze sex appeal from my walk-away. He probably wasn't even looking and I didn't peek back to check. I met up with the sisters and we headed over to our side of the decking.

'What happened?' asked Kirsty.

'He wanted to clear the air and check I was okay, about, you know...what happened.'

'About you *k-i-s-s-i-n-g*!' teased Jade.

'That's great!' said Kirsty, pointedly ignoring her little sister.

'Ooohhhh, that's a good sign!' remarked Suze,

who had been trying to subtly observe our exchange from behind her book.

'Actually, I think he asked me out.'

'What did you say?' demanded Kirsty, barely containing her excitement. She was keener for me to get a boyfriend than I was.

'I said no.'

'Playing it cool, that's the way to keep him interested,' said Suze.

'I wasn't doing it to 'treat him mean and keep him keen'; I didn't want to dump you lot. *Hoes before bros* and all that.'

'Don't worry about that! You should've said yes!' said Kirsty, sounding exasperated.

'Well, he said something about asking me again another time but I'm not sure.'

Annie huffed. 'Jen, have you ever tried to *not* over think things? Not everything has to be so organised. Sometimes you just need to say yes and see what happens.'

'So, is it okay if I say yes?'

'Yes!' they replied in unison.

'Okay, I will,' I said with new found confidence. 'I'll stay cool and say yes... if he asks again that is.'

'You're not very good at this whole dating thing, are you?' said Annie.

'You've only just realised that?' I asked with a chuckle.

I took a sip of water and then said, 'There's something terribly wrong here.'

'What's that?' asked Kirsty, concern furrowing her brow.

'We've all got empty glasses!' I replied and headed back over to the bar.

CHAPTER 16

I leaned on the bar and ordered some more drinks, very aware of my proximity to Michael. I studied the exotic flower and fruit display, desperately trying not to ogle his muscly back as he stood chatting with his friends. Handing over the money to pay for our drinks, I turned to head back to my group, but Michael had spotted me and waved. I waggled my fingers in an awkward wave and tried to make my grin not too goofy. As he approached, I braced myself, giving myself a firm warning, Don't do anything stupid like run away.

'So, are you girls having fun?'

'Oh yes, thanks. We'd run out of drinks so I thought I'd better get the next round in.'

'We can't have that,' he said and then spoke to the barman. 'Keep an eye on their drinks, and make sure they're kept topped up- put it on my tab.' The barman dipped his head.

'Oh no, that's too much.'

He made his dismissive gesture again and said, 'It's fine, it's the least I can do. So, have you changed your mind about grabbing a drink with me? What do you say?' he leaned in seductively.

'Yes, actually that would be great. Thanks.'

He smiled and said, 'Good.' But then didn't say anything else.

The silence made me feel nervous and, in an effort to fill the void, I started babbling. 'I'm pleased we got to clear everything up earlier. I didn't want you thinking that I'm unprofessional or have it reflect badly on me at work or-'

He interrupted my prattling and said, 'Best not discuss work matters whilst you're on holiday.' He raised his eyebrows and swung up and down on his tip toes as he spoke.

'I know, I just wanted to make sure everything was okay with work and...'

'I'm sure there's plenty we need to discuss when we're back in the office,' he said curtly, as if to end the conversation.

It was an odd statement and I was taken aback. His sudden cold, brusque manner was incongruous with his melting hot torso. I was confused, he'd invited me out only moments before and now he seemed, aloof and purely professional.

'So, are you enjoying your holiday?' I asked, at a bit of a loss for what else to say.

'I'm still on call.' He indicated to his phone.

'But I don't start officially until next week so I have time for some... R&R.' He glanced over to the beautiful people he was with.

Michael pursed his lips together in a small, tight smile, his jaw seemed to twitch as if he was stopping himself from speaking.

One of the stunningly attractive girls bobbed up and down, yelling out, 'Miiiike!' Her hefty cleavage bouncing.

Michael waved and I felt a pang in my stomach.

'I should let you get back to your friends,' I said and made my exit.

'What happened?' asked Kirsty when I got back to the group.

I took a big swig from my glass and swallowed hard. 'It was really weird, he asked me out for a drink again but then he turned formal and frosty at the end.'

'Maybe he's worried about a lawsuit, sexual harassment in the office,' said Annie. I raised my eyebrows and pulled a bemused face in response.

'There was something he wasn't saying about work, I've got a bad feeling.'

'I'm sure it's nothing; you worry too much,' said Kirsty.

I had an overwhelming feeling of disappointment and anti-climax. 'Why would he be asking after me and offering us drinks but then go all weird like that a second ago?'

'Maybe he saw you again in the daylight and it

put him off?' joked Annie.

'Not helpful!' said Suze glaring.

'I hope not,' I replied.

'You don't *fancy* him, do you?' said Jade, still in little sister teasing mode. All the girls looked up at me, eyebrows raised.

'No, well, I thought he was flirting in his office but then maybe he was just being nice. I made a bit of a fool of myself at work so I was sure that'd put him off. But, wow, he's hot and then there was that kiss and he seems so lovely and generous...I don't know. The way he turned official... I get the feeling something might be wrong at work.'

In truth, I'd started to stupidly let myself be interested in him. What was I thinking? *My boss indeed!* I mentally told myself off again and pushed the glow of desire I'd been kindling, deep down to the bottom of my chest, trying to extinguish it before I got burned.

Kirsty leaned over and offered me a large juicy king prawn from our platter. 'Seriously, Jenny, you worry too much. I can see it written all over your face!'

I gave her a small smile and took the prawn, nibbling on it slowly; I'd lost my appetite. My phone buzzed, so I wiped my hands on one of the linen serviettes and excused myself from the group. Heading back over to the spot under the foliage I answered the call from Pete.

'Hiya J!'

'Hi Pete, how are you?'

'I'm great, darling, yourself?'

'I'm feeling a bit like royalty at the moment. I hear you helped to organise VIP treatment for us at Breeze.'

'Well it's a long story, darling, but yes I did. Do you like it?'

'Like it? We love it! But, this is crazy, isn't it a bit much?'

'Oh, don't worry. Don't argue. Just go and enjoy, go on, go!' Pete urged.

'Hang on, there's something else I need to ask you about. It's really serious and you've got to promise not to tell anyone.'

'Ooh err, sounds heavy, go on…'

'Say you promise…' I pleaded.

'Alright, alright, I promise not to tell anyone.'

'It's about Mr Henson, I…'

Pete cut me off. 'Oh, that reminds me, did I tell you? I've got a promotion at work!' I could hear him dancing around on the other end of the phone. 'Mr Henson called me into his office after you left the other day and we had a great chat, He's nice ain't he? Well, we had a long chat about what I do and what everyone does in the office and now I'm head of the assistants' section, I've got three people under me! Ha ha, sounds kinky doesn't it?'

'Pete that's fab! I'm so happy for you! Hang on, three? Three people?' My blood started to run cold.

'Yeah, The Witches won't know what's hit them next week!'

'But I'm in the assistants' section, what about me?'

'Oh darling, I'm sorry, didn't you know? You've been…'

'Bleep bleep bleep.'

I looked down to my phone, the screen was blank. Frantically pressing the on button, the screen briefly flashed but then went dark again. The battery was flat. 'I've been what?' I speculated, panicking. Moved? Demoted? Fired? All for a mis-sent email and a bra mishap? My hands trembled with fear and fury, and I gripped on to the tree to steady myself.

CHAPTER 17

The DJ was really heating up, and as the sun was going down the volume was increasing. He was playing the biggest tunes of the moment and the crowd below were loving it. I went back over to the girls, they were already up and dancing.

A fresh order of drinks had arrived and I grabbed a full glass and downed it. I shuddered at the sickly sweet flavour as the sex on the beach cocktail hit my stomach, and stifled a hiccup. It didn't sit well with the champagne and seafood I'd been scoffing but it seemed to help calm my nerves. I indicated to the bar man for another round and quickly downed that one too. I couldn't stop thinking about what Pete was trying to tell me; did I have a job to go back to after the holiday? Maybe Michael buying us drinks was because he felt bad that I'd lost my job?

Kirsty leaned over to me and reading her lips

I could see she was asking if I was alright but the music was too loud to hear. I told her I thought I'd been fired but she couldn't hear me; she nodded and gave me the thumbs up sign. She must have thought I said I was fine.

After downing the cocktails, I was losing the feeling in my arms and I didn't care, if I had lost my job then this would be my last holiday for a while, I best enjoy it. My logic was getting wobbly, as was I. Losing our inhibitions, the girls and I threw some crazy shapes, standing on our sun loungers and dancing in a frenzy. Even Jade loosened up and relaxed her "I'm glamorous and aloof" persona.

Glancing to the other side of the VIP area, I could see Michael and his posse had ordered some magnums of champagne and the bimbos were spraying one over themselves laughing. This enraged me, I was facing virtual poverty status from losing my job and there he was, wasting champagne. That guy must have money to burn.

Anger was rising up from my toes, the heat licking its way up to my chest. Before I knew it, I was off the sun lounger and striding over to the other hot tub. The alcohol had doused any shyness and insecurity I might have otherwise felt. I was furious. He saw me coming. On reflection, the entire VIP area probably saw me coming but I could only see him. Michael braced his hand on the edge of the hot tub and swung himself easily out, all his body weight through one arm. He landed lightly considering his towering frame and he came towards me, smiling.

'Jennifer, good to see you. You having fun?' his voice petered off as he recognised the look of contempt on my face as I reached him.

'Don't "Jennifer" me, you odious bastard,' I hissed over the music. 'Who on earth do you think you are? Coming on my holiday, kissing me, pretending to be worried if I'm okay, organising all this...' I circled my finger round pointing at the VIP area in general. 'When the whole time you were waiting for me to get back to work so you can fire me? Thought you'd rub it in by splashing around expensive champagne with your tarts? Bet that gave you a right laugh, ha! *Jenny won't be able to afford this next week when she's on the dole*," my voice was getting louder and louder.

'Whoa...slow down, I think we've got our wires crossed.' He put his hands up defensively.

'Wires crossed?! Anymore metaphors for me or are you saving them for when you fire me, or should I say "lay me off" or is it gonna be "let me go"?' I stood up on my tip toes to get really close, to try and look him squarely in the eyes.

'Calm down, I'm not sure I completely follow...'

'Don't tell me to calm down,' I said, pushing his broad shoulders.

'Is there a problem here?' Annie had appeared, looking concerned.

'No, I was just leaving,' I announced, casting Michael my most scathing glare.

'Jennifer…' he called after me, but I'd already flounced off. Annie said something to him then left too, quickly catching me up.

'Come on, Jen,' she said. 'We need to go, Suze has been sick in the dipping pool. I think it's best we leave.'

The thought of being sick seemed a pretty good idea to me too, I'd drunk too much and eaten too little today. My eruption had left me feeling heady. Determined to leave with dignity, less make a mockery of my outburst, I rapidly swallowed and held my head high. I grabbed my bag, threw on my dress and strutted off after the other girls. All was going pretty well and I was happy with my storming off technique until I tripped on part of the decking and fell face first down the steps and landed in a tangle of red rope at the bottom. One of the hazards of still wearing sunglasses once it's got dark, I guess.

Annie scooped me up and as we walked off she called out, 'We're just leaving. Thank you.'

'What did you say to him?' I asked.

'I told him I had heels bigger than his dick, so he'd better not mess with you.'

'Wow, that's quite scary!' I said. 'At least one of us left a serious impression.'

Suze was leaning against a rocky wall, while Annie rubbed her back. The rest of us perched on a boulder a few metres away. The entrance of the beach club was behind us as we looked down the road. The cool breeze from the sea flowed over me as we waited for a taxi, and slowly my rage quelled. As I managed to focus, two thoughts jumbled around my sloshy head, ouch, my knee really hurts! And, oh no, what have I done?.

Swaying, I leaned forward and peered down at my legs. A large graze covered one of my knees. That explained the first thought. Now to the "oh no, what have I done" feeling. Yep, I was pretty sure I just yelled at my boss. If I wasn't fired before, I think shouting at him and insulting his friends would probably do it. I rubbed the bridge of my nose with my fingers, despairing. My knee throbbed and another wave of regret washed over me, he probably saw me fall down as well. How humiliating. My drunken group was oblivious to my turmoil, only Annie had been aware of what was going on and she was busy looking after Suze.

'Ouch, that looks sore,' slurred Kirsty, examining my knee.

'Yeah, it is. I fell,' I replied. I was sobering up by the second.

'Sign of a good time!' exclaimed Jade.

'Hmmmm.' I was unable to muster any more of a reply.

'TAXIIIIIIII!' yelled Kirsty standing up and pointing to the vehicle as it drew nearer. A familiar face greeted us through the window and Antonio called out, 'Hola, Señoritas. It is an early night for you, non?'

'I think we all peaked too soon, Antonio,' said Annie as she shoved Suze's behind up into the minibus.

Suze had slumped over a couple of seats so there was still not enough room for me to sit in the back. I clambered into my usual seat in the front and gave Antonio a small smile. Antonio opened the windows to help sober us up and drove off in the direction of our apartment.

'Yenny, you do not seem your usual self. Are you not enjoying your holiday here?'

'I'm having a great time,' I replied quietly.

'Well it must be a man then, non?'

Antonio had such a gentle, easy, way, I opened up to him and before I knew it my story came tumbling out, all higgledy-piggledy and out of sync.

'I think I've been fired and I screamed at my boss which is going to make it really hard when I go back into work especially as he kissed me which was amazing but I hate him.'

'Yenny, slow down! Let me get this right, your boss is here? And he fired you and then kissed you?'

'No. I don't know. I don't even know if I've been fired for sure.'

'But you are mad at your boss?'

'Yes.'

'Because he kissed you?'

'No, because he fired me.'

'You like that he kissed you, eh?! And you do not know if he fired you?'

'I don't knooow Antonio, I am so confuuused!' I wailed.

As we waited at a red light, Antonio turned to me and said, 'You are not making a lot of sense, but I know you are a good girl. I will tell you what I tell my own daughter. You can only do your best and be yourself. If it is work, or if it is a man, this is all you can do.' He patted my arm then as the lights changed he released the break and pulled away. 'Now, you will need to clear all this up, but you can do it in the morning. And do not forget, just do your best and be true to yourself.'

Antonio dropped us off at our apartment and we headed up to bed, rather flat after such a fantastic day. The fresh air and pain from my knee had sobered me up. As I lay in bed, grappling with sleep, I contemplated what Antonio had said to me. I couldn't help but disagree with him, I'd been doing my best and that led to me being fired. And clearly, being myself meant I was a clumsy, unlovable fool. Perhaps what I needed was to NOT be myself, to be better. Then maybe I wouldn't find myself in these kinds of situations.

My phone suddenly flashed into life as the

battery charged. A text came in making it vibrate on the tiled floor and Suze grunted in her sleep. I slipped off the bed and padded over to see what it said. It was from Pete, the time stamp showed he must have sent it straight after my battery died. My heart plummeted as I read the message.

Not sure what happened darling, but I can't get through. Haven't you heard? You've been promoted! ☺ It's a transfer to the finance department. If you want it that is? We can talk more in work. How exciting! Luv ya xx

I was stunned, motionless. When I should've been leaping around the room, overjoyed, I just wanted to crawl into a corner and hide. What had I done? I'd presumed the worst on half a story and made a complete fool out of myself. After chewing out Michael like that he was going to think I was bat-shit-crazy. I wondered if he could take the new job away from me, I felt I almost deserved it. I sunk to the ground and considered my options. Calling Pete was certainly high on my to-do list and as it wasn't too late, I crept out to the balcony to phone him.

'Hiya darling, did you get my message?'

'Yes, thanks. That's why I'm calling you back.'

'You okay? You should be thrilled, you don't sound thrilled.'

'I think I've made a right tit of myself actually. Have you got a minute?'

I leaned on the balcony railing and poured

my heart out to my friend. I explained about Natalia and the bad impression I'd made at work. I told him about the mystery man and *that* kiss and that it was Mr Henson all along. Then the awkward encounter at Breeze followed by our half-finished conversation where I'd stupidly presumed I'd been fired, and then my rampage.

'So, you were upset, got drunk and screamed at him?' summarised Pete as I was finishing up.

'Yeah, pretty much.' I hung my head, ashamed. 'Do you think he's going to fire me?'

'No, darling, he can't fire you. He put me in charge of assistants and it was me who decided to move you to finance. If you want the job that is?'

'Oh yes, Pete, of course,' I gushed. I was so relieved.

'Now, you should know it was Mr Henson that sorted your upgrade at Breeze. He got me to organise it, but insisted I put it on his account. I think it was his way of celebrating your promotion. We've got lots to catch up on when you're back. Now, you enjoy the rest of your holiday and I'll see you in a few days.'

I thanked Pete again and we said our goodbyes. Needing some unconditional love and support I sent a text to my mum, I was a little bewildered and wanted to talk things through with her.

How are you doing mum? Do you fancy a chat? Xx

Stop worrying about me Jennifer and go and

enjoy yourself. Lots of love Mum xx

She must have misunderstood and thought I was checking up on her again. At a loss for what else to do I fell into bed and waited for sleep to take me.

CHAPTER 18

'**M**y hat!' wailed Kirsty.

When we had all roused after our eventful night we started to take stock of what had happened. Kirsty was most put out to find she had left her big floppy hat in the VIP area during our mass exodus.

'Do you think it'll still be there? Will someone have taken it?' she worried.

I struggled to be diplomatic with my answer. 'I don't think it would've been stolen, it'd be quite large to smuggle out…' *and who would want it, it's bloody huge!* '…Let's pop back in later and check, we need to head to the beach today anyway.'

'I don't think I can show my face there again!' moaned Suze, ashen.

'Well, one of us could nip in and check anyway.' As I said it I realised it would most probably end up being me.

Annie, feeling chipper, piped up, 'It's ironic, Suze, if you had the hat you could've hidden your face under it as a disguise.'

There was a thwack as the cushion Suze was hugging landed on Annie.

'I guess I deserve this teasing,' said Suze. 'I made a right idiot of myself last night.'

'It could have been worse,' I replied, 'you could've done something *really* stupid like scream at your boss and then fall down the stairs...'

The girls went quiet for a second then caught my eye and we all started laughing. There's nothing like having good friends around when you have made a complete fool of yourself.

'I'm not sure how we can disguise that graze on your knee though. It won't be as easy as wearing sunglasses,' said Jade.

'I'll try and cover it up with clothing I think.'

'Maybe we could all walk with a limp like we are gangsters?' Jade looked half serious as she said it. I rolled my eyes in response.

'What are you going to do about your boss? You need to get it sorted out,' asked Annie, straight to the point as always.

'I think I'll start with an apology.'

'And maybe try not to have any more embarrassing disasters near him, eh?'

'Thanks for the advice, Annie!' I'm not sure who was being more helpful, Annie or Jade? 'I can presume that drink he suggested is off the table, can't I?' My friends nodded sympathetically in response.

The big plan for the day was to head down to the beach for some water sports fun and then onto a club later in the night. However, my most pressing task was to clear things up with Michael, I gave this a good two minutes consideration and then decided hiding from him for a bit would probably be best. Why put off till later what I could try to avoid forever?

I took a big gulp and swallowed my pride. Sunglasses donned as an extra bit of armour and a floaty maxi dress to cover my knee, I limped up to the reception desk in the foyer at Breeze and smiled at the man on duty. I didn't recognise him so I was quite confident that he hadn't been on duty yesterday. Phew! He spoke good English and I told him about the hat and asked if it had been handed in.

'Can you describe the hat?'

'It's extremely big and floppy.'

'I don't think so,' he said rummaging in a closet behind the desk. 'Where did you leave it?'

'I believe it might have been the VIP area, but I don't want to bother you.'

I was panicking that I would have to return to the scene of my fall. I was relieved when he picked up the phone and dialled what I expected was the VIP bar, he had a conversation in quick Spanish that went right over my head.

Replacing the handset, he looked up

apologetically. 'Sorry, no hat,' he said.

'Okay, thanks for checking,' I said and turned to go.

'You could leave your contact details in case it turns up.'

Smiling, I moved back to the desk. I jotted down our details and a description of the hat. Eager to leave before I got recognised I called out, 'Adios!'

As I left the desk and the man called back, 'Adios! Watch your step, we don't want you to trip and fall...'

Blushing with embarrassment, my limp became more of a lurch as I hurried to leave. I could hear the guy chuckling at my expense. *Thanks girls!* I thought to myself. They were busy getting ice creams while I was dutifully searching for that bloody hat.

I caught up with everyone at the ice cream parlour and, with our cones in hand, we padded across the sandy beach in our flip flops, the sand scorching underfoot. I'd scraped my hair back into a ponytail but the wind off the sea tugged at the tendrils which were loose around my face. Suze had bought me a couple of scoops of rum and raisin and I hastened to eat it before it melted all over me.

A young-looking guy called Connor greeted us at the water sports shack, he had a golden tan and the sun had streaked blond through his hair which was tied up in a top knot, very beach bum chic. I was pleasantly surprised to find that he was Australian, working on the beach all season to fund his travels around Europe. It was a relief not to try and speak Spanish, I always felt so rude that I couldn't communicate properly.

I'd booked us on to a jet ski experience over the internet, but was beginning to wonder why I hadn't gone with something more relaxing such as a spa day. We had our own private session with Connor, I don't mind making a fool of myself in front of my friends but with a group of strangers it's another matter entirely.

'Welcome, ladies, I'm stoked to have you here learning to jet ski today! So, which one of you is the Jenny who's been emailing?'

I waved my hand. 'That's me.'

He seemed to give me a once over before saying, 'Nice to put a name to a face. And the bride to be?'

We all pushed Kirsty forwards.

'So, you're the lucky recipient of this.' He handed her a blue and white L-plate and chuckled. 'It's a little bit of fun we get all the hens and bucks to fix on their PWCs.'

He noted our blank faces and explained, 'Personal water-crafts. After all, if you can handle a jet ski, you can handle a marriage! Go and change your togs and we can get started.'

Connor's enthusiasm reminded me of a puppy. He provided some short wetsuits and we pulled them on over our bikinis in the shack and then headed out. We joined him on the shore with the water lapping on the wet sand and over our feet. He handed out life jackets and gave us a safety talk and a very brief explanation of what on earth we were supposed to do.

'So, when it comes to stopping, you have three options. You can press the stop button.' He indicated to a big red button. 'You can fall off and this will automatically cut out the engine.' The girls and I glanced at each other apprehensively. 'Or you can hit something that's bigger than you.' We laughed nervously. Connor continued, 'Now it's easier to learn all this in practise, so let's stop talking and crack on.'

He hailed us over to the water-crafts and splashed into the sea. Six jet skis were bobbing up and down ready for us to embark and we waded towards them.

'Who wants to go first?' he asked.

We all hesitated, no one sure what to do.

'Kirsty should, she's the bride to be,' announced Jade.

'No, I'd rather see how it's done first,' said Kirsty, a note of panic in her voice.

'Okay, you with the knee, you seem like the adventurous type. You jump on first,' commanded Connor looking at me.

Sod it, let's do this. It can't be worse than all the fiascos that Michael's witnessed. With a renewed sense of confidence, I approached the nearest jet ski. Presuming it would be best to get on it the same way you'd get on a horse, I grabbed at the side of it. As I put my foot up to haul myself up out of the sea it tipped suddenly over towards me and dunked me unceremoniously back into the water. I surfaced quickly blowing the salty water out of my nose to find Connor chuckling along with the girls. My knee was stinging in the brine, and I again wondered why I'd booked something so gung-ho for us to do.

'Your friend here has just given you a great demonstration of how *not* to get on. I think if you try from the back you'll find it a lot easier.' Connor then indicated for everyone to mount the jet skis.

Determined not to be beaten, I stuck out my chin and mounted the damn thing as gracefully as I could muster. The girls, still dry, looked at me smugly and I stuck out my tongue when Connor wasn't looking.

'Where are the brakes?' asked Suze, puzzled.

'There are no brakes, ladies, so you need to read the waves and plan ahead. And you should expect to get very wet!' Connor gave out a throaty chuckle and winked.

We went through some more basics and then we were let loose in a large area cordoned off by colourful floating ropes to have a go. The girls pulled away one by one and practised accelerating and steering around some buoys.

I was last to go and as I gently squeezed the throttle Connor winked at me and shouted, 'Go get 'em, Grommet!'

'It's Jenny, actually,' I called behind me, and accelerated forwards, my back straight and my head held high. I was determined not to be a laughing stock.

The feeling of speed was incredible; I loved the wind in my face and the cooling spritz of water misting me as I sped around. This could be my sport I thought as I whizzed around, I was starting to get the hang of it.

After some more practise, Connor herded us over to the furthest point from the beach and unclipped one of the ropes, we steered through the gap and out into open water. He circled round us a couple of times making our stationary vessels bob heavily up and down in the water.

Cruising to a brief stop he yelled out, 'Follow me and try to keep up.' Then zoomed off, spraying us with water.

We laughed and then raced after him as fast as we could. The hardest part for all of us was slowing or stopping. Turning was pretty hard too. And we'd all capsized at least twice. We were having a lot of fun and Connor's jibes and cockiness had us all trying to beat him and prove him wrong. I'd changed my mind and decided I was very pleased with what I'd booked for us. We had a tour of some nearby coves as well as messing around out in the open water, all the while, Connor gently goaded us into getting better.

'We're gonna head back now,' he called out.

Marencanto was a distant glimmer on the horizon; we'd been carving through the water for almost an hour. I was proud that we'd all improved massively in that time, and that I hadn't lost my faithful sunglasses despite a couple more dunks in the sea.

'Be careful,' said Connor. 'The bay's gonna be a lot busier with other water traffic now it's later in the day, so you should watch out.' Then he careered off again.

We were forever playing catch up with him and it was really winding me up; he was so smug. I don't know what it was, maybe my body had finally got the technique of jet skiing or maybe I had the wind behind me, but as I rapidly accelerated after him, the engine screaming in my ears, I could sense that I was gaining on him. This spurred me on and I squeezed the accelerator even harder, emboldened by my new-found prowess.

We chased him back towards the base and covered the distance much quicker than I was expecting. Watching Connor, I saw that he had slowed down and I seized my opportunity to race in to the lead. As I overtook I looked back laughing at him, but instead of irritation on his face, I could see his eyes wide with fear. I whipped my head back round to see a fair-sized yacht loom into the foreground. *Eeeeeeeek!* I panicked and my mind went blank. My hand was clenched on to the accelerator with an iron grip.

Hit the stop button, I thought but then I remembered Suze doing that and how she went sailing over the top of the handlebars. How else to stop? How else to stop? I frantically tried to remember what Connor had said in the beginning. *Fall off.* Nope, not doing that either, my body was ignoring my mind, and dignity-preservation seemed to be overriding the self-preservation function. I continued to head straight for the boat. My course was unwavering. With a split-second to go I managed to move finally. I turned hard to the left and wrenched the jet ski off its path, moving fluidly with the machine as it dipped to turn. A huge arc of seawater spraying behind me as I went.

Euphoric that I'd avoided what could have been a potentially life-threatening collision, I breathed out and remembered that I just needed to let go of the accelerator to slow to a stop.

I righted my position and gently circled to find the rest of the group. I could hear Connor yelling something. Catching sight of the yacht as I looked for my group, there were four people standing on the deck. Four dripping wet people. I recognised the two girls as the beautiful bimbos from the VIP hot tub at Breeze. I squinted through my salt crusted sunglasses and my breath caught in my throat. Yes, one of the figures had a very familiar frame; Michael was stood there too. Water dripped from his soaking hair and off his muscular body like something out of a men's fragrance advert. Except those models usually smoulder with sex appeal rather than glower with animosity. And they don't usually have seaweed on their shoulders.

CHAPTER 19

Having caught up with Connor and the girls, I beat a hasty retreat back to the water sports base. Mooring the jet skis back on the shore, I uncurled my hand from the throttle and stretched it out. The vibration of the engine felt like it was still running through me. As I made to dismount, my bad knee complained, a lot. I'd been distracted from the discomfort while we were larking about but now we'd finished I could really feel it. I heaved myself off and lowered into the water in a slow, ungainly manner. As I turned I found myself caught between Connor's imposing body and the jet ski.

In a low and scarily calm voice, he whispered, 'If you ever do anything like that again, I swear to God, I...' He trailed off and stared at me intensely. 'Listen, you could have seriously hurt yourself back then. I know you girls are here to have a good time and I don't wanna put a downer on this for you and your friends but I never want you do something that stupid ever again.'

'I'm sorry,' I stuttered, 'I hadn't realised that boat was there and then I… I don't know what happened. I froze.'

'Never again,' he replied quietly. The girls started coming over to join us and after looking me in the eye again he said in his usual cheerful voice, 'Come on, Grommet. You seem to be some sort of disaster area; let's get that knee looked at.' He linked his arm behind me and helped me up on to the beach.

Having been a life guard back in Australia, Connor was well versed in first-aid and did an excellent job of checking my knee and patching me up.

'How did you do this?' he asked.

'You don't want to know,' I replied sheepishly.

'You did it throwing yourself at someone, ay?' He winked at me.

'The complete opposite actually,' cut in Annie.

All the girls were crowded round watching Connor clean me up; I was uncomfortable in the spot light.

'You've done that before,' said Suze. 'Maybe you should come out with us later, in case Jenny gets in to any more pickles.'

Before Connor could answer Jade piped up, 'Yeah, you should look out for us tonight. What's the name of the club we're going to Jenny?'

'Estrella de mar.'

Connor nodded his approval. 'I know it well,'

he said. 'That's an ace night out, I might swing by later.' Connor smiled warmly at Jade and she grinned back.

'It'd be great if you did,' I said, thinking I could maybe help matchmake him and Jade. 'Well, we'd better head off now. Thanks so much for this morning, and for patching up my knee.'

'Yes, it was fantastic, thanks so much,' gushed Kirsty. 'You must come out later, I'm the bride-to-be so everyone has to do what I say! It'll be fun.'

'Of course,' he replied, laughing. 'I'm looking forward to it already.'

He was saying the right things but I secretly thought the idea of seeing our group of crazy women again filled him with fear. I hoped Jade wouldn't be too disappointed, she seemed quite taken with him.

We were all a bit wobbly on our legs after the mammoth jet skiing session so we waddled slowly back to the apartment to put our feet up with a cup of tea. When we got back, we received a message from Beth saying that she'd got back home okay and was spending time with her gran and the rest of her family.

Annie caught my eye, she was looking a bit forlorn. 'I feel bad for how I went on at her,' she said.

'You're only human, you didn't know what was going on.'

'Yeah, but I was a bit harsh.'

'You don't take any nonsense and you tell people how it is; it's a good quality.'

'At the time I feel like I'm doing the person a favour, but afterwards, I feel like I've maybe been…mean.' Annie bit her lip.

'Beth'll forgive you, I'm sure she already has! I might not forgive you though…' I pretended to look annoyed.

'What? Why?'

'Beth was my clearing up and travelling home buddy, now when you guys swan off tomorrow I've got a whole evening on my own.'

'How's that my fault?'

'You paid for her flight back!' I said laughing.

'Why are you on a separate flight anyway?'

'Your flight was full. I couldn't get us all on the same one. So, Beth and I were getting the one the next day.'

'That's a shame.'

'At least it gives me the opportunity to give this place a good clean so we get our deposits back.' With a sigh, I surveyed the mess we had made; girls getting ready sure does spew a lot of crap everywhere.

We didn't end up going out until after eleven as the club didn't open until late. I'd got us on the guest list, so there was no need to queue. Sipping on my tequila cocktail with the wall at my back, I tried not to feel self-conscious, everyone else was here in fancy dress too. It had seemed like a great idea when I was planning the trip. I'd seen that this club was really highly rated and then when I saw they were hosting a sexy fancy dress night while we were here, it seemed as if everything was falling into place. However, Beth, who was bringing out my costume, had also taken it back with her. It didn't even cross my mind until we were getting ready. Jade, ever the fashion savvy problem solver, had jumped to the rescue.

'Why don't you go as a sexy pirate? Then you've got an excuse for your limp and you can wear an eye patch!'

'Jade!' Kirsty shouted. 'Don't be mean!'

'I'm not, I'm being practical.'

'She's got a point,' I defended her. 'I can't be a sexy super hero with you guys, what super hero has a squint *and* a limp?!'

So, while Wonder Woman, Catwoman, Storm and Supergirl were wandering around looking super cute and sexy, here I was in a bandana, eye patch and billowing white gypsy shirt. Jade had accessorised me with some huge chunky gold hoop earrings and other tacky trinkets that looked like loot. Suze donated a baggy pair of beige linen trousers to be butchered into a cropped castaway style. The whole ensemble was synched in with a fat leather belt, one of the many things Kirsty had packed that we never thought she would need. At least my costume accentuated my waist and covered my various injuries. To be fair to Jade, she had worked a miracle with what we had, and had done a really good job of creating me an outfit out of nothing.

Truthfully, it wasn't my costume that had me feeling self-conscious, it was the embarrassment of screaming at Michael that was hanging over me. I needed to confront my fear and swallow my pride and just simply apologise to him. He was so calm, and controlled, I was scared to find him; I was such a wreck in comparison.

The beats of Spanish summer tunes and euro-pop were thumping, mixed in with some sultry house; the club was buzzing. The beautiful people of Marencanto were milling around, sipping their drinks and generally looking magnificent. From my position as chief wallflower I was enjoying watching the throng of revellers and I could see my friends, real superheroes in their own right, having a great time in the centre of it all.

I was brought out of my reverie by a well-muscled arm suddenly pressing against the wall by my head. A bare chest filled my view. Surprised, I glanced up and a roman centurion's helmet was obscuring a familiar face.

Sighing inwardly, I said, 'Hello Brutus,' over the top of the music. 'What are you sniffing around for?'

'That's no way to treat your amigo.'

I snorted in response and tried to shift away from him but his hefty frame loomed over me, blocking my view and my exit.

'Tell me, where is our mutual friend?'

'I don't think we have any mutual friends,' I said, coldly.

'Don't be like this. You know, your friend with the big green eyes and the big…'

I cut him off, hoping to get rid of him as quickly as possible. 'Beth. Her name was Beth. Well done for remembering, that's real classy. She's not here so why don't you go and annoy someone else.'

I sidestepped away from him but he kept pace with me and moved to block me. I was starting to feel more than a little irritated.

'Why are you being like this?' He stroked my face and ran his fingers through my hair; claustrophobia crept over me. 'We are friends, aren't we?' he asked, a sinister note in his voice.

'I'd say we were more like acquaintances. Now, I really had better get back to my actual friends.' I tried to push my way out but he forced me back up against the wall and my head banged on the brick.

My temperature was rising and my heart raced as panic started to set in.

'Is there a problem here?' A deep English voice boomed out over the sound of the music.

'Who are you meant to be?' Brutus laughed, half turning towards the guy, but not relinquishing his position over me. 'James Bond?'

'Yes, if you say so. Now, as I said, is there a

problem here?'

'Non, non. I was just catching up with my... friend,' said Brutus menacingly, turning back towards me.

'Well let's see if your *friend* is okay,' said the voice and then a large hand grappled with Brutus' shoulder and wrenched him away.

Michael appeared before me, completely seething. *Not again!*

'Jennifer?' He sounded surprised.

'Oh, hello, Michael,' I said meekly. 'Fancy meeting you here.'

Brutus tutted and lunged away, shouldering Michael in the chest as he barged off and melted into the crowd on the dance floor.

'Erm, thank you for er...intervening,' I said. 'I had it all under control but it was nice to have some back up.'

Michael raised his eyebrows, maybe I hadn't been radiating the aura of composure and confidence that I was hoping for.

He stood before me for a second, his black suit and crisp white shirt incongruous with the dazzling colours of the lights and other costumes, but cutting a striking silhouette. Seconds ticked past and it began to get awkward. He turned to go.

'Wait.' I reached out to his arm. 'I wanted to say something.'

'Didn't you say everything you wanted to last night?' he said.

'No, I...I mean yes...oh dear.' I paused and took a deep breath. 'I wanted to apologise.'

Michael was staring at me, his lips pursed and one eyebrow raised ever so slightly.

'I'm sorry for my explosion last night; I was completely wrong. I shouldn't have said any of it and I certainly shouldn't have come over and screamed at you while you were with your friends having fun. I...I...I had been drinking and it was unprofessional and I'm sorry.' I caught my breath after my outburst and slowly looked up into his eyes. I'd been directing my whole speech at his chin.

The dark, smoky club, and flashing lights made it difficult to read his expression. My heart raced as I stood so close to him. *Why wasn't he saying anything?*

Ruffled, I carried on babbling. 'I just... I got the wrong end of the stick and I thought you'd fired me and I panicked, and did I say I'd been drinking? I clearly don't make sensible choices when I've been drinking. I really am truly sorry.'

He held my gaze, unblinking, and I stared back expectantly. More seconds passed and still he remained mute.

Taking a deep breath, I ploughed on, 'I'm really sorry, look if there's anything I can do to make it up to you then I...'

Michael started to shake, the corners of his mouth twitched and, as he caught sight of my confused expression, bent forward in full belly laughs.

'What the…?'

As he calmed his laughter into chuckles he managed to say, 'Sorry, I wanted to see what you'd say next. The longer I left it the more flustered you got, another minute and who knows what you'd have been saying?'

'You mean you're not mad?'

'Oh, I was mad.' His face became quite serious suddenly. 'But you have a very good colleague who phoned me this morning and cleared a few things up.'

I mentally thanked Pete. *What would I do without that guy?*

'I'm sorry you got so upset. It must have been pretty scary thinking you'd lost your job.' He rested his hand on my arm and my skin tingled underneath.

His kindness surprised me, guys aren't normally this understanding.

He gave me a very cheeky grin and changed the subject. 'I have your hat, by the way. I noticed you'd left it behind after you made your…er… exit last night.' His eyes shone as he teased me.

'Thanks. It's not actually mine, but Kirsty will be so pleased.'

'Not yours? But I've seen you toting that thing everywhere.'

'Yeah, Kirsty has a habit of forgetting about it.'

'How? It's huge!' We laughed and I felt the ice break for the first time, we were snug in our mutual exasperation of that bloody hat.

'So, are you here with *all* your friends then?'

'Yeah, why do you ask?'

He winced as he said, 'Well, your friend with the afro *and the heels*, she scares me!'

'That's Annie. She scares me sometimes too but I'll do my best to protect you!' I said and laughed.

As we talked, or shouted, over the music I felt a new sensation emerge. Michael had roused many feelings in me over the last few days, lust, anger, hate, but now there was something different. I liked him. I wasn't scared by his power, enraged by his decisions or swooning at his physique, we were chatting normally and it felt great; it felt comfortable. Don't get me wrong, I wasn't about to confess that it was me who gave him a sea water facial. I wasn't that comfortable. He hadn't mentioned the incident so I was hoping that the salt in his eyes and the disguise of a jet ski and wet suit meant he was clueless about the perpetrator.

'Grommet! I almost didn't recognise ya!' said Connor as he approached cheerily. 'Someone prised you away from those sunglasses?'

'Shame I'm not wearing them now, Connor, help me cope with the reflection from your costume,' I snapped back. I was irritated that someone had broken into my cosy conversation with Michael.

I wished he would stop with the 'Grommet'.

Had he misheard my name? Was he comparing me to an animated dog? Whatever it was it, wasn't funny.

Connor wasn't picking up on the 'you are not welcome' vibes and boldly stood there, chest stuck out proudly, grinning at us. With his hands on his hips, he displayed his Silver Surfer costume, which consisted of teeny tiny silver speedos and a hell of a lot of silver body paint.

'You could borrow this one's sunglasses,' he said to Michael. 'Then you'd look like one of the Men in Black.'

'Indeed,' said Michael, stonily. 'So, you two know each other well then?'

I was about to say 'no' but Connor piped up. 'I should say, I gave Grommet a private jet ski lesson earlier today and...'

Michael's nostrils flared and he stared piercingly between the two of us. 'I should leave you to your reunion, my friends will be looking for me,' he announced and strode off.

'What's got his goat?' Connor asked, leaning in to hear me over the music.

'Thanks a lot, Connor! You've scared him off!' I huffed.

'Who? That stuck up pommy bastard? What are you interested in him for?'

'I'm not...' I was getting flustered. 'He's my boss and we've only recently started seeing eye to eye and...' I tailed off. 'Hey, I'm a pommy bastard too!' I said indignantly.

'Yeah, but I like you.' Connor looked me right in the eye and then smirked. 'He doesn't know it was you who almost came a gutser on the jet ski, does he? He doesn't know it was you who dressed him in seaweed?'

'I think he probably just worked it out, thanks to you.'

'Nah, he doesn't know for sure. I could go tell him, clear the mystery up for him?' he teased.

I knew he was only winding me up but I couldn't keep the pleading out of my voice. 'No, don't, please!' I implored. If there was any chance of keeping that a secret I was going to take it.

'What's it worth?' he asked, with a very cheeky lilt in his voice.

Deciding to play him at his own game, I leaned in and coyly said, 'I can think of something to make it worth your while.' I had a plan to distract him.

His eyes lit up. 'Really, what's that then?'

He was flirting big time and he didn't realise I was about to throw him to the wolves. I hooked a finger into the waist band of his speedos and lead him away, scanning the crowd for my girls.

I could hear him chuntering, 'Mind the budgie smugglers.' But he followed me quite willingly.

CHAPTER 20

My superheroes were strutting their stuff in the middle of the dance floor and we squeezed through the masses to join them. I winked at Jade and then shoved Connor in her and Suze's general direction, they pounced on him, as I'd hoped. Connor joined them with a big grin on his face.

The recognizable beat of mine and Kirsty's favourite song peeled out; the cheesy boyband of our youth's biggest hit single. Kirsty grabbed my hands and squealed, and for a good three minutes we boogied the hell out of that dance floor. Decades of practise had led to us perfecting a particular routine and we danced as if no one was watching. Although the circle of onlookers that formed around us certainly implied that we were being watched, we didn't care. By the end of it, our little group had all picked up the moves and it had caught on with other dancers too. More retro tracks were played, keeping everyone dancing.

It was far too loud to have a conversation, so after an epic dance session I mouthed that I was going to get some air, so I could go and search for Michael. Kirsty gave me a thumbs up sign, she seemed very happy in the middle of the dance floor. I limped and wriggled and scooched as best I could around the club doing my best to look out for him but all the while trying to appear cool and sophisticated. It wasn't working.

After my second lap, Connor found me and pulled me over to the bar.

'You look like you could use a shot,' he said.

I nodded in agreement and perched on one of the bar stools. Connor sat next to me and spoke with the barman. After a moment, we were given two tiny glasses and the tell-tale accompaniments of salt and lemon.

Having downed my tequila slammer, I squeezed the lemon into my mouth and caught sight of Michael at the other end of the bar. Or, it would be better to say that I caught sight of *them*. I felt sick. It wasn't the tequila.

Seeing Michael throw back his head and laugh along with one of the bimbos made my stomach pitch, flip and tie in a knot. Her amazing figure was on full display as she wore a sequined strapless red swimming costume and feathered headdress. Finally, Michael's costume made sense, they must have come as a couple, a magician and his assistant. As he leaned in close to her face another pang hit. Not wanting to see, I turned back to Connor.

'Everything alright, Grommet?'

'Yeah,' I replied tightly.

I beckoned to the barman for another shot, he dipped his head in surprise but refilled the glass nevertheless. My mind was racing and my stomach was churning. I kept my eyes focused down on the salt shaker and finally told myself some hard truths.

I was majorly crushing on my boss.

I was a walking disaster area.

I was completely sozzled.

Things needed to change when I got back from the holiday.

Wanting to get my head around this, I was suddenly desperate for some peace. I looked up at Connor and said, 'Thanks for the shots, I just need to nip to the ladies' room, I'll see you back on the dance floor.'

He frowned. 'You sure you're alright?' he asked.

'Of course.' I forced a smile and then slipped down from my stool and gave him a small wave before disappearing into the crowd.

My heart felt heavy; I'd got carried away, thinking I had a chance with Michael. Watching him with that other lady, or bimbo as I'd bitterly thought, brought back all the raw pain from my last relationship. I hadn't been interested in anyone since James, I think that whole experience dented my confidence quite a bit actually. So, well done to me for choosing my boss to be my rebound. *That was sensible, Jenny!* I'd felt a real connection from our tête-à-tête earlier in the night, and I'd discovered more to him than just good looks. But now my heart was feeling trampled again; perhaps being so out of practise I'd misread the signals.

As I walked aimlessly through the mass of people I caught sight of my reflection and realised, *of course he wouldn't be interested in me.* I was a mess and not even a hot one. I was in a makeshift costume to replace the one I'd forgotten about. The ensemble was attempting to disguise a gammy knee and bad eye. At least I didn't break my neck when I fell off the stage, I'd have had to dress as an Egyptian mummy to disguise that. I felt like such a fool. And what could I do about it? Absolutely nothing, except try and shut my emotions off, I'd simply have to find happiness as a spinster. A clumsy spinster.

Returning to the gang of superheroes I did my best to enjoy the night but my heart wasn't in it anymore. Connor had rejoined the group and was doing a grand job keeping Jade and Suze happy, he was dancing with everyone and anyone. The tell-tale smudges of silver rubbing off on people from where he was shimmying around.

He thrust his way over to me and leaned in, shouting into my ear, 'Are you sure you're alright,

Grommet? You look a bit ropey.'

I pulled as big a smile as I could and gave him a geeky thumbs up sign.

'I'm not convinced,' he replied before turning around and bucking his butt in my general direction. Jade and Suze whooped and hollered in appreciation of his moves.

CHAPTER 21

I tried to carry on partying but the feelings of gloom and disappointment were creeping over me. I really didn't want to bring down the mood so I slunk off and sent the girls a group text message.

Don't worry. I feel a bit unwell so I'm going back to the apartment. Have fun girlies. See you in the morning, J xx

The club was heaving as I made my way out, a thrashing mass of sweaty bodies. There was no sign of Michael or his bimbo, but then again, I was trying not to look out for them.

I was feeling hot and gross from my heavy pirate costume and long hair hanging down my back, it was a relief to get outside into the fresh air. As I moved away from the club I could see the stars shining in the sky. An idea came to me, not to go straight back to the apartment, but to head to the beach to catch a breeze off the sea and try to clear my head a bit more.

After a few minutes walking, the sound of the bass from the club had disappeared and my surroundings became familiar; I knew I was almost there. The old town was deserted as I headed through the old cobbled streets down towards the bay. It was so late, even our little bar on the main square was shut.

The silver light of the moon lit my way, shining off the cobbles and reflecting in the glass of the shop windows. I turned the corner and headed down towards the old amphitheatre, but seeing the dark, decaying shadow rear up gave me the shivers and the hairs on my neck pricked up.

My head was fuzzy from the tequila and my ears were ringing from the music but my senses sharpened instantly. My heart beat accelerated. I could have sworn I heard footsteps. I peered back but it was too dark to see anything.

Quickening my pace, I was desperate to get past the creepy old ruin and back towards civilisation. I heard something again, this time it sounded like a can skittering across the road. I still couldn't see anything. It must have been an animal in some rubbish I told myself, unconvincingly. I fumbled in my pocket for my phone and pulled it out to use the light from the screen as some sort of makeshift torch. Having the phone in my hand comforted me somewhat;

I could call for help if I needed it.

Picking up my pace, I scanned around with the dim light, I was passing right by the old ruins. Their shadow swathed the area in darkness. *You'd think they'd put on some security lights*, I grouched. I was treading the line between keeping a sensible reasoned head while walking calmly home and being completely terrified of the dark and running away screaming "help".

What was that? I definitely heard footsteps and they sounded like they were speeding up, and getting closer.

'Is that Jenny all alone there?' A menacing Spanish voice called out.

My skin flushed cold.

Brutus.

The more I encountered this guy the more I realised he was a nasty piece of work. I didn't want to take any chances. Thinking frantically, I remembered back to the dank passageway in the bullring and although it had freaked me out in broad daylight, it would be a good place to hide from him. I switched the light of my phone off not wanting to broadcast a homing beacon to help him find me.

'Jeeeennnnyyyy,' he called, creepily.

Swear words coursed through my head. Gripping my phone tightly I ran, too scared to look back. *Ow, ow, ow!* Every other step was agony. I ripped the stupid eye patch from my eye as I went, blinking in the darkness. With my free hand, I groped for the wall of the ruins and felt for the opening. Once I was in the passageway, the gloom got darker and I could smell the dank.

My ears strained to pick up any noise to indicate he'd followed me. I tried to breathe as quietly as possible, which was hard considering I was also trying to catch my breath.

A singular thought crossed my mind. *Why the hell have I gone into a tunnel?* This was by far the most stupid thing I'd done all holiday. Deciding to go deeper into the bullring I crept as quietly as possible through the passageway with the intention of hiding in the ruins. I felt along the cold rough wall and made my way slowly. Heart racing and paranoia pounding, I convinced myself I could hear someone following me. Picking up speed I sprinted the last few yards but my foot caught on a loose stone and I plunged into the wall, face first.

'Heyyyy,' a voice called out.

'Arghhhh!' I shouted back.

The footsteps stomped up to me and someone grabbed hold of my arms, pulling me up off the floor. Terrified, I shrieked and spouted a tirade of abuse, fighting and punching and kicking my assailant.

'Hey, hey, Grommet. It's me. Calm down. Shhhh, shhhh...' The soft Australian voice brought me back to my senses and I relaxed, it was only Connor.

'Jeez, you scared the absolute bejesus out of

me! I thought you were Brutus.' His grip loosened and he rubbed my arms gently then let go. 'What were you thinking grabbing me like that?' I forced a laugh but I was still trembling all over.

The moon lit up the inside of the bullring giving Connor an ethereal glow. We walked over to low a wall and sat down.

He was definitely drunk, I could smell the beer on him, but he was coherent. 'You know that douche's name isn't really Brutus, don't you? I saw him following you. He's got a certain reputation around here so I wanted to make sure you got home alright.'

'I would have done if it wasn't for you!' I made a show of brushing off the grime from the tunnel.

'It's a good job I did. I caught up with him and had a quiet word. He suddenly decided following you wasn't such a great idea. I guessed you'd gone in here so I thought I'd come and give you the all clear. You've gotta stop these near-death experiences.' Connor turned to me, looking me right in the eye. 'You know hiding somewhere like this is probably the stupidest move I've seen you make so far...'

The thunder of heavy footsteps cut Connor off mid-sentence and I tensed up, fearing Brutus had changed his mind. Connor put a protective arm around me. As I squinted into the dark, a large shape emerged that became more familiar with every stride. Michael.

'Leave her alone, you bastard,' he shouted.

Confused, I twisted around and glanced over my shoulder, he must have been talking to us, we were the only ones there. Connor's grip tightened defensively.

'It's alright, Michael, it's…' I was unable to finish my sentence.

With speed Michael careered into us and yanked Connor off me, then punched him squarely in the face.

'STOP! What the…?!' I yelled.

Connor had recovered from the strike and was trying to stand up with his palms up in front of him, a position of surrender. 'Whoa, easy mate.'

Michael went for him again but I managed to grab him and pull his arms backwards until he calmed a bit.

'What. Are. You. Doing?' I demanded, really doing my best not to swear.

'I'm saving you from this rat,' replied Michael.

'What? I don't need saving from Connor, he's the one that saved me…'

At the same time, Connor was speaking over me. 'Listen, mate, what the hell?'

'I saw him sneak off after you when you left the club. I thought it looked suspicious so I followed as soon as I could get away and it's a bloody good job I did; I could hear you screaming half way across the old town. There's no need to thank me.'

Connor was clearly as confused as I was and

he kept repeating Michael's words but with a very Australian upwards inflection, 'Thank *you*?!'

'I think there's been a massive misunderstanding,' I said. However, two male egos started to talk over me.

'Listen, mate, who the hell do you think you are? You can't go around punching people,' said Connor.

'You can't go around attacking poor defenceless girls,' replied Michael.

'Attacking?' Connor asked, clearly outraged.

'Look what you've done to her face, her eye!' Michael pointed towards me. I felt like an object being appraised.

'Hey, he didn't do anything to my eye. I did that a few days ago. And what's wrong with my face?!' I managed to interject, furious.

'Well, who knows what he could have done to you. I know your sort, you're annoyed I caught you and ruined your little game.' Michael jabbed his finger again, this time towards Connor.

'What the...? What are you raving on about?' Connor asked, frown lines creased his forehead.

'It's unconscionable, preying on girls like Jennifer. What do you know about this man anyway?' Michael asked me.

'We're friends,' answered Connor.

'Are you? Jennifer? When did you meet? What's his last name?' Michael was getting more worked up.

'Err...I...err...' words were lost from me again.

'We met this morning, he's Connor, of course he's a friend.'

'This morning? I rest my case. Really Jennifer, I knew you were clumsy but this is nothing short of buffoonery. You could be getting into bed with a psychopathic murderer.'

Buffoonery? That stung!

'Getting in to bed? What? We were only talking.' I tried to argue.

'Hey, I wasn't trying to crack on to her or anything. I just wanted to make sure she was alright.'

'A likely story. Now come on. I'm going to escort you home safely.' Michael grasped my bicep in a firm grip and attempted to lead me away.

I tried to shrug him off. After all my heart ache earlier, now I had him grabbing hold of me and it was the last thing I wanted.

'Hey now, you leave her alone,' said Connor, raising his voice and taking hold of my other arm.

'Will both of you get your hands off me!' I shouted. Shrugging both arms out of their grips, I huffed and spun on my heel, striding off towards the tunnel. 'I'm going home. Alone!' I called back over my shoulder.

'Wait up,' called Connor as he followed me. 'I'll see you home alright.'

'I'm not having that,' shouted Michael, who proceeded to tail Connor. 'You can't trust him.'

It wasn't lost on me that I was being trailed home by two attractive guys when all I desired now was to be on my own. I felt like we were in some sort of conga procession that hadn't realised the party was over.

Raymon raised his eyebrows at me as I passed his security booth at the entrance to the complex but he didn't say anything other than, 'Buenas noches.'

It was a relief. I really wasn't sure how I could explain being covered in grime, whilst a partially silver surfer and someone in a roughed-up suit looking like something out of Reservoir Dogs trailed me. It had been quite a night. All I wanted was to get back and make a much-needed cup of tea.

CHAPTER 22

When finally alone, I shut the door behind me and exhaled, thankful. Then I promptly went and made some tea and toast. I was glad for a moment's peace and quiet. Although, I wouldn't have minded Connor coming in for a cuppa, he could have stayed and waited up to see Jade again but, I didn't want to have to deal with the rollercoaster of emotions elicited by Michael.

As I devoured my midnight feast and loaded the toaster with more bread, I contemplated the night's events. It was quite an evening of revelation for me and I felt exhausted. After finally admitting that I liked him, I was now confused how I felt about Michael. Maybe he was interested in me after all, why else would he have followed me? But, I hesitated, he'd implied that I was a clumsy idiot. And a slut. It was a bit rich of him to suggest this- *he* was the one who appeared to be seeing someone else. I decided to think of him as an unreasonable jerk, a beautiful, but unreasonable jerk.

It frustrated me that he clearly viewed me as a helpless school girl. *I'll show him, I'll get my head down at work and prove him wrong.* I resolved to stop getting distracted and start pushing myself to do better.

The mirror in the bathroom showed a fairly grizzly spectacle, no wonder he thought I'd been attacked. *Next time he sees me I have to be drop dead gorgeous too*, I thought, *to try and replace this horrifying image of me in his mind.* My thick pirate eyeliner had melted down my face in the sweaty atmosphere of the club, my hair was a bedraggled mess and, although a lot better, my eye was still puffy. I was covered head to toe in tunnel grime and a surprising amount of silver body paint.

I cleaned myself up then poured a big glass of water before getting in to bed. Checking my phone, I blanched, *this is all I need!* There was a text message from James.

It was almost noon by the time I'd surfaced, yet no one else was up. I let the hot shower gush over me and considered my plans for the day. It was the last day of the hen do and all we had on the agenda was to chill out and drink yellow drinks. I thought about making the KIRSTY drink challenge end with saying 'yes' to every drink, but I don't think my stomach or liver, or the other hens, would have been very happy. We also needed to retrieve Kirsty's hat from Michael, I wasn't looking forward to that. Once the girls had gone I planned to clean up the apartment, it was only polite, plus I wanted to make sure we got our deposit back. Oh yes, and there was the tiny matter of dealing with James' message.

After my shower, I towelled off my hair and rubbed a lot of moisturiser into my slightly off white (tanned for me) legs. I put a loose, flowery dress on and a light bit of make-up, not wanting to aggravate my eye any more.

The first port of call was confirming the girls' taxi to the airport. Antonio seemed thrilled to oblige and assured me he would pick them up in a few hours.

My stomach was grumbling so I went foraging in the kitchen. I blitzed up some pineapple, banana and mango and made us a zingy, rejuvenating and very yellow smoothie. The noise probably woke the rest of the gang, who slowly made their way into the sitting room. I passed out the drinks and made a ton of toast. Suze tried to get up to help but I ushered her back to her seat where she flopped into it, a shell of a woman.

'Was it a good night?' I asked. They all nodded weakly.

'Are you feeling better now?' croaked Kirsty. 'We missed you.'

'Yeah, thanks. Sorry I had to go. I suddenly felt really bad and didn't want to ruin your night so I thought it best to leave.'

'You should've ruined our night!' said Suze. 'Then I wouldn't feel so rough now, I'm too old for this.'

'Even I'm too old for this!' exclaimed Jade.

'Did you get back alright?' asked Suze.

I paused and studied them in turn, considering how much to tell them, I didn't want to worry them. However, after what had happened with Beth, full disclosure was in order, so I told them everything.

Suze's face changed to worry as she said, 'That Brutus guy was such a creep. I'm glad nothing bad happened.'

'Yeah, a lucky escape. It was terrifying.'

Plunging me into a hug, Kirsty said. 'Thank God Connor and Michael were there. It should have been us seeing you home safely though.'

Squeezing her back, I forced a smile, not wanting to dwell on it any further. 'No harm done.'

Sensing I wanted to lighten the mood, Annie said, 'So, it sounds like you pulled two blokes last night?!'

'Ha! Not like that. I didn't *pull* anyone. Two guys made sure I got home okay, whether I wanted them to or not.'

'I did wonder where you and Connor had gone,' said Jade.

'He was only making sure I got back okay in the dark.' I could see Jade was looking at me oddly and I wondered if there was a hint of misplaced jealousy, so I said, 'You two looked like you hit it off on the dance floor.'

'I think he wanted to be with some people more than others,' she replied.

'If I was a few years younger!' said Suze.

'Yeah, I thought you'd like him too,' I said winking at her. 'Oh, and when I got home I had a text from James, which was the last thing I needed.'

Kirsty sat bolt upright, smoothie slopping over the edge of the glass. 'What did it say?'

I fished around in my pocket and pulled out my mobile.

Hey Babe, can we meet? xx

I read it aloud and shuddered. 'I hate the way he called me "Babe".'

'What are you going to do?' asked Jade.

'You'd better not meet up with him,' said Kirsty protectively. 'I don't want you going down that road again.'

'Chill out! I'm not sure what I'm going to do yet, but it certainly won't be getting back together with him. He's probably gonna tell me he's getting married or something.'

'Or that he has herpes and he needs to tell all his exes,' piped up Annie.

I threw a pillow at her but a pang of worry

passed through me. *I hope not!*

'No, he's called you "Babe" and put kisses,' said Suze. 'I doubt he'd do that if he was with someone else.'

I locked my phone and chucked it on the table. 'Let's not waste our last few hours on that idiot though, huh? So, who has more gossip from last night?'

We moved out to the balcony and spent the next hour chatting about our antics the night before. Jade couldn't resist getting up and acting out half of it. Annie had taken some fab photos of us all dressed up. We'd been having such a fun trip, and she'd captured everything wonderfully.

'Right, who's my moral support for going to get this bloody hat back?' I asked, looking pointedly at Kirsty.

'I've got your back sister!' She stood up and then cried out, 'Aphrodite, aid me!'

'Oh, don't set her off again,' groaned Jade. 'She was calling out Wonder Woman quotes all night.'

After convincing Kirsty that she wouldn't need her superhero costume, just normal clothes, she got ready and we headed out of the apartment. She linked arms with me and rested her head on my shoulder

'Thanks so much for everything, J,' she said suddenly.

'Don't be silly, I didn't do anything.'

'Don't brush this off like you always do. You've done absolutely tons, you spoilt me rotten and it was perfect and I love you.'

I didn't know what to say so I rested my head on hers as we walked. 'I love you too, chick,' I said after a while.

'You know, you're the best bridesmaid ever.'

'Well, you haven't seen what I've got planned for the honeymoon. I thought you, me and Steve could…'

She gawked at me, slightly aghast, half believing me until I laughed.

'Phew! I love you but…there are some places even best friends shouldn't go!' Then looking around her, clearly disorientated, she asked, 'Where exactly are we going?'

'To get that bloomin' hat!'

We arrived at the security booth and I had mixed feelings as I discovered it was Raymon back on duty. He was so odious, but seeing as he knew us, he was more likely to tell us which apartment Michael was in. After enduring a bit of banter about getting in with two men the night before and then some stomach heaving flirting, Kirsty and I secured the building and apartment number for Michael.

'C Block, apartment forty-one,' I repeated back to him.

'Si.' Raymon double checked in his log book. 'Mr and Mrs Henson. It's the penthouse, so it's at the very top.'

We said, 'Gracias,' and headed off.

As we walked away, I could feel Kirsty's eyes boring in to me. I knew what she was thinking.

'He definitely just said Mr and *Mrs* Henson, didn't he?' I asked.

'Yes!' she replied, her nostrils flaring.

'What the...?' I couldn't even finish the question, I was blindsided. 'His friends said he was single on that night of the...challenges.' *Night of the kiss.*

'Yeah, but I guess guys lie for each other sometimes, douchebags.'

'That's so *not* cool. I'd seen him with a woman a few times, I thought she was just some bimbo he'd picked up along the way but...*wife*?!'

'So, why was he sniffing around after you when you were going home last night?'

'I have no idea! I'd even seen him with someone at the bar. She must've been his wife. Wow, I really dodged a bullet there. To think I was attracted to that guy!'

'So, now it's operation 'recuse hat from the evil bigamist boss', yes?'

'Yes. And then operation 'get these girls a drink'!'

We arrived on the top floor of the building and Kirsty gave my arm a reassuring squeeze before I approached the door. I knocked confidently and we waited for it to open. It seemed like time had stopped. I was convinced it would be Mrs Henson who answered. But when the door finally opened, it was Michael standing there.

'Hi, Jennifer, to what do I owe the pleasure?' he said.

Over his shoulder we could see a glimpse of the grand décor in his apartment, a chandelier glinted in the sunlight. Luckily, I was sober, so I suppressed every urge I had to tell him what I thought of him (again) and went with the simple truth.

'Just hoping to grab that hat please. I hope we aren't disturbing you?'

'Oh no, not at all. I was about to make a pot of coffee, if you'd like to join me?'

'Thanks, but we should really be…'

'Thanks, that would be lovely,' interrupted Kirsty. 'I'm Jenny's friend Kirsty by the way.' She pushed past me and through the front door.

As we entered the penthouse I shot an evil look at her but neither of them saw. *What was she playing at?*

'Ah, the owner of the hat,' said Michael, jovially.

I was astounded by how cool he was with two women in his apartment, knowing his wife could walk in at any minute. *Oh God, what if they're polyamorous?*

'So, this is a big place for you to rattle around in,' said Kirsty as we headed through the huge apartment towards the roof terrace.

'Oh, it's not only me. There's a big group of us, although most of them have gone now. In fact, I'm just overseeing the cleaning team before checking out later.'

'That's what Jenny's doing later.'

'Really? Which service are you using?'

'I'm not employing anyone to clean up after us... I'm just on a later flight so I'm giving the apartment the once over.'

'Oh,' said Michael.

There was an embarrassingly lengthy pause where I felt spectacularly inferior. Michael poured the coffee and offered us each a steaming mug.

'Jennifer, if you're at a loose end this afternoon then you should join me for that drink.'

I *was* feeling inferior and then I remembered he was a scumbag with a wandering eye. I couldn't believe his audacity.

Feeling righteous and empowered, I stood up abruptly and started to say, 'I really don't think that would be appropriate-' *Seeing as you're my boss. And married. And your wife is still here.* However, one of the bimbos wandered onto the roof terrace, surprising me so much I stopped mid-sentence.

As she finished clipping some gold hoops into her ears she glanced up and gave us a striking smile. A pang hit my chest as I realised I'd been feeling resentful, she wasn't a dumb bimbo at all. She looked stunning. I desperately fought the pink glow rising in my cheeks; she probably recognised me as the crazy lady who fell down the stairs at Breeze.

'This is the *hostess with the mostess*, Serena, my sister-in-law.'

'Sister-in-law?' I repeated back to him.

'Yes, my brother's wife. They're to thank for organising this ostentatious pad. I was all for roughing it but they went ahead and booked.'

'Your brother's wife?' I repeated again.

'Keep up, Jenny!' Kirsty nudged me hard, then reached out her hand to her. 'It's lovely to meet you, *Mrs* Henson.'

'Oh, please, call me Serena.'

We shook hands and Michael made the introductions. I used the time to compose myself, I felt a bit foolish for jumping to conclusions; Michael wasn't married after all. And I felt guilty for considering Serena a bimbo, she seemed lovely. Jealousy isn't the best colour on me.

'You were at the party last night, I think I saw you dressed up as Michael's magician's assistant?' I said.

'Yes, I was there. I was supposed to be a burlesque dancer though, and Mikey wasn't a magician. He was in a suit because he'd forgotten his costume.'

She smacked him on the arm playfully and he looked awkward. He passed her a drink with a long-suffering huff.

I could hear Michael mutter, 'It could have been a costume,' under his breath.

Serena's heavily jewelled hand clinked the coffee cup as she clasped it to her chest.

Looking sheepish for embarrassing him she changed the subject. 'So, what have I missed?'

'I was just asking Jennifer here to join me for a drink later.' Michael regarded me, his eyebrow raised, repeating the question.

I hesitated, now I knew he wasn't married I couldn't think of a good reason to decline. I was still uncertain though.

'Oh, you must, Jenny, I feel absolutely terrible leaving poor Mikey here to close up the place on his own. Anthony and I are off very shortly.'

Kirsty helpfully piped up, 'Oh go on, it's not like you're doing anything other than cleaning and waiting for the flight.' *Thanks Kirsty.*

'That sounds delightful, thank you.' I tried to sound demure. 'Now, we really should get your hat and be getting you on your flight, Kirsty.'

Once we'd arranged the meet up later and retrieved Kirsty's hat, we said our goodbyes and headed back to the apartment. I did my best not to be mad at Kirsty but it was a struggle.

'Why did you have to invite us in like that?'

'Didn't you see the chandelier when he opened the door? I just *had* to get in and have a nose around. And, I wanted to put him on the spot in case his wife walked in.'

'Seriously, K, what happened to plan "rescue hat from bigamist boss then get drink"?'

'But we found out he wasn't married after all

so where's the problem? And, we got you a date!'

'It's not a date! It's just a drink…with my boss, don't forget. I'm not sure how I feel about it.'

'Chill out! Operation 'get a drink' was a success. A drink with your gorgeous and clearly rich boss, who's taken a shine to you!'

Exasperated, I groaned and flapped the brim of the hat while Kirsty giggled and batted me away.

CHAPTER 23

The legend that was Antonio came to pick up the girls at the agreed time.

'Aren't you keeping me company too, Yenny?' he asked, calling out of the window.

'I need you to come back for me tomorrow, Antonio. The flight was full so I thought I'd enjoy another evening here and fly back tomorrow.'

'On your own?'

'I was supposed to have Beth with me. It's okay though.'

'But you are all by yourself. Non, non. You come back to my house, and my wife, she will cook for you.'

'Thanks, that's so lovely, but I'm meeting someone later so I can't,' I replied coyly. All the girls whooped from their seats in the taxi.

'I hope it is that man you told me about?' Antonio winked at me then hit the accelerator.

The girls waved from the windows and I watched them drive off until there was only a dusty cloud left.

It didn't take long to throw out the rubbish, and then fling the vacuum cleaner and mop around. I was quite enjoying having the place to myself. The weather was so hot and muggy; I'd stripped down to a little vest top and pants to clean in, like I always did at home. It had been a lovely holiday with the girls but it was a relief to have a bit of peace and quiet, I was used to living on my own.

When I finished sprucing the apartment, I decided to make the most of the sun loungers on the balcony. There was a little bit of wine left over, so I poured myself a cheeky glass as a reward for my efforts.

Checking my phone, I saw I had a message from Kirsty saying:

We're heading to the bar, got through security-no problems! Luv u xx

I caught sight of the message from James in my inbox and wondered how to reply, it intrigued me but, as I kept telling myself, I was over him. I didn't want him to get the wrong idea. And I was plagued with doubts.

What if he didn't mean to text me?

What if he now called someone else "Babe"? Or was he trying to contact a different Jenny and pressed the wrong button?

What if he's heard I'm still single and wants to try and take advantage of me again?

My worries kept running through my head. I thought for a while, carefully sipping my wine, then typed a response.

Hi James, it's Jenny. I'm on holiday at the moment. Maybe you could text me when I'm back next week and I could try and speak to you then, if I'm free.

Satisfied that I'd struck a balance of indifference and inaccessibility, I hit send and hoped I wasn't making a plonker of myself. Noticing the clock, I realised I needed to go and get ready for my meeting with Michael. *It's not a date!* I told myself as butterflies swarmed in my tummy.

Torn between my desire to not be sat waiting on my own, but equally deploring being late, I arrived at the bar on the old town square a minute after our agreed meeting time. Michael was already there, sitting in the corner. I smiled at him and ran my hands over my spotty sun dress to check all was in order as I walked over.

He stood when I arrived and I went to give him a peck on the cheek but he pulled back awkwardly. The wine must have gone to my head, that and being surrounded by lovely, friendly, Mediterranean ways. I would never dream of kissing my boss if I was back home. Cringing inwardly, I tried to move on as quickly as possible.

'This is a great bar, have you been before?' *Very cool Jenny, you might as well have asked 'Do you come here often?'*

Michael's piercing blue eyes studied me closely as he paused before replying. 'I popped in with my brother a couple of times. We were last here when the feria was on.'

It flashed across my mind that the girls had said they'd seen the 'hottie' in here asking for me. This thought was rapidly followed by wondering if Michael was the English guy that caught me when I fell off the stage. Luckily, the barman came over at this exact point to take our order and I was spared from blushing in front of him.

'No special drinks today?' joked the barman as I ordered a wine spritzer.

'You're looking lovely tonight,' Michael said as we waited for our order to come.

'Thanks, I guess anything is an improvement on being a one-eyed pirate covered in dirt,' I replied. The compliment surprised me so I went into self-deprecation mode rather than sit there blushing.

We chatted about our holidays, carefully skirting around discussing anything that may bring up our kiss, or my tirade of abuse. He told me that he was in Spain celebrating his brother's thirtieth birthday with a big group of friends. I was desperate to keep my face straight when he mentioned that they'd spent the day on a yacht. I was well aware of that.

'For Anthony's actual birthday we spent the day out in the bay, on Galateia.'

'Galateia?' I asked.

'Oh, she's just our little family tub,' he told me. Trying to act surprised, I nodded, mute. 'It's beautiful out there and we had a great day, mostly. Have you been out in the bay?'

'Yes, I had a jet skiing lesson out there.'

Michael's face darkened. 'Oh, yes, with that fellow from Australia. What was his name again? Kevin?'

'Connor.'

'Well if you ask me, more people should have lessons before they are let loose on those things. There are some real hooligans out there.'

Yes, like me. 'Really?' I replied, as innocently as possible.

Everything had been going so well, I didn't dare confess. He didn't say any more about it and I wondered if he was too embarrassed to admit the whole incident.

'Speak of the devil and he doth appear,' said Michael suddenly, looking disappointed.

Confused, I turned to see who he was referring to.

'Connor!' I jumped up, pleased to see another friendly face.

He came up and gathered me in a big embrace then planted a kiss on each cheek before offering a hand to Michael. Michael shook it but with little enthusiasm.

'I thought Jade told me you girls were heading home today?'

'The others have gone but I've got one more night.'

'That's ace. You need to make the most of your last day then.'

Connor headed to the bar, he shook the barman's hand as well. I smiled, it was nice to see someone so friendly and happy all the time. As I turned back to Michael I caught the end of a scowl which he was quick to hide. Puzzled, I searched for something to say. Steering the conversation away from jet skiing, I asked him about his friends.

'Ah, we're thick as thieves,' he laughed, 'I've known them all since boarding school.'

Just as he relaxed again, Connor came back over with a jug of Sangria and three tumblers.

He plonked them in the middle of the table and called out, 'Salud!'

Pouring us each a glass we clinked and said 'Salud!' in turn. Michael had tightened up again and Connor picked up on his frosty vibes.

'I hope you don't mind me joining you?'

Silence.

Before the pause got too unbearable I beamed and said, 'Of course not. We were just having a drink as we're both loners tonight.'

This was the truth as far as I could see. Michael hadn't mentioned anything about it being a date, and I thought it best to presume it wasn't. I noticed Michael didn't jump to contradict me. *The more the merrier,* I thought.

Connor turned to Michael and said, 'Listen, no hard feelings about last night, ay? I know we'd all been drinking and were simply looking out for Grommet here. You know, I wouldn't be doing anything to hurt her.'

Again, he reached out his hand in a bid to broker peace between the two men. Michael studied Connor's coarse, water-worn hand, and then reached out with his own, manicured fingers, and shook it.

'Yes, I suppose it was that Brutus fellow that caused the misunderstanding. I feel somewhat protective over Jennifer, working with her and all.' He looked steadily at Connor as if that was the best apology he was going to give. 'Let's hope we can avoid him like the plague tonight.'

Michael's stiff, clipped speech stood out starkly against Connors easy, soft patter. Studying my company for the night was like looking at either end of the entire spectrum of men. They couldn't be more dissimilar and I wondered how on earth the evening was going to turn out. Still, it was nice to have some company.

Connor fiddled with his phone, typing something, before placing it out on the table. A minute later the screen lit up, catching my eye and I couldn't help but see that a new message had come in from Jade. He swiped it up quickly and a smile flitted across his face before he stowed it into his pocket. He hadn't noticed that I'd seen. *I knew they'd hit it off.*

We shared an easy hour together, sipping our sangria and Michael talked some more about his friends and his adventures in boarding school. The alcohol seemed to relax him and he became super chatty, with Michael chewing our ears off and Connor filling us in on his travelling around the world, I could barely get a word in. I was in desperate need of a bathroom break and as the two men finally seemed to be getting on, I nipped to the ladies' room. As I passed the barman he gave me a wink, and feeling merry I gave him a big grin back. He beckoned me over to him.

'You found your English man, si?'

'Pardon?' I said, peeking back over to the table.

'The man that saved you when you fell off the stage. You are drinking with him, non?'

'Oh, am I?' A thrill passed through me to know it was Michael that had caught me.

'Si! You did not know?'

'No, it hadn't really come up.'

'Well, now you have found him!' He winked again and then turned to serve another customer and I carried on my way.

CHAPTER 24

After getting over the initial pleasure from knowing it had been Michael that caught me, the dreaded feeling of humiliation crept back over me. I seemed to be a complete blundering walrus anytime I was near him, it wasn't as if I could say he had "an effect" on me, half the time I didn't even know he was there.

On my way, back I ordered us another jug of sangria and some tapas. Sitting down between the two men I felt pleased Connor was with us, knowing that I was much less likely to throw myself at my employer with a buffer present, and he was so cheerful and easy going. Plus, it gave me the chance to try and work out how I felt about Michael.

With the haze of wine, Michael was looking more and more handsome, if that was possible. Maybe it was because he was my secret hero. I wasn't sure why he hadn't brought up what had happened, but I figured he was sparing me the embarrassment. *It's going to be hard not to fall for this guy.*

The cosy glow I felt didn't last long however, we were on our third Sangria jug when it all went a bit wrong.

'Why on earth do you keep calling Jennifer, Grommet?' asked Michael.

'I've been wondering the same thing!' We both looked at Connor expectantly.

'Well, look at her, she's so young looking, and so bad at water sports...she's a Grommet. Young Grommet. That's what I'd call her back home.'

'Er...thanks!' I said sarcastically. 'I'm not that bad at water sports...' I followed up lamely.

'True, I've never seen you surf, but you almost killed yourself jet skiing the other day.'

'Connor...' I tried to stop him before he said anymore.

'Seriously, I worry about you! You were this close to hitting that yacht, thank God you veered off at the last second.' Connor had raised his hand up, his thumb and forefinger millimetres apart.

My eyes were locked on Michael's face as he processed what he was hearing, his nostrils flared and he looked between me and Connor. Livid.

'So, it was you all along, Jennifer. You know, your actions were really quite immature and downright dangerous. You ruined the birthday celebrations not to mention almost damaging the hull. It could have been a write off.'

'I'm sorry, it was an accident,' I managed to squeak out. I was unable to stop the heat flooding my cheeks.

Michael focused on Connor and said, 'And you should know better. Where's your professionalism? Should you be letting incompetent people loose in the open water? I knew you were bad news.' He stood and threw a large wad of euros on the table. 'Well, I think I'd better call it a night,' he announced and started to leave.

'I really am sorry, there's no need to go so suddenly,' I said.

'We both have a flight to catch in the morning, we don't want any more... misfortunes to happen, do we.' He picked his words carefully.

My mouth gaped, as I searched for a response. I'd been thoroughly told off and I could feel him judging me and my clumsy ways. Michael looked between Connor and I, his eyes narrowed.

'And perhaps you should start calling me *Mr* Henson again.' He turned on his heel and left.

'Oh, sorry. I shouldn't have said anything,' said Connor.

'It was bound to come out eventually,' I sighed, slumping back in my chair.

'After teasing you last night though, I didn't mean for it come out like that. When I remembered, it was too late, I'd already said it.'

'Really, don't worry. Eurgh! I feel awful. I can't believe I ruined his brother's birthday.'

'Honestly, I think that's a bit of an over-reaction, don't you? It was only a bit of spray.' Connor topped up our glasses as he tried to reassure me.

'He's right though; it was dangerous and I could have damaged their boat.'

'I'd be more worried about you seriously damaging yourself! I know he's your boss and you like him and all but, that guy needs to get his priorities right.'

I suddenly felt defensive towards Michael, or should I say Mr Henson? Yes, he had just stormed off but that was my fault really. He was so refined and sophisticated, no wonder getting covered in seaweed ruined their day. I could forgive him his outburst, he did forgive me my tantrum. And he saved me from the fall. He'd been so generous to us at Breeze. Then there was *that* kiss. Oh, I was falling for him and no mistake.

'I can understand why he'd be upset. Hopefully he'll have forgiven me by tomorrow, it seems as though we'll be getting the same flight back, and even if we aren't, I've still got to work for him next week.'

'Jeeez', I don't envy you that! You should try having a more fun job like me.'

'I'm not really in the position to drop everything and swan off around the world.'

'Why not?'

'I've just got a promotion at work and then there's my mum to look after and the wedding to help with...' I trailed off. I couldn't possibly just leave everything.

'Well, you know where I am if you change your mind. For the next few months anyway, then who knows where I'll end up?!'

I rolled my eyes at Connor, he was so laid back he was almost lying down. 'I'd love to have no worries like you. You have everything so easy.'

He gave a short laugh and said, 'Well, maybe I did until you came along. I've done nothing but worry about keeping you alive since then!'

'I can look after myself,' I exclaimed.

'You think? It seems to me as if you're too busy looking out for everyone else.'

It felt so easy chatting with Connor, as if we had known each other for years. I really felt I could open up to him. Or perhaps it was the sangria speaking?

I looked at him earnestly and said, 'I've been thinking recently, maybe I should try and take a bit more control of my life and my surroundings. I seem to be disaster area, especially near Michael. It's embarrassing.'

'Don't you mean *Mr Henson?*' He put on a posh British accent. 'You should take control of your life for yourself, not just him. So, you really like this guy, huh?'

Shy, I shook my head. 'It's not like I expect anything to happen; he's out of my league, on so many levels...'

'Don't go all droopy drawers on me Grommet. If he doesn't like you for who you are, he's not worth it.'

I smiled, I was pleased I'd made a new friend. 'Thanks Connor,' I said softly, 'and Connor...'

'Yes?'

'STOP CALLING ME GROMMET!'

CHAPTER 25

Antonio came up to the apartment to help me carry my suitcase.

'How was your date?' he asked, his brown eyes dancing with amusement.

'It wasn't a date! But I had a nice evening, thanks for asking.'

We headed down to the taxi and before my case was loaded in the boot I quickly flipped it open and rummaged through it, grabbing a cardigan.

'Where's the sun gone? It's so gloomy today!'

'You English people are funny, always talking about the weather.' Antonio chuckled at me.

I sat in the front and chatted with him about his family. About halfway through the journey, a crackling announcement came over his radio.

Antonio let out a low whistle. 'Yenny, it is not good news, there is a problem at the airport. There are massive delays. I am sorry.'

'It's not your fault, did they say what it was?'

'Non, but I think you will have a long wait today. You must call me if you need anything.'

'Thanks.' I was touched he was so concerned about me.

The taxi pulled into the quick drop off area in front of the airport. I paid Antonio and bid him a fond goodbye, hoping, in the nicest possible way, that I wouldn't see him again.

The departure area was a writhing mass of bodies and I began to feel claustrophobic as I pushed my way into the big hall. I was sincerely regretting the large suitcase I was lugging along with me. I made my way towards the check in and joined the back of a lengthy, disgruntled queue. The airline's name was in big lights above an unmanned desk, with a sign saying, "please wait for further information". *Great!*

The people around me had started sitting down so I pushed my case flat on to the floor too and squatted down on it. Minutes seemed like hours. Bored, I idly flicked through one of the magazines the girls had left behind and used it as a fan. The number of bodies around me was increasing and the hall was heating up.

Suddenly the grumpy hubbub increased in volume and I stood up to see what was happening. A tiny lady was stood behind the desk and was clearly delivering bad news but I couldn't make out what it was. I'd turned off my phone to try and preserve the battery but feeling impatient, I switched it back on to try and find out. I was flooded with text messages.

Are you okay J? Have you seen the news? They've cancelled all the flights! Kx

Only you could get stranded in Spain because of a volcano! Call me if you need anything, Annie xx

Stock up on water my dear, I don't want you dehydrating. Let me know when you've got back okay, love Suze

Can you bring back some nice perfume from duty free? I think us bridesmaids need a signature scent xJx

Puzzled, and unable to hear the tiny lady, I checked on a news website and saw the main headlines. Hundreds of airports were closed due to volcanic ash. *Oh my!* Stunned, I reread the article a couple of times and remembered the chaos from a few years before, when an Icelandic volcano had erupted. Looking back over my text messages, I laughed at the variety of priorities my friends had. The news was spreading around the other passengers and I could sense panic and frustration in the air.

'Cancelled until tomorrow afternoon at the earliest?' I repeated back to the check in lady. Palpitations thumped in my chest. 'What am I supposed to do? Where am I supposed to wait?'

She gave me a ticket with a number on it and told me to wait until my turn was called and they would give me more information. I knew it wasn't this poor lady's fault, she was just on the frontline trying to deal with it all. Not wanting to take my frustrations out on her I took a deep breath and tried to calm the anxiety that was building up.

I shuffled through the crowds of people over to a space and flopped down on my case again. Flicking my phone on, I texted my mum to see if she was okay and to let her know what was happening, following up with a text to Kirsty to ask her to check in on her. Mum had been a bit of a recluse since my dad left and then when she did venture out she broke her ankle, a nasty fracture which was taking ages to heal. I'd taken to checking up on her, getting her groceries and generally worrying about her. Having Kirsty on the case put my mind at ease instantly, I knew she would look after her like her own mother for me.

My next concern was work. I phoned Pete and told him I wouldn't be in tomorrow.

'It's alright, darling, it's not your fault, and we can sort it out when you're back. It's all over the news. Do you really think you'll be back by tomorrow night?'

'I hope so.' Although seeing the hordes of people around me did little to reassure me that there would be a quick resolution. 'I'll let you know if it changes, but hopefully I'll see you the day after tomorrow.'

'Don't forget, we need to do lunch. I've got a lot to fill you in on,' he said.

It was like waiting at the deli counter of a supermarket, watching for the number on my little ticket to come up. Although this was a very long wait without the nice cheese at the end. It had been hours and I was getting very bored, having switched my phone off to save the battery and already eaten through my whole stash of inflight snacks. I kept a close hold of the magazine, my only way to cool off in the sweaty atmosphere. It was in tatters, having read it cover to cover, and from me nervously picking at it and using it as a fan.

Finally, my number flashed up and I made my way over to the counter. They told me I needed to wait until a flight in three days' time and that they would be unable to find me accommodation. I was informed they had to give priority to families with children, the elderly and single female travellers.

'But I *am* a single female traveller,' I replied.

'Non, it shows here you are travelling as a party of two people, you and a Ms Beth Wilson.'

'But she got an earlier flight, she's back already. I'm here on my own.' I anxiously raked my hands through my increasingly matted hair.

'That's not what we have on our records. Her flight was never cancelled. Ms George, you've been allocated this flight as the first available one for you, if you don't take it then we will offer it to the next in line.'

'Where am I supposed to stay until then?' I could feel my eyes welling up, threatening to overspill onto the desk. I was feeling overwhelmed.

'We can offer you a room as of tomorrow night, all the local hotels are already full for tonight. Completo.'

On the verge of tears, I sagged down on to the counter, burying my head to hide my tell-tale eyes.

'Now, what's all this?'

I recognised his clipped English voice immediately and swung around. Hastily wiping my eyes and trying to make myself look generally less airporty and yuck.

'Michael.' It came out as more a sob than the cool greeting I was hoping for. 'Sorry, I mean Mr Henson... I can't get a flight back for days and I don't know what I'm going to do. I need to get back for work. Where am I going to stay?'

My voice cracked and I started howling. Seeing a familiar face broke my last ounce of resolve and I couldn't hold it together any longer.

Michael placed a soothing arm on my back, bent forward and said something to the airline clerk. I couldn't hear what he had said over the sounds of my own sobs. The next thing I knew, he was leading me away and I found myself in a cool, air-conditioned room with comfy sofas. I was being passed a chilled bottle of water. I caught my breath then took a swig and looked around.

'Where are we?'

'The VIP lounge. I've called a taxi to take us to a hotel.'

'Wha...what?'

'Well, we can't stay here, can we?'

CHAPTER 26

The giant roll top bath was brimming with bubbles. Water sloshed over the edge as I clumsily stepped into it and submerged myself. I held my breath, feeling the water swamp me all over and soak into my hair. Sitting up with a gasp, I swiped the foam from my face. It all felt like a very strange dream that I was struggling to wake from.

I looked around the huge marble bathroom; it was exquisite, elegant and extremely expensive. Michael had whisked me off to a glamorous hotel. It was, of course, full when we arrived. I'm not quite sure how he did it, but somehow, we were checked in to the penthouse suite and there was a bath waiting for me.

There were some fancy glass bottles of lotions and potions on the side, so I sampled them all. I washed my hair and scrubbed my face and body, removing every trace of disgusting airport sweat and grime.

Lying back to soak in the glorious bath a bit longer, I took stock of my situation. Stuck in Spain. No flight for days. Nowhere to stay. Not good. Michael swans in and saves me - again. Acquires exquisite accommodation. And is generally handsome and wonderful. Very good. He's my boss. Not good.

Our earlier conversation ran through my mind, he'd appeared so embarrassed discussing the forthcoming sleeping situation, he could barely look me in the eye.

'I've secured the master suite. I can't stand the thought of you waiting on your own at the airport so I thought you could stay here with me. We can get through this together.'

'That's… wow…thank you!'

'The trouble is there are no other rooms available and there's only one bed.'

'You should have it. It's your room after all. I'll be fine on the floor.'

'Don't be absurd. You have the bed, I'll be quite comfortable on the settee. If you're comfortable with the thought of us sharing, that is?'

'Of course! That's very generous, thank you.'

'Don't mention it.'

He said it in such a way that made it clear he felt awkward and really didn't want me to mention his generosity again. Ever.

I decided I should probably phone Pete and update him. At least I could relax about work. I could hardly get in trouble for not getting back to work if Michael couldn't get back either.

With wrinkly fingers and toes, I hoisted myself up out of the bath, towelled down and wrapped the fluffy white dressing gown round me. I secured my hair up in a towel and slid my feet into the fluffy complimentary slippers. The steam had cleared from the mirror and I caught sight of myself. Some freckles had appeared across my nose and, despite the harrowing day, I had a glow from the bath and from spending a few days in the sun. I noticed I was looking slightly thinner, perhaps from living off mainly toast and tapas rather than eating properly. I didn't have a smidge of make-up on. All my toiletries and clothes were in my suitcase, which had been left on the case stand, where the bell boy had put it.

Not wanting Michael to see me like this, I glanced around the bathroom to see what I could do. My eyes fell on the pile of grim clothes on the floor that I'd literally peeled off. I wasn't going to put those back on after my lovely bath, no way. It crossed my mind that perhaps Michael wasn't in the room and I could reach my suitcase without him seeing me. Shuffling up to the bathroom door, I pressed my ear against it, I couldn't hear anything. Opening it a crack, I peeked out and could see no sign of him in the room.

'Mr Henson?'

There was no answer, so I pushed the door open wider and scanned around. The room was deserted and I could see my case on the little luggage stand about twenty paces away. *This is where he comes in and sees me when I am half way there, stuck in the open.*

I took a deep breath, peered around and then bolted for the case. I could only take silly little scuttling steps because of the slippers and dressing gown, so I moved my feet extra quickly to cover the ground; I felt like a cartoon character. I grabbed the case and heaved it off the stand, which fell over, of course. Setting the stand back up right, I then dashed back to the bathroom dragging the case wildly behind me.

Once I was back into the safety of the bathroom, I shut the door and leaned back against it, panting. That's when the giggles overcame me. It wasn't only relief over the ninja style recovery of my case, but a sense of relief that my ordeal was over. My situation had gone from the sublime to the ridiculous; almost a homeless mess on the floor of the airport to being pampered in the penthouse of a luxurious hotel. Great thundering snorts wracked through me as I leaned forward onto my case, the towel unravelling from my hair and falling down to cover my face.

I was soon to have even more to laugh about. The door was flung open and strong hands gripped a hold of me, wrenching me up. My guffawing stopped instantly.

'Are you okay? I thought you were having a fit!'

'I'm sorry!' I squeaked, then the hysteria rolled over me again. 'I was just thinking about how ridiculous this all is.' I managed to choke out before being consumed with laughter again.

The severe expression on Michael's face did nothing to calm me down. His no-nonsense persona made me relish the nonsense all the more.

'Pull yourself together,' he said as he looked me up and down.

'Yes, give me a second to compose myself.'

'No, I mean your dressing gown; you might want to pull it together,' he said curtly, before turning on his heel and striding out.

CHAPTER 27

My dignity was in a heap on the floor, as was the towel from my hair. I was fully aware I'd just flashed a man who I wanted to respect me. It was only a glimpse of belly button but still... I spent a while blow drying my hair, applying careful make-up and choosing a conservative outfit to try and claim back a scrap of decorum.

When I finally left the bathroom, I seemed that Michael had gone out, but I thought it was only sensible to walk around the suite to double check. I didn't want any more surprises.

The drapes around the huge four post bed were gently flapping in the breeze, which was drifting through the open doors to the balcony. I went through the French doors and could see that outside was deserted too. A cold cafetière sat, mostly empty, on the table; Michael must have been on the balcony when he heard my laughter. He must have thought I was having a seizure or something. I winced at the recollection and then shrugged at the thought of how much worse it could have been.

My maxi dress billowed as I leaned on the edge and looked over at the view of the lush manicured gardens which led down to the hotel's own private beach. It was still quite overcast and I felt a bit of a chill with the breeze from the sea, so I headed back into the room. Hauling my case back onto the stand, I rummaged through it and found a pashmina. Slinging the soft silky fabric around my shoulders, I felt much better.

Carrying on my tour of the suite, I went through an archway that took me into a large living area where there was the entrance, a kitchenette and beyond that, a social area. I hadn't been able to take in all the sumptuous features when I'd first arrived. There was even a chandelier in the sitting area, and in the corner was a baby grand piano with a huge orchid display on the lid. I let out a low whistle as I wandered slowly around.

On the little table by the front door I found a note from Michael, telling me that he'd gone down to the business centre. Thinking of work jogged my memory and I remembered that I hadn't yet updated Pete. I dialled our work number and a familiar voice answered. It was Natalia, my office nemesis and leader of the coven of work bitches.

'Hi, can I speak to Pete please?' I did my best

not to let my voice wobble but I felt a bit sick at the memory of our last encounter.

'Who can I say is calling?'

'Natalia, it's Jenny. I'm calling from Spain.' I could hear her readjusting the hand set.

'I'll just see if he's available.'

I could have kicked myself as soon as I said that. I spent the next several minutes on hold, cursing, and, unsurprisingly, when she finally came back on the line, she hadn't been able to locate him. I pictured her laughing as she kept me on hold unnecessarily.

'Could you give him a message, please?'

'Of course.' I could hear the spite in her voice.

'Please tell him that I will try and phone again but, just so he knows, I won't be back in work for at least two more days. And tell him that I'm sorry.'

'Of course,' she said and hung up.

I was highly dubious that the message would ever get through. To cover all my bases, I sent him a text as well.

I was toying with the idea of going to find Michael, but I didn't want to come off as needy. Opening up the fridge I found a bottle of champagne, and although I would have dearly loved a drink, the several hundred euro price on the little card propped next to it put me off. Feeling safer with tap water, I poured some into a cut crystal tumbler and then went and perched on the edge of the sofa. I couldn't get comfortable. The room was so unbelievably beautiful I felt out of place. Tweaking the cotton of my dress, I felt cheap and scruffy. Noticing my trusty magazine poking out of the bin, its corners curling up, I reached for it and felt instantly better. Michael found me an hour later as I was chewing on the end of a pen, struggling over the last two answers to the crossword at the back.

'Hi,' I squeaked in surprise.

'I'm pleased to see you looking much more errr, much less erm, much more yourself.' He glanced at my glass and said, 'You've hit the vodka already?!'

'No, it's just water,' I replied earnestly.

'I was kidding. Let's see if we can find a proper drink after the day we've had.'

I padded over to the kitchen area to help, grabbing two flutes while Michael popped the champagne. We headed on to the balcony to see the purple and orange glow of the sunset in the weird, overcast sky.

'So, I guess you should go back to calling me Michael, if you want? We're camping out in Spain together after all.'

He seemed nervous and I wondered if perhaps my wardrobe malfunction had ruffled him. It's not like he'd seen any more than he would at the pool, I think it was perhaps the unexpected revelation more than anything. I found his awkwardness cute. He was so dominating normally, that it was endearing when something flustered him. I flustered him. I glowed inside with the thought. Although, perhaps part of that was the champagne.

'Okay, but only if you call me Jenny,' I replied.

'I'd prefer Jennifer.'

'Sure.'

'Jennifer, I feel we need to clear the air.' He waved his hands in front of his face.

Not entirely sure about which incident he was referring to, I played it safe and said, 'Really?'

'Yes. Now, I've forgiven you for almost crashing into Tia...'

'Tia? Who's Tia?' I interrupted, slightly outraged at the false accusation.

'Galateia, my family's yacht. We call her "Tia" for short. Anyway, you shouldn't be held responsible for that, you were under the leadership of that Australian chap, Colin, was it?'

'Connor. And it was definitely my fault and not his. I'm so sorry. Thank goodness no one was hurt.'

'Yes, and finding a decent yacht repairer can be such a bore. It's a good job I bumped into you at the airport; I hate the idea of you being stranded alone and I don't trust that Conrad.'

'It's Connor. And why? He's only ever been nice to me and my friends.'

'I found him irresponsible and immature,' he replied abruptly. 'You're better off avoiding him.' His tone softened and he looked me in the eye.

'Now, I've tried to be understanding about your outburst at the club and the near miss with the boat. I'd really appreciate it if you could forget about him and perhaps we could… start afresh.' He moved nearer to me, holding my gaze.

My breath caught in my throat; he was so close. His voice sounded earnest and in that moment all I wanted to do was please him. Although I didn't understand his problem with Connor.

And did he want wo start "afresh" professionally? Socially? Or perhaps more intimately? I didn't want to get carried away but, wouldn't I be a fool not to take this opportunity? Especially after James showed no interest, even when we were together. He didn't move, every nerve ending in my body was screaming from his proximity.

I took a moment and then said, 'Connor's harmless, but I doubt I'll bump into him again before I leave anyway.'

He smiled. 'I've been thinking, it's great we have this chance to spend more time together. What with our flight being grounded, at least I get the opportunity to get to know you a little better.'

'That's definitely the silver lining,' I said.

'To silver linings,' he announced, clinking his glass into mine.

I swigged the last of my champagne and pulled my pashmina more tightly round me. Wearing only a thin cotton dress underneath I was getting chilly.

'Are you cold?'

'A little now it's dark.'

Michael started to say, 'Would you like…' and my brain immediately tried to fill in the blanks. *To borrow your jacket like in a cheesy rom com? Yes please!* But it was not the question I was hoping for. '…me to get your coat?'

'No, it's okay, I can get it.' I wobbled up from my seat and made my way back in to the suite, as the effects of the drink hit my head.

In my room, I sorted through my case searching for my warmest jacket, sadly passing over my old, comfy pyjamas, which I dearly wished I could put on. I didn't want to scare the guy. My stomach grumbled as I was heading back to the balcony so I grabbed the room service menu as I went.

I passed it to him and a zing of thrill skittered across my skin as our hands brushed together. Studying the menu next to him, I could feel his chest rise and fall. My heart picked up pace and I desperately hoped he wasn't as aware of me, as I was of him, at that moment. We browsed the selection, but I was struggling to concentrate on the food. With a rather loud gurgle, my stomach cheated on me and Michael startled at the sound.

'We need to get you something to eat.'

Embarrassed, I concentrated harder on the words, making myself focus on food certainly made me feel hungry again. The club sandwich with a side of sweet potato fries caught my eye but before I had a chance to say anything, Michael had snapped the menu shut and said, 'I'll go and order us a couple of house salads.'

'I was thinking more along the lines of...'

But he didn't let me finish. He thought I was offering to pay and he talked over me, saying, 'Nonsense, I'll put it on the room.'

'Wouldn't you fancy a dessert?' I asked.

He laughed at me and said, 'No thanks, a moment on the lips and all that.'

Errr, what? How disappointing! Although his abstinence from desserts did help to explain his amazing physique. I watched him walk inside to make the call, and admired him secretly from the dark balcony. He came back out with the rest of the champagne and topped up our glasses. While we waited for room service we chatted some more. He told me more about his upbringing and following his father's footsteps going in to "business". Between the yachts and penthouse suites, personal chefs and private schools, it was apparent he came from a completely different world to me. He was so refined. I wondered if he was out of my league.

We heard a knock and both jumped up. I answered the door and welcomed in a man pushing a trolley with two silver domed platters, he parked it up by the dining area. Michael tipped the waiter and said something to him in Spanish.

Listening to his deep voice speak the language perfectly made my stomach flip.

Yep, he's completely out of my league.

Pulling out my chair, Michael gave an alluring smile and I was thankful I'd turned away from him to sit down, I could feel my cheeks heating up and a goofy grin snuck across my face. I'd composed myself by the time he'd sat down. *Best behaviour, Jenny. Things seem to be going well, don't blow it.*

The junk food addict that I am never thought I'd eat a salad for dinner, but I was enjoying it. There was a flirty atmosphere; we kept reaching for the condiments at the same time, skin tingling as we brushed hands together. We were full of polite giggles and awkward "sorrys". Michael told me more about his past, he really had a lot of stories to tell about the places he'd been and the adventures he'd had. My little life spent mostly worrying about my mum would have sounded very tame, so I didn't mention it, afraid I'd sound dull.

While Michael was rummaging through the fridge for something else to drink I checked my phone. There was still no news from Pete, however, Kirsty had replied to the message I'd sent, filling her in on my unexpected situation.

So J, you're telling me you've only been on one date with Mr Handsome and you're already spending the night in a hotel together?! It's not like you to move so quickly ;)

I rolled my eyes. I wished this was the case.

Seriously K, I think I really like this guy. I don't know what to do. I don't want to do anything to ruin my position at work but- WOW, he's incredible. P.S. THAT WASN'T A DATE!

Seconds later came the response:

I think you should jump his bones.

I shut my phone off and tossed it to the side, Kirsty clearly wasn't going to be any real help and I couldn't get hold of Pete, so I was on my own. I decided that playing it cool was probably my best option. Flights seemed to be going nowhere so I had plenty of opportunities to make a complete fool of myself.

I wandered over to the piano and casually tinkled two keys up and down. Absentmindedly, I settled on the bench in front of it and let my fingers roam up and down the keys.

As he brought the drinks over Michael said, 'I didn't know you played,' a hint of genuine surprise in his voice.

'There's a lot you don't know about me,' I replied.

He came and perched very close to me on the bench and I was reluctant to shift over and give him more room. I mentally quashed the recollection of the piano scene from Pretty

Woman from my mind. *Concentrate Jenny!*

There was another knock at the door, and he got up to answer it, leaving me rather breathless.

CHAPTER 28

Sleep was fitful. It was one of those nights where you wake up more tired than when you went to bed. I needed to get back to work to distract myself from overthinking every little thing with Michael. After our lovely evening of chatting I'd lain awake tossing around questions. Did he like me? Did it matter that he was my boss? Will I lose respect at work? Should I make the first move? Being out of the dating game for so long had dented my confidence, had the rules of The Game changed? I was never very good at playing it anyway. I'd eventually managed to fall asleep thinking about the trail of tingles on my skin that Michael's hand had traced as he played the piano next to me.

Skipping a plunge in the bath, I showered to help myself wake up. It could have been my sleep deprived state or because I had no knowledge of fancy plumbing, but it took me a while to find the right knob to pull and button to press. I only wanted a constant stream of warm water at the right height from the right nozzle. By the time I'd finished, everywhere was soaked. Thank goodness it was a wet room. I was running out of outfits, not expecting to be away so long, but I dressed in a cute sundress and applied some light make up before daring to venture out to find Michael.

He was in his usual spot on the balcony with an empty coffee pot, indicating he'd been up a while.

'Morning,' I said, trying not to be too shy.

'Morning. I've taken the liberty of ordering up breakfast. We're in a bit of a rush this morning, and I thought it might save you time.'

'Thank you,' I said. I was a bit surprised by this, but flattered that he'd been so thoughtful. 'Do you want more coffee?'

'I'll phone down and add it on to the order.'

While Michael was inside, I checked my phone and saw a message from an unknown number, I wondered if it was from the airline with news of my flight.

I heard about the problem with flights, did you get home okay? Connor

Astounded, I couldn't work out how he had my number. Perhaps he checked our booking details to get it. I felt a little flutter in my stomach and I put that down to feeling guilty for telling Michael that I'd avoid Connor.

Hi, my flight was cancelled so I'm still in Spain.

I got an immediate response.

Jeez, that sucks! Do you need a place to crash?

I'm okay thanks. I'm staying in the Penthouse at the Marencanto Del Rey Hotel.

Twit-twooo. Gimme a shout if you fancy a drink.

Michael poked his head around the door of the balcony and said, 'Room service is here. What are you looking so happy about?'

'Oh, erm, nothing.' I stuttered, confused at the blunt question. 'I was replying to some texts.' I stood up and followed him in and over to the dining table.

'Any news on your flight?'

'No, it was only a message from Connor seeing if I'd got back okay.' I could see Michael stiffen on hearing his name. I was annoyed with myself for even mentioning him, he seemed to rub Michael the wrong way and I wasn't sure why. Trying to appease him I added, 'It was nothing really, he offered me somewhere to crash, that's all.'

Michael rolled his eyes. 'That loser couldn't offer you any more than the sandy floor of his beach hut to sleep on.'

'He was just trying to be nice...'

'Nice? He needs to think about getting a proper job, not bumming around on the beach.'

I cursed inwardly, why was I still talking

about Connor? It was clearly winding Michael up further. I decided not to defend Connor and just change the subject. 'What's the plan for today?'

'I need you for a conference call, in your new capacity as Finance Assistant. Get yourself ready after breakfast and then meet me in the business centre. Oh, and I got you this.' He held up a bag with the hotel boutique's logo on it.

Michael flashed me a smile as he passed the bag over, grabbed an apple off the breakfast cart and left the room. Looking down, I was slightly affronted that he hadn't considered that I was "ready". And I was disappointed he wasn't joining me for breakfast. *Stop overthinking things,* I chastised myself.

In the bag was a silk blouse, all billowing and ruffly. It really wasn't "me" but I guess it was the thought that counts. I figured he wanted me to look smart for this video meeting. Adjusting my attitude, I felt a thrill that perhaps he did appreciate my professional input after all.

To prepare for the meeting I phoned Pete to get the lowdown on what it was going to be about, so I had the chance to think of something valuable to add. Luckily, he answered this time.

'It's a good job you texted me yesterday, somehow your message was buried under a pile of papers.'

'Hmmm, sounds like Natalia's been *helpful* again. I'm so sorry I'm not there.'

'Don't worry! Now, listen darling, a lot's been

going on here, while you've been away. I need to discuss some things about Mr Henson with you.'

'Well, that's partly why I've phoned. He's invited me to sit in on this conference call and I want to give a good impression.'

'You mean professionally?'

'Yes, I want him to respect me, especially after my last day in the office.'

'Well, in that case, I can probably help. But don't forget I've got a long story to tell you at some point. There's some things I think you need to know.'

'Okay, I'll call you back when I can, but please give me some quick pointers. I don't want to be late for the meeting.'

Dressed for the occasion and armed with some interesting insights and suggestions for the discussion, I headed down to the business centre. I was excited to be part of the action, rather than passively recording the minutes and keeping my mouth shut.

Michael's eyes twinkled appreciatively at my change of clothing, but the warm flutters of butterflies were kept at bay by my nerves. This was my chance to redeem myself and *finally* make a good impression.

Our legs touched lightly as we needed to sit close together so we could both fit on the screen. Thank goodness for the air-conditioning; I was sticky with the stress and I didn't want to melt onto Michael. The call began well and I spoke up, clearly greeting the other people present and introducing myself, as I'd seen done many times when I was an assistant. During the meeting, I couldn't help but keep notes in the back of my organiser, old habits and all that. My moment came as the participants started brainstorming and I thought this was as good a time as any to contribute my ideas.

'With regard to the Olaf account, how about...'

'Thank you for reminding me Miss George,' Michael interrupted me, 'the Olaf account...' He went on to discuss this at length, leaving no room for me to contribute anything further. *At least I'm on the right track with my ideas.* I waited for the next opportunity to offer a nugget of wisdom.

'May I suggest a...'

'That's a good point Miss George.' Michael cut me off again. 'Let's pause and reconvene after a brief coffee break. Okay everyone, see you in five.'

Flustered, I didn't know what to say, conscious to avoid a gaping fish impression, I pursed my lips while I picked my words carefully.

'I didn't mean to suggest having a break there Michael, I wanted to suggest...'

'Now don't concern yourself with all the technical things, Jennifer. Why not sit back and observe the intricacies of business a little longer before plunging in to the deep end.'

'Well, yes that's why I wanted to suggest...'

'You want us to make a good impression, don't

you?' Michael patted my hand affectionately. 'Best leave it to me.'

His voice was so kind as he said this that it wasn't until he was calling the front desk to send refreshments, that the full implication of what he'd said hit me. I didn't know why I was here, he didn't want my input at all. I clearly had a long way to go to prove myself to him. I resolved to impress him at the next opportunity, I was feeling desperate for him to respect me.

As I walked into the room I caught the tail end of Michael's phone call. 'Yes, I'll do my best...no I understand...leave it with me.' He turned to me and beamed. 'I knew I could trust you to look stunning, your smile is positively distracting.'

The compliment made me glow inside and I became preoccupied, thinking about what he'd said. *Concentrate Jenny, he's still talking!*

'...so they don't pay too much attention to the 'Barts account'. Is that understood?'

I was lost, unable to listen and swoon simultaneously, I hadn't taken in anything he'd said. Michael was staring at me intensely and I didn't want to disappoint him. I remembered what Annie had said. *Just say yes, and see what happens.*

'Yes.'

'Now, I'm glad that's cleared up. Leave the rest of the meeting to me, you've done your bit.'

As I sat there, the thoughts in my head drifted back and forth like the lapping tide outside. I was frustrated that I wasn't allowed to contribute, but the compliment gave me a glimmer of hope that all was not lost. Although I'd prefer to be respected professionally at least I'd superseded the memory of looking like a shipwrecked pirate.

I clutched my organiser to my chest, a kind of comfort blanket as we rode up in the lift to the top floor.

Michael briefly rubbed my silky shoulder and said, 'You did a good job today.'

I could feel my skin tingle where his hand had been. I thanked him but it crossed my mind that I hadn't done anything at all, and he was starting to seem a tad patronising. I was disappointed in myself for not being more assertive too.

A "do not disturb sign" was hanging from the door knob, which Michael must have put there. No one would have been into the suite since we left and I blanched, remembering the mess I'd left in the bathroom. Slipping my heels off inside the door, I made a beeline to go and tidy it up before Michael could go in and see what a slob I was. As I rushed in to the still wet wet-room, I slipped on a puddle of water that hadn't dried from my earlier shower fiasco. I skidded and careered into the bath, stopping with a thump, barely missing the little table filled with glass bottles. *Phew!* I could hear a distant knocking mingled with Michael's shouts as he ran to see what had happened.

'What's going on now?' shouted Michael.

'It was just a little slip,' I said as I put my hand up and grabbed hold of the table trying to lever myself up. Instead I pulled the whole thing down on me and the smash of breaking glass rang around the room only partially obscuring Michael's exasperated curses.

'You really are the clumsiest person I have ever encountered-' A different clattering interrupted Michael.

'Jeez, Grommet, what a mess!' Connor had thrown himself through the door.

'What the hell are you doing here?' demanded Michael.

'I came to see if Grommet was alright, it's a good job I did. I could hear the commotion from outside the suite.' Connor started to pick his way over to me.

'Well, as you can see she's fine. You're not welcome here. I suggest you leave.' Michael clapped a hand onto Connor's shoulder.

'She's not fine man, look she's bleeding.'

While Connor and Michael were bickering, I was doing my best to gracefully heave myself off the floor, without causing further mess. The shard of glass sticking out of my foot was hampering this plan somewhat. Connor shook off Michael's restraining arm and crunched his way over to me in his flip-flops.

'Mind your feet, you might cut yourself,' I worried.

'Even a shark couldn't bite through these tough old things,' he laughed. Scooping me up effortlessly, he made his way out of the room, and lay me on the bed.

'Watch out, you'll get blood everywhere!' I heard Michael moan.

'Hey *Mikey*, why don't you channel your concern into locating a first-aid kit and finding someone to clean up that mess, ay?'

Looking angry, Michael left the bedroom. Connor sat carefully down by my foot, and delicately eased out the shard of glass, then applied pressure to the wound with a towel.

'Don't look so worried, Grommet.'

'He seems really mad. I can't believe I'm such a disaster area.'

'Really? I could have placed money on finding you in a pickle. That's why I came over, I had a feeling you might need saving again.'

A first-aid kit came sailing into the room. Calmly, Connor plucked it out of the air with his left hand before it hit him square in the head.

'Thanks, mate,' he called out and I heard a huff from next door. He leaned in to me, conspiringly. 'Do you get the impression he doesn't like me much?'

I caught his eye and laughed. 'I'm pretty sure you're the last person he wanted or expected to see.'

Connor quickly and proficiently tended my wound, he was so gentle, I barely felt any pain. Or was that because I was becoming numb to escape the embarrassment of forever being in trouble?

'Thanks,' I said as he smoothed the plaster down on my foot. 'What would I do without you?'

Connor winked and moved his hand towards mine, I could have sworn he was about to hold it but at that moment a lady walked in with a mop and bucket and announced, "housekeeping". Michael followed her in, and suggested, in no uncertain terms, that Connor leave.

'I'll go when Grommet wants me to go.'

I really didn't want to referee another argument, and feeling guilty about the mayhem I'd caused, said, 'Actually, I could do with a rest, Connor. Thank you so much for visiting me.'

'You sure you want me to go? Don't let this guy bully you.'

'No, no, it's fine. Thanks again for coming over.'

'Listen, you know where I am if you need anything, yes?'

I nodded appreciatively to Connor, but I could feel Michael's eyes boring in to me so I didn't say anything else.

Once Connor and the maid had left, I was alone in the bedroom while Michael was making another business call from the lounge. I could hear his raised voice sounding cross but I couldn't make out what he was saying. I limped over to the door to go and get my phone from my bag, still lying by the front door. Michael saw me coming out of the bedroom and hung up hastily.

'You should be resting,' he said, trying to usher me back into the room.

'I'm fine. Anyway, I just came out to get my stuff.' I scanned the area and asked, 'Have you seen my organiser?'

'No, what does it look like?'

'The binder I had in the meeting, it has an elephant on it. I must have thrown it somewhere when we came in.'

'I'm sure it will turn up.' He helped me limp back to the bed. He seemed to have softened again since Connor had gone. 'Let me get you a drink.' Minutes later he came back with a mug of herbal tea.

I took a sip and winced. 'Thanks, but that's really bitter, proper tea's more my nectar.'

'You've had an ordeal today, this should help relax you,' he replied.

I took another sip, unconvinced. He climbed up onto the bed with me, and a jolt of excitement ran through me.

'Here, let me give you a massage.' His large hands cupped over my shoulders and he gently squeezed and rubbed them. It was heaven. I leaned in as an intense relaxation took hold of me.

CHAPTER 29

Waking up groggy, I looked down, confused. I'd fallen asleep in my clothes. A vague sensation of having missed something passed over me. The last thing I could remember was cutting my foot and Connor being here and then Michael being angry, and then Michael being...oh my, had I fallen asleep while he was giving me a massage? That's so typical!

Michael's voice floated through from the next room, I caught a snippet of what sounded like yet another business call. '...I've had to improvise... no it won't be a problem...'

Standing up, my foot didn't hurt. I mentally thanked Connor, he'd done an excellent first-aid job. My bedside table was empty, which was odd, I normally had at least one half-full glass of water on it. Gasping with thirst, I figured nothing could be more embarrassing than falling asleep mid massage so I went out to forage for a drink still wearing yesterday's clothes and make up.

Michael smiled at me as he hung up the phone and said, 'Morning sleepy head.'

'Morning, everything okay?' I indicated to the phone in his hand.

'Oh yes, I was filling in head office about being stuck out here.'

'Sorry about yesterday, I don't know what came over me.'

'Not to worry, you must have needed the rest. Now, I've ordered us breakfast again, save you having to go down to the restaurant with your bad foot.'

His blowing hot and cold was very confusing. In fact, he had one of the most contrary personalities I'd ever known. Michael was like a different man without Connor around. Suddenly, a little thought kindled in my head, *What if he was jealous? What if he did actually like me?* I tried to stop myself getting carried away, but the more I thought about it, the more it seemed plausible. The extravagant hotel room, the room service, the massage...the bitter hatred whenever Connor seemed to surface.

My phone pinged and I searched for it. After a while I found it stuffed under some cushions. *What was I on yesterday?* I wondered as I picked it up and scanned the message.

'Who is it?' asked Michael, seeming concerned. 'The airline?'

'No, it's Connor, he's asking how my foot is. He said he might pop over later, is that okay?'

The tendons in Michael's neck tautened like rigid cords. 'Actually, I had plans for us later. I thought we could go out on Tia.'

Busted! After seeing his visceral response, I was surer than ever that he was jealous of Connor.

'I think he's trying to get in my good books so I talk him up to Jade. I'll politely decline,' I told him.

I went back into the bedroom to get ready and came out as breakfast arrived. Something had changed with Michael, he seemed moody and stressed again. Slightly deflated, I suggested a breakfast themed drink, to see if that helped lighten the mood.

Eyeing up the tomato juice I asked, 'Would you like a Bloody Mary?'

'Absolutely not, I need a clear head to work,' he snapped back.

He was being like Jekyll and Hyde, we'd been getting on when I first got up, but once more, Connor somehow ruined the moment. Despite his thoughtful ways, I was starting to feel slight resentment towards Connor; he reminded me again of a loveable puppy- a puppy that kept peeing on the carpet at the least opportune moments.

The sky was still a weird hue and the humidity was close. I put it down to the volcanic ash that was keeping the flights grounded too. Michael didn't need to convince me to escape the clamminess and come out on the water with him. Well, who would say no to the chance of heading out on his private yacht?

The more I learnt about Michael, the more I realised we were from *very* different worlds. I mean, he owned a yacht and had a retainer on some of the crew, you know, just in case he wanted to head out at short notice. Hoping to not seem too out of place, I was wearing my bikini under a stripy nautical sun dress and had twirled my hair up into a huge top knot to stop it scruffing in the breeze. However, I felt completely inadequate.

Looking out at the turquoise sea there was a banana boat bouncing through the waves in the distance and I could see some people messing around on jet skis, I briefly wondered if it was Connor leading them. I thought back to when I was on the other side of the gunwale and how I'd drenched the "beautiful people", now I was on deck and I certainly didn't feel like I should be here.

I indulged myself in reliving some *Titanic* fantasies; spreading my arms out over the bow and feeling the wind fly over me. If only Michael would take me down below deck to mess around in a vintage car, then the day would be perfect.

Instead, Michael was busy below deck, working. He seemed to have been working very hard over the last couple of days.

Heading to see him in his office there was a brass sign on the door which read "*SALOON*". Smartly dressed crew were stood at the side, and I shot them a warm smile as I walked through. He was sat behind a grand wooden desk, the type you would expect to see with large maps spread out on. Instead, this one was scattered with A4 paper and piles of folders and binders.

'Can I help with anything?' I asked, optimistically.

'No, I'm just checking over the minutes from this morning's meeting.'

'Can I see? I should have been in that meeting this morning.'

'Yes, to write the minutes. I don't need your input on the project, thank you very much.'

'Oh, okay,' I managed to say, swallowing hard. 'I thought after the conference call it would be good to follow up on what was discussed. I'd like to be kept up to date so I know what's going on when we get back.'

'Why don't you leave the hard work to me and go and relax,' he said.

He patted my hand. There were no sparks on this occasion, just another impression of being patronised. The smile on Michael's face didn't reach his eyes and I felt uneasy.

I headed back to the deck, lonely and confused.

My phone had no signal so I couldn't phone Pete to get caught up on the office affairs. He'd said he had a long story to tell me, and now I finally had the time to hear it. It would have been nice to talk through my feelings for Michael with someone too; he'd turned cold all of a sudden and I wasn't sure if it was because he was stressed or if I was simply being paranoid. I missed my friends and felt very alone.

Standing on the deck, gazing out at the horizon, I started to wish I had Kirsty's hat. Despite the overcast cloud, I was convinced I was going to burn. I decided I should find something to do inside. Boredom was setting in, with nothing to do and no one to talk to.

I popped up to the cockpit to see the Captain but he told me, 'Mr Henson does not like me socialising with his guests.'

So that ended that conversation.

Disappointed, I headed back below deck to see Michael in the saloon again.

'Would you like a drink?' I offered, feeling like I needed to do something.

'Don't be ridiculous, Jennifer. We have staff for that.'

'Oh, well, I was going to get one, so I just thought I'd offer.'

Michael rolled his eyes at me then clicked his fingers and a crew member jumped forward.

'Si, Señor Henson?'

'Get us two bloody marys,' he said sharply.

The lady nodded and scuttled away.

'Erm, thanks. I was thinking more like a coffee but a cocktail is great too. Where's the kitchen?'

'You've not been on a yacht before have you.' It wasn't so much a question as a statement of my naivety.

'We did a couple of ferry trips to France when I was younger.'

Michael made a 'pfft' noise. 'It's called a galley. And where is she with our drinks?' He shuffled the papers aggressively.

I left Michael and went to see if I could help, still feeling a bit awkward at what I should be doing. I couldn't work out why I was unable to relax. As I stepped through the door into the darkened corridor there was a sudden crash. A terrible flash back to my last day in work jarred through me and I relived the office coffees splashing up in to the air as the cocktails rained down.

'Perdon, perdon,' I exclaimed as I tried to help the poor crew member recover. We were both soaking wet.

'What's all this commotion?' said Michael coming out to see us in our sticky predicament. 'What a mess.' There was a derisive sneer on his face.

'It was my fault,' I said, trying to defend the poor lady.

'Maria, you are on a warning. Any more mistakes and you're fired.'

'Michael, it was an accident, there's no need to...'

'Go and get cleaned up, Jennifer. You look a state. Again.' He turned on his heel and went back inside.

I helped Maria pick up the broken glass and fetched a wad of tissues to soak up the tomato juice, despite her efforts to stop me. I followed her back to the galley, the tray of chaos dripping all the way. In the stark false light below deck we looked like we were extras from a horror film; the red streaked across Maria's starched white uniform and had soaked into my dress as well.

'I'm sorry for causing you trouble. I was coming to see if I could help you, but ended up causing all this mess.'

'De nada, Señorita. Please do not worry.'

'But what about your job?'

She clicked her tongue and said, 'Señor Henson has threatened to fire me many times, but I am still here. I work for his brother, so when Anthony fires me, then I will go.'

I raised my eyebrows and, not sure what to say, did my best fish impression.

'So, have you worked with the Hensons a long time?'

'Si. I was first employed by their father, when he and their mother died a few years ago the boys inherited the boat and all the staff. Anthony kept us all going, he has worked hard to keep alive his father's pride and joy.'

'I hadn't realised his parents had died,' I said, shocked. 'Maybe that explains why Michael can be so grumpy sometimes,' I said, more to myself than Maria.

'No, he has always been as he is. That is his way. Although, this trip he seems more sensitive and stressed than normal.'

'Trying to work while stranded here must be stressful.' I tried to defend him.

'You are different though, you are like Anthony. You treat us like people, not servants.'

'I feel a bit out of place to be honest.'

'I know my opinion is not worth anything, but I do not think it is bad, you not feeling like you fit in. I would not want to fit in.'

'Thanks Maria, it's worth something to me,' I said giving her a shy smile. 'Can I stay down here with you? I've been a bit lonely up on deck. I can't even get signal on my phone.'

'I do not think Señor Henson would like that,' she replied, looking apologetic. 'But I will see if I can sort something out for you.'

I lay sunbathing on the deck in my bikini, my dress next to me, drying out. Maria had found me some sun cream and an old captain's hat so I wasn't worried about burning. Listening to the waves and the engine of the boat I'd drifted into a daydream, reimagining my tumble off the stage at the feria but with Michael heroically catching me. The nice non-stressy version of Michael. My beeping phone startled me. We must have crossed in to an area with some signal. Surveying the shoreline on the horizon, I could see that we had, indeed, changed direction.

The message from Kirsty told me she'd checked on my mum and all was well. James had texted to say he wanted to meet me when I was back. Connor had texted again to see if I wanted another jet ski lesson. It felt so good to be back in touch with civilisation. The next message was from the airline, confirming my flight for the following afternoon. I flicked through my contacts list to Pete's number.

'Hiya J, please tell me you're back.'

'Afraid I'm still stuck here, I'll be back in the office the day after tomorrow. I'm feeling terrible leaving you in the lurch like this.'

'It's not your fault darling, don't worry. How are you, you alright out there?'

'I'm a bit lonely, but Michael's around. That is when he's not working,' *or shouting at staff and being weirdly jealous.*

'It looks like he's been cracking the whip with you too.'

'What made you think that? I'm feeling a bit surplus to requirements really.'

'Well, you were in that conference call and a ton of paperwork has just crossed my desk with your name all over it.'

'Really? What paperwork?'

'The Olaf account. The Barts account...'

'Oh, I guess we did discuss that in the meeting.'

'You need to be less modest, it seems like you are doing a great job,' said Pete.

'I don't think I am...'

'While I think of it, you must let me tell you something. I'm sure it's something and nothing but as you're stuck out there with him, I thought you should know.'

'What?'

'There's been a rumour about Michael...'

'Go on,' I said, nervously.

'Well, I've heard that there was a complaint about him in his previous role. Apparently, one of the assistants accused him of stealing their bag, but then it appeared under a desk a few days later so they put it down to being misplaced. And something weird about some stationary going missing. I looked into it, nothing official was ever reported, but I wanted you to know. Has he been alright with you?'

'Yeah, fine. That's weird, he's clearly loaded, why would he steal stationery? I'll be honest, I thought you were gonna dish something a lot bigger than a paperclip thief.'

'Well, it's dead boring around here without you shaking things up. Literally.'

'Are you saying I'm clumsy?'

'I'm saying your refinement could be... refined.'

'Thanks a lot! I miss you too! I should probably go.'

'Okay darling, lovely to speak with you. Let me know when you hear anything about coming back.'

A few things about our conversation were niggling me while I pulled on my dress. Why would Michael be accused of stealing stationery? That was equal parts strange and dull. And why would my name appear over paperwork for accounts that I had barely heard of? There had to be a simple explanation so I went to find Michael, to ask him out right.

CHAPTER 30

I told myself it was an accident waiting to happen. Anyone could have tripped over the threshold of the saloon and fallen head first into the room.

'Crikey Jennifer. I didn't know you were so accident prone.' Michael stood over me, smirking.

I peeked up from my disadvantaged angle. 'Didn't falling off the stage not give you a hint?' I replied curtly.

'Falling off the stage? How embarrassing. When did you do that?'

I was confused. If Michael didn't know I'd fallen off the stage, if he wasn't the person that caught me, then who was?

He flopped down behind the desk, looking tired. His face was pasty after a few days spent inside. A pang of empathy passed over me, he'd been working so hard. I picked myself up and sat opposite him, peering over a stack of binders.

'How can I help?' Michael said, flatly.

'I wanted to ask a few questions about…hey, is that my folder?! The one with the elephant on it?' I pulled out a familiar looking binder from near the bottom of the stack.

'For heaven's sake, woman!' Michael cried out, while the pile slid onto him.

'Ooops, sorry. But seriously, this is my folder. Why have you got my folder?' *Maybe he is a stationery weirdo and gets off on sniffing envelope seals?*

'It must have got caught up with my paperwork back in the hotel,' he replied.

Michael was busy setting the stack of folders up again, when he looked up his face was quite innocent.

I popped it under my arm and tried to continue. 'So, as I was saying, I spoke with Pete and he mentioned something about the O…'

'When did you speak to Pete?'

'A minute ago, when we finally got back into some phone signal.'

Michael jumped up and ran to the window. Swearing, he left the room abruptly and I heard him thundering away up the stairs. There were several bangs from doors swinging shut and then muffled shouts drifted down from above. Wandering out of the saloon I found Maria and some other staff congregating there, listening in. Maria was looking worried.

'What's happening?' I asked.

'Jenny, it is all my fault.'

'No, of course it isn't. He just stormed out.'

'Yes, because he realised the Captain changed direction. He wanted to get away from Marencanto but the captain changed course and headed back towards the shore.' Guilt flooded Maria's face.

'Why?'

'I asked him to, I knew you were lonely. The captain is sweet on me; he'd do anything for me. I only asked him to go back to where you could get signal for the phone. I hadn't realised it would mean he was disobeying orders.'

'Don't worry Maria. I'm sure it will all be okay,' I replied confidently. Although I wasn't sure at all.

I went back into the saloon, shutting the door behind me. Something didn't feel right but I couldn't place my finger on it. Michael, the perfect English gentleman, seemed to have developed a nasty temper, but it wasn't only that. I walked behind the big desk, almost tripping again, this time over a canvas holdall.

It seemed that Michael had packed for longer than a day trip out on the water. A glance in the holdall confirmed he was up to no good. Who carries around three phones and an envelope stuffed with money? I became more uneasy. Studying the desk, most of the paperwork on it was gobbledygook to me. However, documents for the two accounts caught my eye. Not caring that I was breaking at least a dozen company rules I took photos of them on my phone, particularly any which seemed to have my name on them. For just sitting in on a meeting and not being allowed to speak, it certainly looked like I'd been pretty busy. One document seemed particularly interesting and I hastily grabbed it. What on earth had I stumbled upon?

The arguing stopped. I had no idea how much time I had left before he returned. Carefully, I stepped back round to the front of the desk and managed to sit down and open up my organiser to an old half written to-do list when Michael walked back in.

'Oh, you're still here?' he said.

'Yeah, just catching up on some personal stuff while I had the chance.' I smiled up to him serenely. 'Everything okay?'

'Yes, yes.' Michael went behind the desk and sat down. Over the top of the page I could see him trying to inconspicuously survey all the papers, perhaps to see if he'd left anything incriminating out in front of me. 'What did you want to speak to me about?' he asked.

'Oh, it was only that Pete had mentioned...' I paused, I didn't want Michael to find out that I knew something was up. Thinking quickly, I improvised. 'He mentioned the office was now a bit short staffed, I wondered if I could help interview for my replacement.'

'Don't worry yourself with these things, that's

for Pete to sort out now.'

Michael appeared to have taken this as proof that I wasn't suspicious and seemed to relax. Maybe his presumption that I was completely worthless in the office was going to play to my favour.

He shone his dashing smile at me and in a soft voice said, 'With all this uncertainty about flights and everything, you must be really stressed. Why don't you go and relax some more?'

I wasn't fooled by his act anymore. Playing along, I replied, 'Actually, that would be great, if you don't mind?'

'Not at all,' he said. 'I have an important call I need to make.'

'Let me know if you need anything,' I said, trying not to look too relieved to have an excuse to leave.

Standing in the corridor, I was out of sight of the door but, with my ear pressed against the thin wall, I could catch snippets of the conversation. It was worse than I imagined.

As I headed back up, to go out on deck, I passed Maria. She was carrying some ice and a towel.

'Is everything okay?' I asked.

'Non, he has punched the Captain,' said Maria, her eyes wild with fear.

'What?! That's awful. Can I do anything to help?'

'Non, non, gracias. You need to look after

yourself though, Jenny.'

CHAPTER 31

A large hand bore down on my shoulder, gripping it tightly. I was so pent up I almost shot a foot into the air with fright.

'I didn't mean to alarm you, Jennifer'

Turning, I found Michael looming over me, his tall stature now intimidating rather than alluring. *Keep calm, don't give anything away.*

'I was in a world of my own, no harm done.' I forced a smile. 'Have you come out for some fresh air?'

'I'm not staying for long, better get back to the grind stone and all that. I wanted to let you know that I've just heard from the airline; the flight's been delayed a few more days. So, I thought we could cruise and do a bit of the Spanish coast while we've got the opportunity.'

He's lying. HE'S LYING! Is he trying to kidnap me? What have I got myself into? Play it cool, Jenny, and say something- he's looking at you!

'That sounds lovely.' I paused, trying to pick my words carefully. 'But could I pop back to the hotel and get a change of clothes?'

'No,' he said sharply and then with a softer voice, 'we're half way there now, there's not really time. I'll see if Maria can rustle up something for you.'

'That'd be great!' I beamed at him, blinking hard so I didn't do anything stupid like cry. Michael smiled and finally released his grip on my shoulder. He went back below deck and I released the breath I didn't know I'd been holding.

He was clearly trying to get me on my own, away from the outside world. My mind flicked back to all the room service he'd ordered, maybe he'd been trying to isolate me for longer than I'd realised. I shuddered, feeling sick and betrayed. I only let myself feel anxious for a second, then I took a deep breath and resolved to get myself out of this mess.

I had to get away. I was somehow ensnared in this crazy plot. Putting together all that I'd seen and heard, it looked like I was about to be framed for embezzling a huge amount of company funds. As far as I could see, the best-case scenario would be that I lost my job, the worst case being that I got sent to prison. Or Michael could discover my amateur sleuthing and get really mad, violent even. My mind was reeling.

The yacht had changed direction again and I

was eager to try and get help before we were too far away. Glancing over my shoulder to check I wasn't being observed, I took my phone out and dialled the only person I could think of to help.

'Connor?'

'Grommet! To what do I owe the pleasure? I thought you were out sunning yourself on Michael's yacht?'

'I need your help.'

'I don't doubt it!'

'Seriously, I'm in trouble.'

'How can I help?'

'I need a ride.'

'Are you back at the hotel? I can come and get you, no problemo.'

'It's not quite that simple...'

I checked the time, he'd said to wait half an hour. It had been maybe thirty seconds. All I needed to do was keep a low profile for thirty minutes longer and I would be okay. If Michael got wind of my plan before then, I was going to be in big trouble.

Paranoid, I scanned the area and out of the corner of my eye, something moved. I looked harder, the deck was clear, but a sun shade flapped against a stack of sun-loungers being stored at the side. I was definitely paranoid. I turned back to check the time, twenty-nine minutes to go. I heard a squeak. I spun around to see Maria coming slowly out from the shadows. I clutched hold of my folder tightly- organiser, weapon, shield. I wasn't letting it go.

'I did not mean to scare you,' she said.

I didn't say anything, but held on tighter to the organiser, it helped to stop my hands from shaking.

'I heard your conversation, I think I can help. But, please don't tell Señor Henson.'

Maria beckoned me inside towards the galley and, reluctantly, I followed.

'I'm scared, Maria,' I confessed. 'I'm not sure what's going on but I'm definitely in trouble. I mean, there's all this stuff with work and...I think he may have drugged me last night. Is he crazy?'

She didn't say anything at first, just pulled open a drawer full of kitchen sundries- scissors, knives, cling-film, foil, and such.

Then she winked at me and said, 'Like I said before, you need to take care of yourself. Something in here might help. Don't forget, I have nothing to do with this.' And then she left.

Time to get prepared.

Five minutes to go. I stood on the deck craning to see as far as I could out to the horizon. There was a little dot which, if I squinted hard enough, seemed to be getting bigger. *That's him! That's got to be him!*

Ears straining, I listened for any sound of his approach. The last thing I needed was Michael to be tipped off early and stop me. All was quiet so far. I clenched my hands around the safety barrier of the gunwale, joints straining, knuckles turning white. *Come onnnn.*

Adrenaline pounding, I squeezed the rail and tried not to literally jump up and down with impatience. I could see Connor's hair streaming behind him from the speed, his sunglasses glinting. Taking deep breaths to try and calm myself I waited for the perfect moment, my foot up on the lowest rung. I was ready.

Glancing over my left shoulder I checked all was clear in the direction of the cabins. Nothing. *Phew!*

'Going somewhere?'

Fear choked me. Michael had silently approached me from the right. I hadn't seen or heard him coming.

'No, no,' I said, sounding as innocent as possible. Stepping back, I subtly tried to move out of his range. He took a step forward.

'Don't lie to me, Jennifer.'

'I'm not, I was just enjoying the view.' I forced my features into an expression of serene innocence and tried to keep calm.

'I've been studying you, I know you better than you know yourself.'

I'd been holding Michael's gaze but I had to take a peek to see where Connor was. He was close, the engine was off and he was watching us, ready. Luckily, Michael still hadn't noticed him.

I looked back, Michael had stepped closer again.

'I think there's been a bit of a misunderstanding,' I said, trying to keep things light. I took another pace back.

'Oh no, Jennifer. I understand you perfectly. Ditzy Jennifer who's desperate for a man. Clumsy Jennifer who wants to move up at work. You were the perfect mark. Poor, distracted, Jennifer, always so worried about her friends and family, too busy to see what's going on around her.'

I took my bag off my shoulder.

'Is that supposed to scare me? Ohhhh, the little girl wielding a bag? You're the one that should be scared.'

I'd had enough of him belittling me, I retorted, 'Why? Because you've implicated me in your embezzlement plot, I know what you've been up to. You've used me as your decoy so I'll get all the blame and you can get away scot free. I've got it all recorded on my phone in here, when I get back I can clear my name and reveal your true plan.'

'In this bag?' Michael said, grabbing my bag and yanking it out of my hands. 'You never were the nimblest, were you?' He laughed right in my face as he tossed it over the edge without even looking.

I don't know, I'm not so bad, I thought as I flung my legs over the bar and dived in after it. The salt water burned my nose as it filled up my sinuses. I'd gone down deep into the water, having jumped from such a height. I was stinging all over; I hadn't belly flopped since I was a child. Kicking upwards I surfaced and strong rough hands reached out to me. Looking up I could see Connor's tanned face grinning at me.

'You could have used the ladder on the side, Grommet.'

CHAPTER 32

I approached the jet ski from the rear and clambered on behind Connor. He passed me the bag he'd fished out from the water and I nestled it between us before gripping him firmly around the waist. He sped off and I clung to him, relief and sea spray washed over me. Things were, by no means over, but at least I was safe. Michael's shouts rung in my ears but I didn't look back. A pang of worry for Maria and the other crew on board hit me, and while we skimmed across the waves I tried to figure out how to help them.

Recovering the rest of my luggage from the hotel was uneventful. I had visions of a hitman or kidnapper waiting for me, but there was no need to worry. Connor had offered to take me back to his pad but I felt like I wanted to be near lots of people, so we found ourselves in our usual bar on the old town square.

'What can I do about Maria? I'm so worried about her being stuck with that lunatic. He assaulted the captain!'

'I'm sure she's fine, try not to worry.'

'But he might find out that she helped me. I can't abandon her.'

'Well, I'm not sure what you *can* do. I'm not having you put yourself at risk and you can't really phone the police and say 'There's a guy with a bad temper on a boat, oh yeah and I think he might have been trying to rip off his business. No, I have no evidence, it got thrown in the sea!''

'I'm not as stupid as I may seem. I had a contingency plan I'll have you know.'

'Oh yeah?'

I pulled up my damp bag from its puddle on the floor.

'Nice, Grommet. You should have left that at my place to dry out,' he said, pulling a face.

'This isn't leaving my side,' I said as I opened it up and pulled out a white plastic bundle.

Connor stared curiously as I painstakingly unravelled it. Meter by meter of cling film piled up on our table, until my, mostly dry, elephant organiser and phone were revealed in the centre.

'That's brilliant!'

'Maria gave me the idea. Well, she showed me where the knives and scissors were stored in the kitchen. I thought I should maybe get tooled up, but then I thought he could easily use a weapon against me... then I noticed the cling-film.' I smiled at Connor and he grinned back. 'Impressed?'

'Defo, but I'm smiling because I never thought I'd hear you use the phrase *'tooled up'*!'

'Don't underestimate me, Connor,' I replied, with one eyebrow cockily raised.

'Shall we order another drink?'

'Sure, although, I'm going to nip to the toilet to freshen up first. Can you watch my stuff please?'

'Of course.'

When I came back I felt sick. *How could I be so stupid*? Connor was gone and so was my folder and phone, he must have been in on it with Michael the whole time. *Stupid, stupid, stupid.* My eyes welled up and as I pointlessly checked underneath the table, they overspilled. My tears splashed in the puddle already on the floor. I pulled myself up and slumped on the chair, my head in my hands.

'Ehem,' coughed the barman. I looked up to see him baring a jug of wine and two glasses. 'Is everything okay, Señorita?'

Sniffing heavily, I nodded and then gestured at the tray. 'I think there's been a mistake, it's just me.'

'Oh no, your friend ordered it. Here he is now.'

Peering over to where the barman's head had indicated, I could see Connor coming back through the door. There a plastic bag in one hand and my wet bag was slung over his shoulder.

'Everything alright, Grommet?'

'You'd gone...I was worried...I...'

'Sorry, it took me longer than expected. I thought I'd be back before you; I know how long you can take in the bathroom.'

The barman poured us a glass of wine each and then left. I grabbed the nearest and took a big swig.

Seeing Connor's eyebrows raise, I gave him a guilty grin and said, 'Salud,' as an afterthought.

'I know it's been a helluva day, but go easy, ay?'

I bobbed my head and forced another smile, tight-lipped to stop from trembling.

'Aw, you didn't think I'd left you, did you?' said Connor.

I paused, on the brink of not being entirely in control of my emotions, then I gave a small nod. 'All my stuff was gone, you were gone. I panicked.'

'Hey,' he said as he rubbed my arm soothingly. 'I'd only nipped out to get you a present.' He pushed the plastic bag over to me. 'Sorry about the wrapping.'

I pulled out a large bag of rice, and then looked up at Connor. 'Thanks...I think.'

He rolled his eyes at me. 'It's for your phone, in case it got a bit damp. Put it in the rice and it'll help it dry. Keep going there's more.'

Next out of the bag was a new binder with a dolphin motif on the front.

'Thanks, is this so I can remember my dramatic sea escape?'

'Ha! No. I noticed your elephant one is curling up a bit at the corners from where it got slightly wet. So, I thought you could transfer all your important stuff to a new one. Did you know dolphins have incredible memories? They're awesome creatures, much smarter than humans.'

I was genuinely touched. 'That's really thoughtful, thank you.'

At the bottom, neatly folded up was a new, navy, tote bag. I pulled it out and held it up.

'It was all I could find quickly.' He looked apologetic. 'I thought it was better than hauling that dripping sack around.' Connor pushed my old drenched bag away with his toe.

'It's perfect, thank you. I love navy, it goes with everything! Thank you so much.' I leaned in to give him an awkward hug and peck on the cheek.

He batted me away, embarrassed, and said, 'Don't thank me, just buy the next round.'

Transferring the pages over to my new binder, I came across Antonio's number and a thought flashed in to my head. *Perhaps his brother in the police could help?*

'I'm too scared to switch my phone on yet, in case it's wet inside. Can I borrow yours please?'

'Sure,' he said, tossing me his mobile.

I dialled Antonio but it just rang and rang.

Placing Connor's phone back on the table, I

said, 'He's not answering, I'll try again in a minute.'

We drank some more wine and I filled Connor in on my plan to try and save Maria and the rest of the crew. It wasn't long before impatience crept over me. I wanted to try and ring Antonio again. To save time I went into the recent calls list on the phone. Antonio's number was at the top, but a couple of numbers down I noticed Jade's number and my stomach gave a little flip. *This is stupid, I knew he'd be perfect for Jade, I even had an inkling that he liked her. Why am I so disappointed?* Brushing off my jealousy as some sort of misplaced white knight syndrome, I ignored the pitching in my stomach and dialled Antonio again.

Somehow, I needed to explain things to the people at work. It was late in the evening so no one was in the office and Pete wasn't answering his phone. I was annoyed I couldn't clear the whole thing up, yet relieved I didn't have to begin to work out how to explain it.

Turning to Connor, I said, 'Do you fancy a bite to eat?'

'Sure. What were you thinking?'

'I'd like a last taste of Spanish cuisine before my flight back.'

'I know a great little tapas place on the sea front. We'd get a good vantage point of the marina from there. We could see if the Galateia makes it back.'

Waving cheerily to the barman as we left, we wound our way through the old town down to the waterside. The humidity had settled and there was a lovely feel to the evening air. We strolled companionably along and I realised, despite my ordeal, that this was the most relaxed I'd been in a while. I wasn't worried about my mum, or work, or executing the perfect hen do. I felt good.

Connor led me to a tapas restaurant that was just to the side of the marina, close enough to be in a great spot but far enough away so it wasn't extortionate. It was jam-packed with locals, which I always think is a good sign. We grabbed the last available table outside and ordered enough tapas for ten of us. Stabbing his fork into some juicy chorizo fried in cider, Connor splashed his shirt in the greasy orange goo.

'Aw Jeez, look at the state of me.'

'Don't worry, it makes me feel better not being the only clumsy one.'

'I'd like to say that it was being around you that's made me clumsy but I've been in the hospital enough times for that to be a lie.'

'How many times?' I asked, intrigued.

'Eleven. Six broken bones and about fifty-four stitches so far.'

'Eight. Two breaks, thirty-two stitches and

two concussions,' I replied, counting off my score on my fingers.

'Not bad, Grommet. Not bad.'

We chatted a bit more, comparing war wounds and clumsy encounters. I found myself more and more drawn to him. He was kind, thoughtful, funny, and friendly; everything that Michael wasn't. He was attractive in a fit, outdoorsy, care free kind of way. The opposite of Michael's clinical, tailored suit and manicured good looks. Oh yeah, and he liked Jade.

Before I could over think things, my train of thought was interrupted by a loud, 'Yenny!'

'Antonio! Fancy meeting you here!'

'This is my regular, it is the best in town! Here let me introduce you to my brother, Jaime.'

I went to shake hands but, again, the friendly cheek kissing caught me out.

'Jaime, I must thank you for your help,' I said earnestly.

'De nada! When Antonio explained the situation I knew we would have to do something creative to get them to come back. Luckily, the coast guard owed me a favour. I have just heard back from him; he approached the vessel and made them return to the harbour over permit violations. Nothing major, but they had to turn around.'

'We thought we would see how it all played out from the comfort of our favourite restaurant,' added Antonio.

'Please join us,' said Connor, pulling a spare chair up to the table.

'I would not want to interrupt your date,' Antonio said to me with a cheeky glint in his eye.

'We were here to watch the spectacle too,' said Connor.

Following his lead I said, 'Yeah, it's not a date. We'd love for you to join us.'

As they sat down Antonio whispered in my ear, 'So that's two dates you *haven't* had?'

I tried to convey a expression which said 'don't remind me'.

Antonio and Jaime had just been served some cold beers when the gates to the marina opened and in sailed the Galateia. The captain docked her in a nearby berth. We had a clear view of everything from our cosy vantage point. We had the benefit of being hidden in a dimly lit crowd of people while we watched Michael and the crew file off, out in the open, under the screaming bright lights of the marina. Michael crossed straight over the boardwalk and after glancing over his shoulder, he got into a waiting taxi and drove off onto the dark roads. I saw Maria and the captain holding hands as they disembarked; they seemed to have all her limbs intact so I figured my job was done.

'Phew, I'm glad Maria's back okay! Who wants another drink? They're on me,' I announced cheerfully.

'I wonder where Michael's headed?' Connor

mused.

'What if he's heading back to the office? What if he's on my flight?' My moment of relief was quickly replaced by panic.

'Hey, hey, it's okay. You'll square it with work tomorrow, try not to stress about things you can't control.'

'I might be able to find out where he's gone,' said Antonio with a mischievous grin on his face. 'I know all the taxi drivers around here!'

CHAPTER 33

While we were sat waiting for Antonio to return we chatted a bit more with Jaime. Suddenly, a large shadow loomed over me and I turned to see what was causing it.

'Brutus,' I breathed. Remembering my recent encounter with him filled me with dread.

'Jenny, you always seem to be surrounded by different men. I can't seem to get you on your own,' he said. I could hear the malice in his voice.

I'd been through enough in the last few days, I wasn't going to be intimidated or pushed around anymore. I sat up straight, squared my shoulders and said levelly, 'Let me introduce you to Jaime, he's a member of the Policia.'

Grasping Jaime by the shoulder I beamed up at Brutus, while Jaime breathed in, sticking out his chest. He seemed to triple in size. Brutus took a step back, I could see the sinister leer on his face drop.

'Your reputation proceeds you, *Brutus*. I think you and I need to go for a little chat,' said Jaime as he stood up.

He matched Brutus in height and stature and led him off to the edge of the restaurant. I saw Jaime make a call, although I was unable to hear or understand what was going on, but I could see lots of gesticulation.

At that moment, our table was approached by a woman about my age, who also seemed to be on holiday.

She smiled shyly and then said, 'Sorry to interrupt, do you know the man that was just here?'

'I wouldn't say I know him well,' I replied. Something about her eagerness worried me, I could tell she was interested in Brutus, perhaps angling to know if he was "with" anyone. A moment of boldness overcame me and not wanting anyone else to get treated like Beth had been, I said, 'I've bumped into him before though, at the sexual health clinic.'

'Sexual health clinic?' she stuttered back.

'Yeah, a few times actually.'

She visibly paled, 'Oh, okay...thanks...' she replied before heading back to her friends shaking her head.

Connor leaned over to me, chuckling, and said, 'Good onya, Grommet, that's two drongos dealt with today. You're on a roll!'

I raised my eyebrows and grimaced, to me it

felt like there was still a lot to do.

'Are you happy staying here a bit longer?' I asked, anxious to find out what had happened to Michael.

'Sure, we've not even had any dessert yet,' he replied.

When Jaime returned, he beamed at us and said, 'Antonio told me about that man; I'm glad I bumped into him. He won't be bothering anyone for a while.'

'No,' I said. *Especially after the lie I just told to his next potential conquest.* I didn't feel even a little bit guilty.

At that moment Antonio came back and said, 'Señor Henson is heading to the hire car place by the airport. If he can't get a flight, I imagine he's going to try and drive somewhere he *can* fly from.'

'It sounds like he's trying to get back too then,' I said as a steely resolve settled over me. I knew I was going to have to fight this through to the end so I could clear my name and regain my self-respect.

The sunlight filtered in through the curtains and I blinked myself awake. I lay motionless, wrestling with the dilemma of feeling both really comfortable, but needing to get up to pee. Decisions, decisions. The warm duvet around me stirred and I peeked over to see Connor, lying angelically, beside me. If anyone walked in to see us now they'd think I was a complete cougar, this handsome guy, barely in his twenties, holed up in bed with me. They probably wouldn't believe that nothing had happened. And precisely nothing had happened. He was a gentleman, and besides, he was into someone else.

When we crawled in from the bar, I made us drinks while Connor set about trying to blow up his inflatable mattress. It had a huge puncture, and while trying to fix it with sticky tape seemed like a great idea at the time, needless to say it was unsuccessful. He wouldn't hear of me sleeping on the floor and I wasn't going to turf him out of his bed so we came to an impasse and agreed to both share the mattress. When it came to bed time, I went to the bathroom to change into my comfy, baggy, pyjamas, and then skipped quickly across the room and self-consciously got into bed. I rolled on to my side, facing away from Connor and fell asleep to the sound of him requesting that if we were going to spoon, he wanted to be the little one.

My brain felt like it was lurching in my head as I leaned down to pluck my phone out of the bag of rice, I was relieved to find it was working. I wanted to check the time and saw it was ten past nine, I figured, even with the hour change, there should be people in the office by now. I swung my legs out of bed and crossed the room to the balcony and went out to phone work. I perched on a big terracotta flower pot to keep from wobbling; I drank too much last night, as much in relief as celebration.

My call was answered by Eve, one of The Witches. 'Mr Thompson's office, who can I say is calling?'

'Hi, it's Jenny. Can I speak to Mr Thompson please?'

'Oh, hi Jenny. How's your holiday going?'

'It's been a bit of a nightmare. Look, I need to speak to Mr Thompson urgently, is he there?'

'No, he's in a meeting all morning and then straight after he is in another meeting with all the directors; he's slammed all day.'

'Do you know what that meeting's about?'

'Yeah, I do actually. Mr Henson called to confirm the details a few minutes ago. He said he was going to email some important documents. The girls are waiting to compile it all now when they receive the email. Jenny, what's all this about?'

'Oh, Eve, this is really important...'

'Are you talking to Jenny George?' I could hear Natalia's scathing tone in the back ground.

'Yeah, she's just...'

'Give that to me.' A loud clunking sounded in my ear as I heard Natalia wrestle the phone from Eve. 'How can I help, Jenny?' She almost spat my name at me.

'Natalia, I really need to speak to Mr Thompson, it's important.'

'I'm sorry, he's unavailable at the moment. Please call back again later.'

There was a click and the line went dead.

A guttural growl welled up in my throat, I'm not a violent person but Natalia was driving me to the edge. Taking a deep breath, I dialled Pete.

'Hi love, any news for me?' he said.

'Yes, I'm on a flight back today.'

'That's fantastic. Can't wait to catch up with you tomorrow.'

'I need a favour, it's urgent. Can you get in to see Mr Thompson? I need to give him a message.'

'No, I can't I'm afraid.'

'Please, this is really important, I wouldn't ask but...'

'I would if I could, darling, but I'm not in work today. Jeremy and I have booked a day off together.'

'Oh...' I replied, I was crestfallen. 'I can sort something I'm sure.'

'You sound upset, darling, what is it? It can't be that bad, can it?'

I explained it all to him and there was silence on the end of the line, I started to think we'd lost the connection.

'You've actually left me speechless... I don't know what to say... I have no words...' he eventually said.

'It's not your problem though, I'm flying back today. I'm sure I can go to the office and set everything straight.'

'Good luck, chick. I think you're gonna need it.'

Connor had put a pot of coffee on when I came back into the apartment. It was a simple self-catering holiday let, but with some family photos dotted around and his paddle board propped by the door, it had a homely feel. The smell of coffee was incredible and made me feel hungry.

'Shall I go and grab us some breakfast?'

'I've got toast if you want?'

'Mmm, yes please.'

'Vegemite or PB?'

I wrinkled my nose at the thought of Vegemite and said, 'Peanut butter, please.'

Connor laughed. 'You Brits don't know what you're missing!'

'Trust me, I've had Marmite, I hear you either love it or hate it. Why don't you save it so you've got a taste of home,' I suggested, trying to be diplomatic.

He laughed and then juggled the two jars he was holding, tossing them over his shoulder.

'Woah! I thought you were clumsy?'

'I'm fine if I'm doing sport or a game. It's in life in general that I'm a butter fingers. It's why I became a water sports instructor. I was supposed to be a doctor like my old man but I didn't fancy slipping with a scalpel.'

I poured the coffee, while Connor carried on making the toast and we chatted more about his passions and plans.

'But what about you, Grommet? What's your dream?'

'I haven't thought of one really.'

'*What?!*'

'Well, I've been busy thinking about other things.'

'You're not supposed to *think* of a dream. It's what you want deep down, your heart knows it before your head does. I know you've been preoccupied with your mum and organising the hens party, but you need to take some time to yourself...'

'How did you know I've been worried about my mum?'

'I got your email, you do know you sent it to *all* the people in your contacts?'

'That's not at all embarrassing!' I replied, stunned at the extent of my email error.

'Don't worry, I thought it was kind of sweet what you'd organised for her. And it's not like I hadn't noticed you were a bit...'

'Stupid?'

'Don't put words in my mouth, I was going to say "accident prone"!'

'Before I can even begin to plan any hopes and dreams, I've got to sort out this fiasco with work. Then I'll sort me out. I've made a resolution.'

'A "new you's resolution"?' he said with a cheeky glint in his eye.

'I like it! But this mess at work needs to get sorted first.'

Connor nodded thoughtfully, crunching his toast heartily.

'Can anyone back at home help out?' he asked.

'I can't get hold of the boss. The other assistants won't help me. My colleague and ally, Pete, is on holiday. I'm just gonna have to run there straight from the airport and hope for the best.'

'What about your friends? Can't any of them help?'

'No, they all work. Except Beth…yes, Connor, that's it' I jumped down from my stool and sprinted to my phone.

CHAPTER 34

My flight was early in the afternoon so I had a couple of hours until I had to be at the airport. Connor said I could hang out at his place until I had to go, he'd gone in to work to service the equipment while business was quiet.

I sent Kirsty a text and she said she was on her break so I decided to forget my rapidly mounting phone bill and call her.

'I'm so glad you're okay J, that all sounds really scary.'

'Well, hopefully it's almost all over now. Is my mum okay?'

'Yeah, she's great. You worry far too much about her. I'm taking her to a book club today, she's having a whale of a time.'

'Okay, that's great, thank you. So, how are the wedding plans coming on?'

'I've had enough talking about it, let's talk about you some more. So, *how's Connor*?' Kirsty put a silly singsong note in her voice.

'What are you insinuating? That I'm a cradle snatcher?'

'No, but I've heard his name a lot.'

'It's 'cos he's been helping me! Anyway, even if I wasn't old enough to be his much older sister, he's not interested in me.'

'Well, if you want to invite him to the wedding then please do. He was fun, it would be great to see him again.'

'Okay I will. Jade will be pleased.'

'Why do you say that?'

'They've been texting and chatting on the phone, didn't she say?'

'No, she hasn't mentioned it. I'm gonna do some digging,' Kirsty sounded intrigued.

'Well, I can verify that he's a complete gent, a real catch.'

Kirsty made an ambiguous 'hmmm' and then said she had to get back to work. I sat holding my phone for a moment trying not to feel jealous that Jade had found such a lovely guy. *If only I was a few years younger.* I gave myself a firm talking to and decided to be pleased for Jade and to stop mooning over something that would never happen.

Right, best go and be a good 'honorary' big sister and get Jade a date for the wedding. And stop talking to myself. Must stop talking to myself.

The sky was bright and the sun was scorching. I could see the silvery white trails of aeroplanes criss-crossing the heavens again and I was relieved that things were getting back to normal. My case bounced and rumbled loudly as I jolted it down the board walk over the beach. I was grateful for my huge sunglasses as they shielded my eyes from the dazzling sea.

'Grommet, this is a nice surprise.'

'I just thought I'd call in to say bye and...' I felt shy suddenly. '...Thanks for...everything.' I slid my sunglasses up on to my head, needing to do something with my hands.

'You're welcome, you big sop. Come here.' He engulfed me in a big sweaty hug and I could feel his muscles, tense under his clinging tee-shirt.

Reluctantly I pulled away and gazed up into his twinkling eyes, squinting in the bright light, they reminded me of something.

'It's gonna be strange, not having you around to bail out all the time. I meant what I said in the bar the other day; if you fancy a change and wanna come back out here and work with me for a few months, then you're welcome. I'm probably gonna be here until the end of the season.'

'Can you take holiday?'

'Sure, are you thinking of planning another girly trip?'

'Kirsty wanted to invite you to the wedding, she doesn't have your address though.'

'That'd be bonza!' Connor was clearly chuffed to be invited.

We heard a toot and looked back up the beach to the road. Antonio's taxi had pulled up and he waved as he made his way down the boardwalk to us. Suddenly I felt rushed, I didn't want to leave. I swallowed hard. Connor grabbed my shoulders and squared me up to him. My eyes were level with his collarbone. I stared at the smooth nook, the small recess flanked by the taut bands of muscle in his neck. Forbidding myself to look in his eyes until I had composed myself, I memorised this little piece of him. His hands squeezed me comfortingly.

'Listen, Grommet. You'll be great later don't worry.'

I shook my head. *That's not why I'm getting upset. Pull yourself together, Jenny.*

'So, I'll email you the details of the wedding?' I managed to ask.

'Yes please, I really am stoked.'

'I think Jade will be *stoked* too.'

'Jade?'

Feeling like an awkward older sister putting my foot in it, I hastily tried to be more subtle. 'Well, we all will.' *Why am I even mentioning Jade?* I could see Antonio getting closer and I waved to him. 'My ride is here.'

'See you soon, Grommet. I just hope the venue doesn't have a stage…' His sentence got cut off by a cheery Antonio.

'Hola Yenny, hola Connor!'

'Hola!' replied Connor giving him a hearty hand shake. 'You get Grommet here to the airport safely, you hear?'

'Si, si.' Said Antonio, laughing, as he picked up my case. 'Estas listo? You ready?'

I nodded. *As ready as I'll ever be.*

Not knowing what to do with my hands I gave Connor a small wave and clutched my navy tote close to me. Reluctantly following Antonio back across the boardwalk, I walked backwards a few steps, so I could keep looking at Connor. He was staring back, the sea breeze ruffling his long hair and wrapping his clothes slickly around him. *Wow! Why am I leaving again? Oh yeah- to save my job.* I gave a final wave and turned back, determined not to stack it as I made my exit. I didn't know if Connor was watching me leave, but I wanted him to be.

Scurrying, elegantly of course, to catch up with Antonio, Connor's question crossed my mind. *Why would he ask about a stage?* Antonio heaved my case in to the boot and opened the passenger door for me. I clambered into my usual spot in the front and sat there, while the cog wheels in my brain whirred.

'Que tal?'

I looked into Antonio's kindly eyes as it all clicked into place.

'It was Connor all along,' I said.

CHAPTER 35

The holiday was most definitely over. I sat in the tight grey aeroplane seat, nursing a slimline tonic. I was determined to keep a clear head. I clutched my precious binder to my knees and tried to get everything straight in my head.

I need to write a list, I thought. Life's always better with a list. Riffling through the binder I found an old scrap of paper and wrote:

1) Evidence: Need proof Michael used me to be money mule in his scheme to defraud the company and embezzle money. See- Photos on my phone, document I 'borrowed'. Email sent.

2) Defence: Need to get back to work to show them his plan before he can frame me. Once he's planted the seed that it was me, who are they going to believe? Need to get to them first. – Beth to collect me from airport.

3) Phone police: Who knows what else he's capable of?

4) Long term: Find new job and/or a lawyer. -Ask Beth for recommendation.

Stop blundering around. -Become less clumsy.

Don't overthink things. -Be more spontaneous and live life for me.

Have confidence in myself. Stand up for myself. -Be more assertive.

= ULTIMATE GOAL: NEW ME'S RESOLUTION!

I wrote the last point in bold and scribbled the exclamation mark with a flourish. Then I leaned back in my chair and nervously read through my list. Once I was happy with the plan there was nothing else to be done, not in this metal tube, thousands of feet up in the sky, so I decided to tidy my organiser, to keep myself busy.

We were about to land as I turned to the last page which had writing on. It was the top sheet of minutes from our conference call. Except that was just it, one sheet. I flicked forward and back, the second page of notes I *knew* I had written wasn't there. The ragged, tell-tale shards of a ripped-out page lined the spine of the A4 jotter pad. This must have been why Michael had my folder, he was destroying the evidence.

A recollection of many teen detective books I'd read when I was younger crept into my head. I could gently shade over the next page with a pencil to reveal the imprint left from writing on the page that was now missing. I snorted to myself. *Don't be ridiculous, that'd never work... except... all those books can't be wrong.* I wanted to catch the attention of the air steward but the fasten seatbelt sign was on. *They probably couldn't help, who has a pencil these days anyway? Actually, I do- in my make-up bag.*

Rummaging in my tote I found my make-up, and indeed, I found the eye pencil but it was black and seemed far too dark. Studying the contents again I came across the bronzing pearls. Taking a pink creamy chalky ball between my finger and thumb I squeezed it until it crumbled into a fine dust and then carefully smoothed it all over the page. My scruffy, barely legible handwriting was revealed and I read it closely, scouring for the tiniest detail to help. The moment we touched down I found the rest of the evidence I needed. *Bingo!*

'Beth, you're such a star. Thank you for this,' I said.

'It's the least I can do after bailing on the hen do. It's a relief to get away for a bit to be honest- now I'm just helping mum organise the funeral and trying to work out what to do with my life.'

I squeezed her hard. 'I'm so sorry about your nan.'

'Hey now, don't be too nice to me, I'm not

ready for that! Distract me so I don't break down and cry again.'

'Alright, drive me to work already! Chop chop!'

Beth swallowed hard and blinked away her tears. 'That's more like it, Jenny, be mean to me!'

'Come on, you old witch.' Beth gave me a grateful look and grabbed the handle of my case. Between us we got it to her car, loaded it in and headed straight to my office.

I was breathless from the adrenaline and my run from the car. I say run, I was trying to appear professional and unflappable, so it was more like a prance. I headed for the main meeting room, but as I burst through the door I could see it was empty. Everyone had gone except for Chantelle, who was clearing up some papers.

'Don't tell me I've missed it, Chantelle?'

'What are you doing here? I thought you were in Spain?'

'I was but... it doesn't matter. I need to speak to Mr Thompson. Is the meeting over?'

'They moved it to Mr Thompson's office...'

'Great thanks!' I called over my shoulder, I must have interrupted her telling me it was strictly confidential in my haste to get away.

Eyes focused on the door, I completely missed Natalia and Stan the burly security guard standing to the side. No sooner was I opening the door and going in, did I find myself tussled to the ground. What an entrance.

'What's the meaning of this?' shouted Mr

Thompson.

With my face pressed into the scratchy industrial carpet, it was hard to reply.

'Ah...vyoung Jenny... I thought you were on holiday.'

Stan relaxed his grip on me, realising who I was and that I wasn't some sort of threat; I wasn't even half his size. I heaved myself up to stand. I'd read somewhere being stood up gives you more power, psychologically speaking. The effect was probably ruined somewhat by the fact I was now only wearing one shoe and Stan still had his hand on my shoulder.

The group of men were huddled around a large document, pens in the air poised to sign. I was just in time. Now I was there, and finally had Mr Thompson's attention, I was at a loss for what to say. My heart was battling to get out of my chest.

'Unhand my client!' said Beth from behind me.

'And this is?'

'I'm Beth Wilson, Miss George's legal advisor.' I turned to beam at Beth and she gave me a wink. Moral support to the rescue.

'I need to explain something to you, Mr Thompson, it's quite serious,' I said.

'Well, this is a bit...ah...unexpected. It's not really the best time...'

'Michael, I mean, Mr Henson, is stealing money from the company and laundering it through the Barts account.'

'Well, that's absurd and quite frankly

slanderous, do you have any proof?'

'Yes! It's all here. I've emailed it to you too, in case something happened to me.'

He looked stunned and appalled. 'In that case, you'd ah… better join us…'

I'd laid out all the evidence on Mr Thompson's desk and he and the other partners pored over it, brows furrowing deeper and deeper. One of the men in suits seemed vaguely familiar, I must have passed him in the hallway at some point.

'We've certainly dodged a bullet here. This is all quite complex, young Jenny, well done for putting it together.'

I sighed inwardly at the patronising old goat, but I didn't let my irritation show on my face.

'Well, I had the motivation of fearing for my job, and my life. Did I mention that he turned violent on the boat?'

'Did he now?' said Mr Thompson, he appeared almost overwhelmed by the deluge of information.

'You know making copies of classified company documents can get you in serious trouble,' said one of the suits.

'Yes, but so can being framed for syphoning away company funds so I thought I'd take a risk.'

Mr Thompson gave me a long look. 'I don't think I can call you *young* Jenny anymore, can I?'

Not sure how cheeky I could be, I just raised

my eyebrows.

Beth spoke up for me. 'I don't think referring to one's age is relevant to whether or not they can complete their role efficiently. I would advise you to refrain from referring to any characteristics, age or otherwise, unless you would like a review of your company's equality and discrimination policies?'

Beth kneed me under the table as I struggled to keep a straight face, I'd never seen her in legal work mode before.

The door to Mr Thompson's office was flung open again and in hurried Pete and Jeremy, waving a stack of papers.

'Mr Thompson, we have proof of Michael Henson's embezzlement schemes,' announced Pete, by way of introduction.

'Well, yes, Peter, ah... Jenny here, she's brought it all to our attention. We are reviewing it now.'

'There's more, Sir. Jeremy and I have been digging and unearthed more from when he was at head office.'

As Jeremy laid out what they'd discovered to the board of men, Pete leaned in to me and said, 'You alright, darling?'

'I think so,' I whispered in reply. 'Isn't it your day off, what are you doing here?'

'I knew there was something fishy about him. Jeremy and I got talking after your call and he looked into some files. I'm so sorry I couldn't warn you about him sooner,' he said in a hushed voice.

'Please, you don't need to apologise. It was my fault. If I hadn't been so distracted, trying to impress him, it would never have happened.'

'Don't be too hard on yourself, he's been doing this for a long time. While Jeremy was examining at the numbers, I made some calls, spoke to that assistant who'd made the complaint before and a couple of her colleagues. It looks like he's been using one assistant after another, small amounts at a time to keep under the radar. Filtering it through petty cash and stationary budgets and such. Little things that people don't really check. You should be proud of yourself for working it out when you did!' Pete elbowed me playfully and said quietly, 'We're gonna need one helluva lunch to go over all this.'

Mr Thompson and the suits were all nodding at what Jeremy was saying and looking very grave. A noise grew steadily louder and we could hear shouting in the corridor, we all twisted in our seats to see Michael barge his way in to the office. He had red shiny eyes, his mouth curled into a snarl and I could see the sweat on his brow. I can't believe I was attracted to this monster.

Seeing him here made me flush cold. I could feel myself starting to shake as I comprehended the magnitude of what *might* have happened on the boat if I hadn't been so lucky as to escape. Clutching on to Pete's hand, he gave me a reassuring squeeze.

Natalia followed him in, almost glowing with excitement at the impending showdown. It was starting to feel very crowded in Mr Thompson's office and I clung to Pete, suddenly feeling tiny and vulnerable.

'Arrest her!' he shouted, dramatically pointing a finger at me. 'She's conning the company out of thousands of pounds, but I've uncovered her plan.'

'Now now, Michael,' said Mr Thompson calmly. 'Let's not conduct ourselves like this. We know the truth of what's ah... going on here.'

'It's no good, Michael,' said one of the suits. 'We know it was you. Calm down and let's talk through this and see if we can work this out.'

Michael seethed, outraged. 'Don't turn this all on me, Philip. You're as guilty as I am.'

'Nonsense,' said Philip, the suit I'd recognised. 'The man's clearly lost it.' There was a nervous edge to his voice and I took a closer look.

Determined not to lose my nerve, I forced myself to remain cool and speak clearly. 'Actually, I think he probably is in on it too. It's taken me a while to place him, but I recognise him from the conference call.'

'Thank you, Jenny,' said Michael.

'Don't thank me. Don't even look at me,' I replied, letting go of Pete's hand and standing tall. 'You disgust me.'

'Yes, I'd be surprised if Michael had pulled this off by himself. You girl, Natalie, is it? Call the police,' commanded Mr Thompson, suddenly direct and assertive.

Natalia, most disgruntled at being bossed around, flounced out of the room like a teenager.

'I don't understand why you did it, Michael? You had such a promising career here. With some hard work you could have done well,' said Mr Thompson.

'Pish!' sneered Philip. 'He's never done a hard day's work in his life; living off his family money. That is until he frittered it all away. He couldn't even seduce a dumb blonde properly.'

'She's not my type!' spat Michael. Clearly, they'd had this argument more than once.

'That's the worst excuse I've ever heard! You were supposed to distract her. Flirt a little. Just enough so she wouldn't think about any funny business at work,' Philip replied.

'I did my best. And she was so desperate to make a good impression on me, I thought it was in the bag. It was that Kenneth's fault, that Australian who kept sniffing around.'

'Er, talk about me as if I'm not here if you want?' I said, outraged. Although this did explain why he kept blowing inexplicably hot and cold.

Natalia had come back into the room and I could see her smirking at my character assassination.

'It's because you went renegade. You blew it,' huffed Philip.

'I told you, it was that damned Australian.'

The men bickered on like this until the police arrived and arrested them, we could hear them carry on down the corridor as they were led away. The rest of the room stood stunned for a moment.

Then, breaking the silence, Beth said, 'Now, I expect my client to be appropriately remunerated for her efforts to save your company. Bear in mind, she has saved you a lot of money and prevented a media scandal. Plus, you will be covering my fee of course.'

Mr Thompson could only nod; he was dumbfounded.

'Now, as a side note, I've had an anonymous tip to request you to investigate work place bullying. I trust you will comply fully with this.' There was more nodding, Natalia, however, paled visibly.

CHAPTER 36

Pete hugged me and said, 'Darling, Jeremy and I were talking last night, we think you've lost far too much weight since your Spanish escapades.'

'Er, thanks. I think.'

We sat down at our usual table in the restaurant, which was right by the window, I could see Pete had already ordered us some wine and olives. It was a week after the big showdown in Mr Thompson's office, and Pete and I had only just found the chance to meet up for a proper natter away from work.

'Thank goodness we're meeting for lunch finally, I can try and feed you up.'

I rolled my eyes, and exclaimed, 'I've got a bridesmaid dress I need to fit into!'

'So, other than escaping a fraudulent megalomaniac, how was your holiday?'

'It was great thanks, and thanks so much for what you organised at Breeze.'

'Oh, don't thank me… as a matter of fact I've been feeling a bit guilty. Maybe I put you in more danger with Mr Henson by organising that?'

'How were you to know? I've been wondering if he knew I was going all along or if it was a pure coincidence that he was in Spain too.'

'I think he'd already chosen you as a target. On his first day in the office he was interviewing everyone, that was when he singled you out. But then it was ridiculously unlucky that you were both on holiday at the same time. Although that probably helped in a way.'

'What do you mean?'

'Well, Jeremy heard from Paul who heard from Dave who heard from Stan-'

'Get to the point. I get that the whole company is talking about me.'

'Well, Stan from security had to work closely with the police after the arrests, and he heard that Philip was really annoyed with Mr Henson. He said he'd ruined all their plans by *improvising* in Spain. Looks like he rushed it with involving you and that, ultimately, led to you working it all out.'

'Don't repeat this, Pete, but I almost didn't work it out. He had me sucked in for a while,' I admitted, knowing I could trust him.

'He had us all sucked in for a while.'

There was a sad glimmer in his eyes and I could see Pete was disappointed with how things had ended up at work.

Trying to lift his mood, I raised up my glass and said, 'Let's forget about the past and toast to the future…'

'To the future!' repeated Pete and we clinked glasses. 'Now, speaking about the future, I've got something I need to ask you.'

'Go on,' I said, intrigued.

'Well, I've been thinking about asking Jeremy to marry me…'

'That's a great idea,' I said, bubbling with excitement for him. 'I think you should definitely do it.'

'Hang on a sec, darling, I haven't got to the bit I want to ask you yet.' Pete paused and then grinned at me as he said, 'I've been thinking about asking Jeremy to marry me, and if he says "yes", will you be my best woman?'

I leapt at Pete and hugged him tightly. 'I'd be so honoured.'

'Well, I'll let you get over your bridesmaid duties for Kirsty first before I get you to do anything else!'

Kirsty handed me the colour swatch and said, 'What do you think?'

'It's um…it's lovely. It's very orange.'

'It's called peach whisper. Do you like it? I want you to be happy, you and Jade have to wear it.'

Whisper? Peach scream more like. 'What does Jade think?' I asked.

'She helped choose it, she said it's right on trend and loves the colour.'

'Me too.' I smiled as a little piece of me died inside.

Must be a good bridesmaid. Must be a good bridesmaid. I couldn't abide the colour orange on me. I had absolutely no problem with other people wearing it. Loved the fruit. But I didn't want to wear it myself and look all pasty and washed out. I knew it wasn't about me though, it was Kirsty's day and, therefore, I'd do whatever she wanted.

Kirsty rolled her eyes at me and said, 'You really are the worst liar, J! I know you hate orange. I'm your best friend, I've known you forever. I would *not* make you wear this.'

'What?' I asked as relief flooded through me.

'I'm messing with you. I wanted to see how you were getting on with the whole 'I'm going to stand up for myself and live my life for me' promise you've been going on about.'

'But it's your wedding day, if you want me to wear it, I'll wear it. It's what a good bridesmaid should do.'

'But we're best friends too, J, and best friends don't make best friends wear orange.'

I hugged her. 'So...what colour is it?' I was virtually bouncing up and down with excitement and relief.

'I've booked us all in for fittings in an hour, you can see then. Now, I can't do any more wedding organising until the last minute. So, let's talk about you and how your *new you's resolution* is going.'

It had been chaos in the few weeks since I'd been back and I'd barely seen Kirsty for a good catch up. We were sat together on a big plump sofa in the pub nursing a couple of glasses of lime and soda. Coffee and tea were gateway drugs to cake and we were trying to avoid all unnecessary calories before the wedding.

'Well, work is the same as ever. They charged Michael with fraud, embezzlement, a whole host of crimes so, obviously, he's been fired. I got a massive bonus for my help in foiling his scheme but they demoted me back to general assistant. Any decisions Michael made in the short time he was in the office were reversed. I think Pete is more gutted than I am though. Mr Thompson is still a patronising bore. Oh, and Natalia left, so that's one good thing to come out of it all.'

'Thank goodness for that. How did that happen?'

'Beth, the one-woman-legal-whirlwind. She instigated a work place bullying investigation and so many people came forward that I think it freaked her out and she left suddenly.'

'She's probably terrorising some other poor office now.'

'Yeah, knowing my luck I'll change jobs and end up where she is again!'

'Are you leaving?'

'I hate it there. I've handed my notice in.'

Kirsty sat up straighter. 'That's sudden.'

'I'm trying not to overthink things, remember?'

'But… it's your job.'

I shrugged. 'I've got the pay off from work to tide me over for a while. I'm not going anywhere there, and I kept thinking, there must be more to life than this, right?'

Kirsty agreed sagely. 'Good for you, we spend so much time at work, we should at least be able to tolerate it, even if we aren't ecstatically happy about it.'

'Exactly. I have no idea what I'm gonna do yet, but I'll work something out. Beth's an inspiration, she's doing so well.'

'I'm glad. I haven't seen her since the funeral,' said Kirsty with a guilty look on her face.

'Don't worry, no one has. She's setting up her own legal consultancy service. I've only spoken to her when dealing with her through work. Mr Thompson has taken on her services, we're her first customers!'

'That's fab! What else have I missed?'

'So, in other news, my mum can't stop singing your praises.'

'Well I am wonderful!' replied Kirsty smugly.

'Seriously, she's saying you saved her life when you popped in to check on her and then made her go to that book club.'

'I didn't make her go, I just suggested it.'

'She tells it differently. She said that you picked her up, drove her there, threw her and her crutches out of the car and yelled, "pick you up in two hours" as you sped off.'

'And?' Kirsty asked, raising a cheeky eyebrow at me.

'And she hated you at the time but now she'll love you forever for it. She met a guy there. He's helping her with her rehab. They go for walks together. It's adorable.'

We clutched our hands over our hearts and said together, 'Old love!' Before falling about, laughing.

'The upshot is, she's fired me as her PA! I don't even need to do her online shopping anymore because he has a car and takes her.'

'So, what are you going to do with all this extra time you've now got? Perhaps you could invest it in your own love life?'

'Seriously, don't suggest sending me to a book club. Mum's been banging on that I should go and that I might meet someone. I've started going to yoga, although, the only guys that go there tend to stick to the back of the hall and keep farting; it's not the best way to meet someone.'

'It's a shame Michael turned out to be such a...' Kirsty paused, I could sense she was trying to be diplomatic.

'Criminal? Megalomaniac? Weasel? ...a cad and a bounder?' I offered.

'You've been reading too much regency era

romance.'

'Never!' I replied.

'I was thinking more 'scheming, arrogant arse',' said Kirsty.

'Yeah, that covers it.' I sighed. 'It was all a bit of a pipe dream, the handsome boss taking an interest in me.'

'Don't forget rich!'

'Ha!' I laughed sarcastically, 'I didn't even know about that at first. Not that he *was* rich, it was his family. He totally squandered all his inheritance, it's why he was trying to embezzle the money.'

'Oooh, I did wonder about that. He wasn't really your type, was he? I know you've never been into rich guys or material stuff. I was only teasing.'

'I know.' My voice was low and level.

'You sound sad. Is it too soon for teasing?'

'I'm not sad about Michael. I just got swept up in the fantasy of being pampered for a while. It's the real-life stuff that's bringing me down.'

'Go on, is there someone else?'

I toyed with the idea of telling Kirsty about Connor. I'd spent most of my free time dripping around thinking about him, wondering what he was up to, wondering if he'd really come to the wedding. I couldn't get him out of my head. It was funny, I'd thought I'd found the reverse of James in Michael, being smart and motivated compared to lazy and selfish. But in truth, it was Connor who was opposite, to both of them. Someone kind and thoughtful is who I should have been on the lookout for all along.

'Yes, no, well, nothing ever happened. He likes someone else anyway.'

'Oh my, it's not James, is it? He was sniffing around again, wasn't he? What happened there?'

'Absolutely not! That's a whole other story, he keeps trying to meet up. I was trying to think of excuses not to go, now I've resorted to ignoring him. He really won't get the message.' I checked my watch, 'Eeek, we better go. We might be late for the fitting!'

The bridal shop was a gorgeous little boutique, which feasted the senses. The air was spritzed with lavender, we perched on the crushed velvet, throne-like chairs, sipping our sparkling elderflower drinks, while dresses dazzled and glowed around us. Harp music was tinkling in the background. I don't think I've ever felt more weddingy before.

Jade had met us at the shop and we sat together while waiting for the curtain around the little stage to be thrown back, revealing Kirsty in her dress. With a swish, the purple drape was pulled to the side and we could see Kirsty peeking down to us, smiling nervously.

'What do you think?'

Stunned, Jade and I gaped.

Finally, I managed the eloquent phrase, 'Wow!'

'Yeah, wow!' said Jade.

'You like it? Do you think it's okay?'

Almost speechless, I eventually managed to string some words together. 'Oh Kirsty, you look stunning!'

Kirsty's grin broadened with relief. 'Phew!'

She was wearing a simple, strapless, princess style dress, it was slightly off-white, complete with a sweetheart neckline and layers and layers of flouncing tulle. Her dark hair was sculpted back with a pearl hair slide. A string of pearls, just perching on her collar bone, finished the ensemble. Classic. Elegant. Breathtaking.

'Can't you see how beautiful you are?' I asked. Kirsty blushed.

Lightening the mood, Jade said, 'Well at least we won't have to wear ugly-ass dresses to make Kirsty look better!'

'Oh yes- your dresses! I hope you like them. We have two weeks to alter them if there's a problem.' Kirsty nodded over to the sales assistant who went behind the scenes and then came back with an armful of puffy dress bags.

As the zip was pulled down, out of the bag unfurled one of the dresses. Jade and I both gasped. Soft nude chiffon tumbled down. The sales assistant held the dresses up for us to see, they echoed the sweetheart neck line of Kirsty's frock, but with a rouching of the fabric criss-crossing over the corset.

'What do you think?'

'Nude is dangerously close to orange, but... *I love it!*'

Jade had already stripped down to her undies and was climbing in to her dress. I nipped behind the curtain on the stage area to slip into mine. They both fit us perfectly.

'K, it's so easy being your bridesmaid. You've been so low maintenance and you're not making us wear anything horrendous. This is great!'

'What about the shoes?' asked Jade, walking around on tiptoes, pretending.

'Oh yes, in those boxes,' Kirsty pointed to the edge of the tiny stage.

Flipping open the lid I was greeted by some nude peep-toe heels. Six inch heels. *Oh hell, I knew I'd spoken too soon.*

'Cute!' cheered Jade.

'Perfect!' I looked up, beaming. And made a mental note to spend every free, waking moment wearing them in.

CHAPTER 37

I rang Kirsty and Steve's doorbell and stood back, looking up at their mid-terraced town house. I smiled to myself. I was so pleased for my friend, she had a wonderful fiancé, a nice house, a good job; she had it all. I, on the other hand, had a chilled bottle of champagne in my bag so, we were all winners in our own way.

'Hello, trouble,' said Steve, holding the door open for me. 'What's with the goofy grin?'

I held the champagne aloft. 'Thought I'd kick off the celebrations a bit early.'

Waltzing in to my home from home, I kicked my shoes off, turned to Steve and said, 'I've also got a couple of beers in my bag so you and your bro don't waste the good stuff.'

'You know us so well,' said Steve laughing, and then tilted his head gesturing into the house. 'She's in the lounge.'

I was engulfed by a huge hug when I walked in, I lifted my assailant off the ground and spun her round.

'Somebody's getting married!' I sung.

'*Tomorrow*!' squealed Kirsty.

When we calmed down, I found Matt, Steve's older brother sat in an armchair watching us, slightly bemused.

We exchanged much more demure hellos and then Matt said, 'Did I hear you mention beer?'

I nodded. 'And Champagne!'

Kirsty said, 'As part of your best man duties, please can you go and get us some glasses?'

'Of course.' Matt sighed in a way that could only mean he had been asked to do many things "as part of his best man duties", none of which probably had anything to do with being best man.

I caught his eye and said, 'Why don't you have a final drink with us and then, *as part of your best man duties*, can you and Steve please bugger off so I can start on my bridesmaid duties?'

'Of course!' he replied.

'So, how was your last day?' asked Kirsty.

'Strange actually. The last couple of weeks have flown by and I couldn't wait for it to all be over and then today I started feeling sad about it. I'm probably just sad about leaving Pete really, but I know we'll stay in touch.'

'It's the fear of the unknown,' said Kirsty, suddenly solemn. I could tell we weren't only talking about me right then.

'Hey, you shouldn't have *fear of the unknown*.

You've known Steve forever; you've been living with him for yonks. Surely you've got fear of the...known?!'

Kirsty tucked a loose lock of hair behind her ear. 'Pre-wedding jitters, probably.'

'Where are those glasses?' I asked; we needed some liquid courage.

The boys emerged with a couple champagne flutes and, after popping the cork, we clunked the cans of beer and glasses together, shouting out, 'Cheers!'

The boys left and we dived right into the final bits that needed to be sorted before the big day.

'What's left to do?' I asked, presuming Kirsty would have finished nearly everything. The wedding was tomorrow after all.

'So, we just need to ice the cake, finish the seating plan, print out the name cards, and work out what to give our mums.'

'Is that all?' I was internally cursing Kirsty's desire to have a homemade wedding. Other than the dresses and suits, she'd done virtually everything herself.

'It's not too much, is it?'

I took a deep breath and grabbed my phone out of my bag. 'It's all going to be fine, I'm just summoning back up.'

After I sent out a call to arms, I turned to Kirsty and asked, 'What do you mean by gifts for your mums?'

'It's tradition to give flowers to the mums at

the wedding, but I'm not sure what to do. It doesn't feel right but I don't have a clue what else to do so I was gonna go to the supermarket and see what they had.'

'That sounds a bit crap, we can do better than that. Leave it with me, I'll have a think.'

'You don't mince your words these days, do you?'

'I thought I'd try *channelling Annie* to try and be more assertive. You know, trying to be blunter and to the point, like she is.'

'How's it going for you so far?' she asked, an eyebrow raised.

'Well, it gets things done, but I think my friends are beginning to hate me!' I replied and we both laughed.

'Maybe just channel her fifty percent, I can only cope with one full Annie.'

'Alright,' I said, grinning.

Within half an hour, Kirsty's mum, Christine, and all the hens had arrived. Suze no longer looked like Cruella, she now had a severely asymmetrical chocolate brown bob.

'I thought it would be classy for the wedding,' she said, plumping the bottom of it.

'I bought more champagne as requested,' announced Annie.

'Okay guys, no time to chat, we've got a wedding to finish!' I called out. 'Right, I'll sort out drinks and food to keep us going. Christine and Suze, you're on cake icing duty. Jade and

Kirsty, you sort the seating plan. Beth and Annie, print those name cards like you've never printed before.'

'How long's she been like this?' asked Annie, just loudly enough for me to hear.

'She's been getting steadily more assertive since her *new you's resolution*,' replied Kirsty.

Beth added, 'She always has been organised though, but now she's bossier.'

I flashed them a smile in response.

While Christine was distracted, I grabbed Kirsty and whispered, 'I'll pop out and sort the flowers now.'

I returned with a piping hot bundle of fish and chips for everyone and two potted rose bushes. Keeping out of Christine's way, I dragged Kirsty into the study, across the hall from the lounge.

'I went *off-piste*, are they okay? I thought they'd last longer,' I asked Kirsty as I showed her the gifts for the mums.

'This is so much better than a couple of bunches of flowers, thank you! It's all coming together.'

'Time for a dinner break then?'

Kirsty nodded and said, 'Can I smell...'

'Fish and chips!' I held the bag aloft. 'There's no point calorie counting now.'

We all sat around on the sofa and the lounge floor, sipping on champagne and munching our dinner out of the paper. It was a lovely atmosphere and Kirsty seemed really content.

'Is everything done now?' asked Suze.

Kirsty listed off on her fingers. 'Cake's done. Name cards are printed but they need folding. J accomplished her secret mission, and the seating plan needs finishing.'

'I'll clear up,' I suggested. 'Suze, you help with the folding of the place cards, while Christine checks on the seating plan to make sure there are no faux pas.'

'Great! Thanks so much for all your help everyone. I love you all!' gushed Kirsty.

'K, don't go getting all emosh'!' wailed Jade.

Kirsty and I went to stand up but Christine stopped us by saying, 'While I've got you all here I think it's a good time to do this... I've got a little something for you, my love.' Christine then presented Kirsty with a light blue silk hanky that had been her grandmothers and a pearl bracelet. She said, 'The hanky is old and blue. I want this bracelet back so it's only borrowed. And I want to pay for your dress so that's your something new.'

'Oh, Mum, this is wonderful, thank you so much,' said Kirsty, tears spilling down her cheeks.

Us on lookers ohhhed and ahhed, honoured to be part of their special moment.

'Get your blubbing done now!' said Annie. 'You don't want to ruin your make up tomorrow!'

With big sniffs, Kirsty wiped at her face and said, 'Right, we're almost done, let's crack on and finish it. Then I need my beauty sleep.'

I came back from cleaning up in the kitchen to quite a row over the seating plan.

'But I don't even know him!' protested Christine.

Jade was passionately arguing back. 'But he doesn't know anyone else; he should be on the top table.'

Curious, I wandered over to have a peak at who they were arguing about. I could see Kirsty sat with her head in her hands, clearly despairing at the politics of arranging who sits next to who. Sticky notes with names on were scattered everywhere. It was a mess.

'Jade, stop being spoilt. He can sit on this table at the back, and he'll get to know people.'

'But Muuuum, Connor needs to sit here.'

At the sound of his name my heart beat quickened and I could feel the heat rise in my cheeks. I felt sick with excitement. However, he was going to be there for Jade, and she clearly wanted him to sit with her on the top table. I needed to get over this absurd crush on him.

'What do you think, Jenny?' They asked simultaneously, startling me out of my contemplation.

It flashed through my mind that I would love him to sit on the top table with us. *God, I'm going to regret saying this...*

'Maybe the top table isn't the best place for him, he might feel a bit overwhelmed. What about with Beth, Annie and Suze? Is there space there? He knows them.'

Jade rolled her eyes at me and I could feel disappointment radiating from her.

'I'll take care after him,' shouted over Suze, who'd been earwigging on the argument.

'Well, that's settled,' said Christine firmly.

In a huff, Jade grabbed the large ornate mirror and pen and started copying over the rough seating plan on to it. I could hear her muttering about Kirsty's sloppy handwriting under her breath.

Eventually everyone began to leave and it was just Kirsty, Jade and myself left. As we shut the door on the last of them, Kirsty leapt on the quiet moment in the hallway to grill me.

'It's Connor, isn't it? That guy you were talking about? I knew it! I saw this coming a month ago!' She wrung my hands in hers and was nearly skipping with excitement.

'It's completely ridiculous. We're from different countries. I'm far too old for him. He's into Jade and she likes him; nothing will ever happen. I'm being a complete idiot.'

'Did I hear my name?' called out Jade from the sitting room.

I shot Kirsty a "don't say anything" look and replied, 'We're talking about walking Kirsty down the aisle tomorrow, I think you should go first as I might make an idiot of myself.'

Jade bounded out to find us and we practised our "walk" up and down the hall until she was satisfied with how Kirsty and I performed it. We fell into bed a bit before midnight, but I couldn't sleep and when I did I had weird dreams of Connor and Jade riding on the backs of dolphins together.

CHAPTER 38

My face was aching from all the smiling. This was a good thing, it was distracting me from my throbbing feet, which had been teetering on ridiculously high heels all afternoon. All was going well so far. The yoga class I'd started, in a bid to stop my mum banging on about book club, seemed to be seriously helping my balance. I'd made it up and down the aisle without tripping and helped Kirsty pee in a tiny toilet cubicle more than once. Although we probably didn't fall over due to the sheer amount of tulle and counterbalance from the walls rather than any skill on my part.

Busy helping Kirsty and posing for photographs, time had flown by. I'd only caught the odd glimpse of Connor, I'd barely seen anyone properly. From what I could gather, squinting across the room, Connor had scrubbed up *very* well. Although I liked how he was unscrubbed too. *Keep your mind on the job, Jenny.*

Christine, or 'Mothzilla of the Bride' as I'd begun to think of her, had wanted the whole wedding party to form a greeting line to welcome the guests before the wedding breakfast. So, I found myself dutifully in the lineup. Shaking hands and making pleasant small talk, mainly with people I didn't know, while wishing they'd move faster as I was so hungry. The teeny tiny canapés that had been passed round were clearly the caterer's idea of a joke, teasing us with the idea of food. Then I saw him, right near the back of the queue, eyes twinkling in the soft glow of candles. Feasting my eyes on him, I couldn't look away. His suit fit snugly to his athletic body, giving the beach bum an air of suave sophistication.

Why do men always look so damn fine in suits? This is torture.

He gave me a warm smile and a casual wave and I waggled my fingers back, feeling nervous. I barely paid any attention to the pleasantries I was exchanging. I was too busy glancing over to him, gauging him getting closer, only to look away quickly so he didn't catch me ogling him. Then he reached Jade and the beginning of the greetings line, and I saw her lean in for one of his warm hugs. My heart felt like it was plummeting into my stomach. They were having a long chat and were laughing; I couldn't tear my eyes away.

'Jenny, Jenny.' There was a frantic tugging at my arm which brought me back to the here and now.

'James? What the hell are you doing here?' I hissed at my ex. 'You were specifically not invited.'

'I just had to see you. Please can we talk, then I'll go. Please?'

The procession had come to a standstill and Mothzilla and the other parents were looking over to see what was causing the hold up. Scarcely containing a growl, I grabbed hold of his elbow and marched him away. Away from where he would cause an unwelcome disruption. Away from my chance to see Connor.

Out in the foyer, I let go of his arm and turned to face him.

'What do you want? You'd better not cause a scene.'

'I'm not going to cause any trouble. I needed to see you, you weren't returning my calls.'

'I didn't want to see you. We're over. You made that quite clear a couple of years ago. What's this sudden interest?'

'It was a mistake, Babe, I made a mistake.'

'Don't call me *Babe*!'

I leaned in close to hiss loudly in his ear, I didn't want to cause a disturbance by shouting, but I was struggling to keep my cool. 'How did you even know where I'd be?'

'I saw their wedding announcement in the local paper. I knew you'd be here too.'

'This is tantamount to stalking.'

'No, I just had to see you. After I saw the pictures online, I realised the mistake I'd made.'

'Pictures?'

'Yeah, I saw all Annie's holiday selfies on her social media. You looked amazing. You look amazing.' He feasted his eyes over me and made me feel like I'd been visually groped. *Yuck.*

'You've got to go, James. It's not going to happen. It's over. *We* are over.'

It had taken a long-time pining, wishing and waiting until I'd realised I was so much better without him. And now the fact that he was finally paying me some attention made me want to laugh if anything. This was too little, much too late. Over this last month I'd really started to have faith in myself, in my convictions, and now I'd finally found the confidence to tell him no.

I ushered him out of the hotel door and it shut heavily behind him. After checking my reflection in the mirror, I stalked quietly into the dining room, slinking into my seat as subtly as possible. Kirsty leaned around to peer at me, with a questioning eyebrow raised. I gave her a small shake of the head and smile, my way of saying, "don't worry". Then I grabbed the wine glass that had already been filled by the attentive waiting staff and took a giant slug of pinot. *I did it!* I felt jubilant inside.

'Cheers!' I said heartily, leaning both ways and toasting my dining companions. I had Steve's dad and brother on either side of me.

I couldn't help myself, I peeked over at Connor. I shouldn't have done that. He seemed to be swapping a meaningful eyebrow conversation with Jade. *Now I just need to get over Connor too.*

My bridesmaid duties were finally over, or so I thought. I'd laughed at the father of the bride's jokes, come on to the dance floor at Kirsty's signal after the first dance, and kept her dress out of the toilet bowl on a number of occasions. Clutching a glass of champagne, I surveyed the room for my friends. The disco had started, and unsurprisingly they were centre of the dance floor with Connor shimmying between Jade and Suze.

Bracing myself, I sidled over to them and stuck myself in the middle of Annie and Beth, my buffers. I was nowhere near as drunk as this lot, so I was doing a simple two-step dance, my air guitar needed tuning by way of a lot more drink before I'd get it out. Connor strutted over to me, doing some sort of chicken imitation to an old dance classic.

'Grommet!'

'Hi Connor, it's good to see you. You having fun?'

'Absolutely, this lot are looking after me well.'

Jade caught my eye and winked. *I bet they are.*

'Can I get you a drink?' he asked.

'I'm okay thanks,' I replied, holding up my

glass. Then I changed my mind. After knocking back the rest of my drink, I said, 'Actually, yes please.' *I'm going to need more wine.*

We stood at the bar and Connor asked if they had any Sangria, 'for old time's sake'.

The puzzled barman politely said, 'No, it's not a wedding favourite.'

'Oh well, I guess we'll have to make champagne our new usual.'

Sipping our bubbly, we passed polite conversation, talking about work and people we both knew from Spain. I was trying to keep it light and detached. I could feel Jade's heavy gaze and looked for excuses to get away. It was becoming increasingly hard to control myself and I didn't want to upset Jade. Luckily, at that moment, Mothzilla grabbed a hold of me.

'You need to go and help Kirsty out in the entrance,' she said.

'I'll be right there.' Downing the rest of my drink I looked to Connor and said, 'See you in a bit.' Gladly leaving and walking out to the venue's foyer.

Raised voices told me Kirsty was there arguing with someone. I rushed over to help, bridesmaid back in action. Cringing, I found James and he was super drunk.

'Isssbabe, tell her, Babe.'

'James, go home. You're not welcome here,' I said and then turned to Kirsty. 'I'll sort this, you go back to your wedding.' Kirsty squeezed my hand then headed away.

'I knew youssssstill wanted me, ssssent her offfso we could be alone.'

'No. You've got to go. I'll call you a cab.'

James stood swaying next to me while I dialled the taxi company and ordered one to come as soon as possible. I hung up and without warning James lunged at me, scooping me in his arms and planting a big wet, alcohol fume-y, tobacco tarnished, kiss. *Blurgh!* It took me a moment to fight him off.

'No, James. It's over,' I said, more softly than he deserved.

He started to cry. I sat him on the leather sofa and watched for the cab. When it arrived, I bundled him inside and apologised to the driver about the state he was in. I watched it drive off, taking a deep breath of cool night air before turning to go back into the reception. An angry looking Jade accosted me before I could go back into the function room.

'What the hell are you playing at with Connor?'

'What?'

'Connor. What. Are. You. Doing. With. Connor?'

'Nothing, nothing. I haven't done anything with him. I wouldn't do that to you.'

'To me? What are you talking about?'

'I know you like him. I wouldn't go there.'

'*I* don't like him. I mean I like him. But not

like *that*. You like him! So why haven't you done anything about it?'

'Because you like him and he likes you.'

'Errrr...no! He likes you. Why else would he have come all this way? He wanted to see you and you've basically ignored him all night.'

'But all those texts and calls to you...'

'He was asking me for advice about you. Now, why have you been rude and ignoring him?

'I haven't, I've been doing bridesmaid duties and...and...'

'And avoiding him as much as possible. Yeah, I noticed. Now get back in there and sort it out. Jeez, I've done nothing but try and get you two together. I can't do anymore, you're on your own.'

Jade slapped me on the bum as she ushered me away and I almost tripped into the room. Almost.

A sense of elation was rising in my chest. *He likes me!* I caught sight of his handsome face laughing. He was in the middle of a dance off circle, which he'd most probably started. He looked so young and vibrant, bouncing away, doubt nibbled into me. *It doesn't matter if he likes you, he's far too young. Or you're far too old.* I berated myself.

I hung back and found my mum and her boyfriend sat on the edge of the dance floor.

'Hi love, it's so lovely Kirsty invited us to the evening do. She looks so beautiful.'

'Yes, she does,' I replied, distracted.

'Everything alright, love?' asked mum.

'Yes and no.'

'Who's that man dancing with all your girls?'

'That's Connor. We met him on the hen do.'

'*That's* the Connor I've heard so much about? Seems like a nice chap.' My mum looked at me meaningfully.

'He is.'

'Why aren't you up there?'

'I'm just…'

'Jennifer Louise George. I know you. I've heard you talk about him for a month. I've seen the way you've looked at him all evening. Go on…or you'll regret it.'

'Muuuum, I don't need relationship advice from you!' She looked offended and I felt bad. 'Sorry, I know you mean well, but he's far too young for me. Look at him, he's barely out of his teens.'

'Yes, yes and you're a woman of the world. I know. Well, age doesn't matter one jot. But, if you need to measure it, I think you could go at least ten years either way, and no one would bat an eyelid.'

At this point her boyfriend leaned in and said, 'And in fact, I'm thirteen years younger than your mum, but she still went for me. Ohhh, she's such a cougar!'

My mum scuffed him on the arm and said, 'I never even asked him. When you love someone, nothing like that matters, you just know.'

I laughed. Perhaps I did need relationship advice from my mum after all. With renewed confidence I headed back onto the dance floor. Connor locked in my sights.

Connor saw me coming and his face fell. This wasn't the reaction I was hoping for. He bent his head down and headed over to the bar. I followed him and stood next to him leaning on the polished wooden counter.

'The usual?' I asked him, trying to make a joke.

'You must be in the mood for celebrating,' he replied, his voice was even, cold in fact.

'Yes, my best friend just got married. Everyone's here having fun. I've quit my job, the world's my oyster.' I was affronted and confused.

'Don't forget your boyfriend, you didn't mention him earlier. That must be worth celebrating.'

'Boyfriend?'

'Yeah, I saw you sneaking off with that guy earlier. You could've told me you know.'

'That's not my boyfriend... that's James.'

'Listen, it would have been nice to have known before I came out here, that's all. I don't want to be the jerk mooning after someone who's already got a boyfriend.'

'You were mooning after me, huh? We should talk about that some more.'

'No, no, no. I'm not into cheating or two-timing, everyone gets hurt. I don't want any part of it.' Connor tried to move away. I grabbed his rock-hard bicep.

'I haven't got a boyfriend.'

'I saw you kiss that guy!'

'No, you didn't.'

'You mean I didn't come into the lobby to see if you were okay, only to find you snogging him.'

'No, I mean, yes, I mean… he kissed me. He was drunk. Didn't you see me push him off?'

Connor's interest piqued. 'Noooo,' he said. I could tell he wasn't quite sure if he believed me.

As I filled him in on the pertinent facts of my relationship with James I could see the severe furrowing of his brow relax.

'So, you shipped him off home? And it's over?' he repeated back to me.

'Yes! It's been over for a loooong time.'

'Well now, that *is* a reason to celebrate.' He turned to catch the attention of the barman. 'Barman, our usual please. We have lots to celebrate!'

CHAPTER 39

As I lay in Connor's arms, everything seemed okay with the world. It could be because I hadn't caught up on any news for two days; I was oblivious to the misdeeds of mankind, safe in our cosy hotel room. It could be because I was still in a food coma from the copious amounts of room service and mini bar raiding. It could be because I'd convinced Connor to let me be the little spoon and his warm arms wrapped around me, fitting my curves perfectly. Made to measure. It was most probably because I'd just decided that I was completely, utterly, and unswervingly in love with him.

'You're thinking again, Grommet,' his husky voice whispered in my ear.

'I'm just thinking I'm happy.'

He curled his fingers around mine. 'Good, I'm happy too.'

'Good.'

'You're still thinking though, stop thinking.

We have another hour before we need to check out and get back to the real world.'

I couldn't tell him the truth, not yet, so I asked him about something that was niggling at me. 'I was thinking- does it bother you? The age difference between us? I mean, I thought it might bother me, but it really doesn't. But does it bother you?'

'What, dating a younger woman? Can't say I mind but I wouldn't mind if you were older either. It doesn't matter,' he said as he kissed my ear.

I sat up on my elbow and half turned to him.

'*Younger* woman? You think I'm younger?'

'Yeah! You're *Young Grommet!*'

'But you're the young one! Look at you, you must be what, twenty, twenty-one at the oldest?'

'No way! Jeez, I hate it when people think I look young for my age.'

'So how old are you?' I asked.

'I'm twenty-eight, twenty-nine next month. You?'

'A lady never tells.'

He laughed at me, a dirty laugh, implying I was no lady. Then he said, 'I'd guess you were twenty-four.'

'Outrageous, people normally think I'm about eighteen!' I paused then said, modestly, 'I'm twenty-seven.'

'Woah, you do look young for your age. So, I was right though. I *am* dating a younger woman.'

'You haven't actually taken me on a date yet.'

'Hmmm good point. What are you doing later today?'

'Going to the job centre to get some careers advice and to work my options out. I've got that bonus from work so I'm not in a rush, I want to make the right decision.'

'Let's go together.'

'To the job centre? That sounds like the worst date ever.'

'No, to the airport. My flight back is this evening. Come back with me to Spain. I'll take you for tapas.'

'You're not serious?'

'For real. Or if you don't fancy Spain again, let's head off on an adventure together somewhere else. You can think about your options anywhere in the world.'

I paused. 'You're serious, aren't you? I don't know what to say.'

'Well, when a fella knows he's in love with someone, he's not gonna let them get away from him, is he?'

He flipped me over and pulled me in closer, our bodies slotting in perfectly together.

'Did you just say…'

'Love. Yes. I love you. I think I've loved you since your first email booking the jet ski lesson- all that effort for your friend, I thought you must be very special. Or maybe it was the email I got that was only meant for your mum…'

I mock punched him and replied, 'Hey, that was an easy mistake to make!'

'Or, maybe it was when I saw you dancing beautifully on stage and then you fell off into my arms, how did that go again?'

He scooped me up in his arms lifting me off the bed, then proceeded to drop me unceremoniously onto the mattress and plunge down into a tickle fight. I managed to flip over on top of him and pin him down, straddling him.

'I love you too.'

I bent down and kissed him and, in that moment, I knew what I was going to do.

I was stripped down to my pants and vest top, as I always did to clean, scrubbing my house like it had never been scrubbed before. I felt a great responsibility subletting it and I wanted it to be nice for the tenants when they arrived. The last couple of days since the wedding had been a whirlwind of activity. Boxes of my belongings had been shipped over to my mum's spare room and my suitcase was packed and standing by the front door. Ready for my adventure to begin.

So far, I'd cleaned the ceilings, walls, floors and windows but I was still not happy with the result. I couldn't work out why I couldn't get the grime off the windows. Looking closer I noticed the dirt was on the outside- *duh!* Without a second thought I popped outside and gave the windows a once over.

The sunlight positively sparkled off them and I stood back, proud to admire my handy work. A van went by and honked, absentminded, I waved without even looking. Months ago, I would have spent hours dissecting that toot. Did that mean they liked me? Was it an ironic toot? Did my bum look big? I grinned, pleased that I'd learned to just accept myself; to believe in myself more. Everything I'd been through, and how I'd handled it, made me really proud. I had really started to respect myself.

There was a bang and my smile froze on my face. *Aw, crap!* That sound was the front door shutting. I'd locked myself out. Half-naked.

Considering my options, I saw that I'd left the awning window propped open in the lounge. *That'll do.* I nodded to myself and with a false sense of confidence in my strength and ability, probably brought about by my new yoga addiction, I hoisted myself up on the window sill. I braced my hands around the edge of the frame and pushed my head up and through the window, my boobs were squashed against the glass. As I began to slide through my hips got caught in the narrow gap, I couldn't lever myself forwards or back. I was stuck. At that moment, I heard some feet crunch on the gravel.

'I'd come over to celebrate with some champagne, Grommet, but this wasn't the bottoms up I had in mind!'

'I've got everything under control,' I called back.

'Sure you have.' Connor boosted me through the gap in the window and I managed to wriggle through, landing in a handstand on the couch and forward rolling off onto the floor.

I could hear him calling out, 'And the young woman from England scores a ten from the judges!'

I stood up to take a bow, and through the window Connor said, 'So, are you gonna let me in, or do I need to crawl through here too?'

After throwing on some clothes, I let Connor in, glancing at the bottle in his hand. 'This is a lovely surprise, what are we toasting this time? We already celebrated my decision to go travelling round Europe with you, booking our flights and then my last night in the house yesterday.' I counted them off on my fingers.

'It's Friday, you've got to observe the sacred tradition of *Fizz on a Friday*!'

'This sounds like a very serious matter indeed, but all my stuff is at my mum's. I've completely gutted the house, and we can't drink champagne out of the bottle. That would be sacrilege, surely?'

'Well, let's head over there now, she can help us drink it.'

'Are you sure you don't mind hanging out with my mum?'

'Of course not! Then I can fill her in on your

unconventional cleaning uniform, she likes it when I keep her up to date with your antics.'

'When do you fill her in on my antics?'

'We've had our moments; her favourite story is hearing how I saved you from breaking your neck falling off the stage.'

'I've been meaning to ask you about that. Why on earth did the barman say the guy that saved me was English?'

Connor laughed, and replied, 'That guy! He always insisted I was English. He couldn't tell the difference between an Aussie and an English accent.'

'If only he could, I'd have known it was you much sooner!'

'Would it have made any difference?'

'Well, I doubt I'd have given Michael so much credit if I didn't think it was him…'

'And risk me not being able to help you make your epic getaway on my jet ski? Nah, I'll take being mistaken for a Pom, thanks very much.'

'We should have got that hat its own seat on the plane,' grumbled Connor the next day. We were crammed into the back of Steve's car, the hat covering both our laps. The four of us were headed to the airport.

'It'll bring you luck,' called out Kirsty from the front.

'Luck? This monstrosity caused nothing but

mayhem on your hen do,' I scoffed.

'Yes, but the hen do was where you met Connor. See, it's lucky,' she replied, giving a little shrug.

'Well, *I* feel lucky now that Jenny's got it!' Steve joked.

The rest of the car journey passed in happy banter. Mainly about the boys being relieved that Connor and I weren't heading off to the same place as Kirsty and Steve were for their honeymoon.

'So, how did you pick Germany?' Kirsty asked.

'We went to the travel agents and spun around their giant globe, then I shut my eyes, put my finger out, and it landed there.'

'What no planning, no research, no nothing?'

'Yep, it's the final step in my "new you's resolution" transformation.'

'So, you and your trusty binder? It's over?'

'Yep. Spontaneity is my new middle name.'

'You're travelling round Europe with no plans at all?' Kirsty clarified.

'We'll just see where the wind takes us,' chipped in Connor.

'Romantic, huh?' I beamed.

Kirsty looked to Steve with a grimace. 'What could possibly go wrong?'

To be continued...

BOOKS BY THIS AUTHOR

Second Thoughts

Find out where Jenny goes next - Second Thoughts is available now!

How well do you ever really know someone?

Jenny George is living her best life. Travelling around Europe with her wonderful new boyfriend, Connor, everything feels perfect.

But then her savings run out.

And Connor has to dash back to Australia.

Determined to fend for herself, she takes a job at a Bavarian ski resort. By the time Connor returns she'll have the funds to pick up their adventures where they left off.

But when Connor doesn't call, doubts start to

creep in, and things go from bad to worse when she bumps into an old rival who once made her life a misery.

However, when her nemesis turns out to be nice, Jenny wonders how good a judge of character she really is. And with no news from Connor, she starts questioning everything.

Connor wouldn't ghost her, would he?

Soon Jenny is wondering just who she can trust, including herself…

Step By Step

Sometimes big changes begin with small steps…

When Zoë Beaufort inherits a cottage in the quaint Somerset village of Honeygrove, she hopes she'll find the new start she desperately needs.

She doesn't expect to find the cottage in a sorry state of repair.

Or a runaway pig.

And she definitely doesn't expect to find the delectable Theo. Kind, gorgeous… and unavailable. Despite the chemistry between them, Zoë knows better than to risk her fresh new start with romantic complications.

Settling in to village life, she can't believe her luck when she finds herself with the job of her dreams and lovely new friends. But the discovery of an old family photograph leaves her reeling. There's a mystery surrounding her inheritance and she's determined to get to the bottom of it.

Will Zoë find the answers she's looking for? Has she finally found a place to call home? And, as her life unexpectedly entwines with Theo's, is it possible she might just get a chance at love?

Two Turtle Doves - A Christmas Anthology

Full of fairy lights, flirting and festive cheer, this delightful Christmas anthology presents all the fun and romance that the season has to offer.

A Partridge in a Pear Tree:

If Holly can pull off the event of the century, she's sure to get a promotion. But when disaster strikes Cherrywell Manor's Christmas Gala she mustn't let the enigmatic gardener, Rory, distract her from her rescue efforts. It's not just her job at stake.

Two Turtle Doves:

Douglas Whittaker really ruffles Angela Hart's feathers; he's nothing but a common thief to her. But when they are forced together to save more than Christmas, she finds the only thing he's stolen is her heart.

Three French Hens:

Greenway's Bookshop holds thousands of old tales on its shelves, but a new romance is in the air this Christmas. The pursuit of an antique recipe book stirs up Gabrielle's love life, but will she find her own happy ever after, or are they only for the pages of her beloved books?

Four Calling Birds:

Pour a glass of fizz and reunite with Jenny and the gang for an unconventional Christmas party. There's a lot to celebrate.

Curl up and discover what true love will bring this Christmas.

Candlelight And Snowball Fights

Grab a hot chocolate, tuck your toes under a loved one and curl up on the sofa with this sweet winter romance…

When Nancy arrives in Denmark to visit her best friend, Tessa, everything seems perfect; the fire is roaring and the snow is gently falling. It's a winter wonderland.

As the snow gets thicker she discovers that things aren't as perfect as they appear. Eager to reconnect with her friend, Nancy is hurt when Tessa is wrapped up with her new beau, leaving her lonely and out in the cold.

Tessa's mysterious colleague, Torben, steps in to keep Nancy company. He could easily be mistaken for a Nordic god but can Nancy melt his icy demeanour?

Will romance kindle as Nancy and Torben get cosy at the fireside? And will Nancy and Tessa's friendship weather the storm? Find out in this warming winter novella... a tale of friendship, love and woolly jumpers.

ABOUT THE AUTHOR

Sarah-Jane Fraser

Sarah-Jane Fraser lives in the English West Country with her husband and two daughters.

She's a book worm and loves losing herself in books, both reading and writing. If it's good escapism she loves it, chicklit, fantasy, anything. She knew at the age of six that she wanted to be an author but it took her a few years to realise that she should listen to her six year old self.

Her debut novel, The Spanish Indecision, was a finalist in the Wishing Shelf Book Award 2018.

For news on forthcoming releases and other bookish things you can follow her on Facebook, Instagram and Twitter - @sjfraserauthor. She loves to hear your reviews and reading recommendations so please don't hesitate to get in contact.

ACKNOWLEDGEMENTS

Massive thanks to all my beta readers, your insight is so appreciated and I couldn't have done this without you. Your suggestions were always helpful. I loved hearing the bits that made you laugh out loud and I hope you'll help me with the next book as well?!

Firstly, Hannah Ellis, how can I ever thank you enough? You've been an inspiration. You're the font of all writing knowledge and you've been endlessly patient with my random musings. Thank you for sticking with me from the beginning!

To Lisa West, thank you for 'getting it'; you're the first who could see what I was doing and why, and I hope I've made you proud.

To Alexandra O'Malley, thank you for totally getting my sense of humour. I'm sorry though, you helped me write a book and all you get is this lousy acknowledgment. And a t-shirt. I'm definitely getting you a t-shirt.

To Gillian Baxter, thank you for your positivity and un-ending patience with my spelling.

Thanks also to Andrew Fraser and Laura Tait for

looking at my initial attempt and giving me the encouragement to keep trying.

To the people on ChickLitChatHQ, thank you for your positive comments and for answering many questions, with particular thanks to Jen Collin and Monique McDonell.

Thanks to Kathryn Fraser and Tiffany Mogg, I will always appreciate your honesty and feedback.

Finally, thank you to my editor, Jenny Kane, who has helped me finesse this story.

Printed in Great Britain
by Amazon